T0149193

THE ARTISTS' HAVEN

Doris Dorwart

authorHOUSE®

AuthorHouse™
1663 Liberty Drive
Bloomington, IN 47403
www.authorhouse.com
Phone: 1 (800) 839-8640

Published by AuthorHouse   09/22/2015

ISBN: 978-1-5049-5145-6 (sc)
ISBN: 978-1-5049-5143-2 (hc)
ISBN: 978-1-5049-5144-9 (e)

Library of Congress Control Number: 2015915557

Print information available on the last page.

Any people depicted in stock imagery provided by Thinkstock are models,
and such images are being used for illustrative purposes only.
Certain stock imagery © Thinkstock.

This book is printed on acid-free paper.

ACKNOWLEDGEMENTS

What you cannot see, in between the wods in this book, is the advice and counsel given to me by friends. While writers like to pretend that they know just about everything, the truth is that they must recognize when they need help and where they need to find it.

In this story, a ballerina plays a pivotal role. So when I learned that a real ballerina was living only one floor above me, I realized that I had hit the jackpot. Harriet Attig took me under her wing and patiently explained what I needed to know to bring my ballerina to life.

When I introduced a master goldsmith in my story, Lynnette Spadea, came to my rescue. She explained how jewelers choose the materials they use in making their pieces. Of course, the jeweler in this story uses only 14 carat gold!

It would have been impossible to write this book without the advice and guidance of my editor, Jane Lloyd. This woman has the patience of Job! Not only did she help me with grammar and punctuation, she understood my characters and loved them just as much as I do—even the despicable ones. The two of us have been through some rough times this year with health issues. However, we are both still here, plotting and delighting in creating characters—some you may love—some you may dislike.

I love the cover of this book. The collage was designed by Linda M. Adams, my artistic niece. She used various symbols found in the story in an amazing collage.

Without these remarkable women, it is quite possible that my story might never have seen the light of day. Thank you ladies—my characters thank you too.

So, come along with us and discover how accomplished artists interact with one another in the beautiful haven that sits in the middle of a Christmas tree farm.

CHAPTER 1

The early December wind was making itself known as it tossed the last of the fallen leaves around. All day long the clouds seemed to be threatening the first snow storm of the season. Local prognosticators were presenting their estimates, regarding the number of inches of snow that the residents of Harrisburg could expect by early morning. However, none of this had an effect on the customers, who had crowded into the *Dirty Frog Saloon* that stood alongside the busy highway, carrying those who were headed to the state capital. Although the outside of the bar was certainly unappealing, it was the only one within several miles, so it was never at a loss for customers.

When one stepped into the bar, the environment didn't get any better. A long, cloudy mirror occupied the entire wall behind the bar. Here and there, pictures of naked women had been taped onto the smoky glass. But one of these beauties, clad in a one-piece white bathing suit, had her own spot—Betty Grable. Only the older patrons appreciated this photo of a forties Hollywood beauty, whose portrait had even been painted on some of the planes that had been used in World War II. In one corner was a pinball machine, whose lights blinked almost synchronously with the little bells that kept ringing as the metal balls found their way to the return mechanism. Some of the tiles were missing from the floor, making walking around the room treacherous for those with any physical disabilities.

In the far corner, underneath a dirty-looking ceiling fan, sat two men who appeared to be studies in opposites. Ray Caltigarone was impeccably dressed. Gold cuff links peeked out from the sleeves of a tailored-made suit. Dark black hair, neatly sleeked back off his face, was expertly cut. His right cheek had a scar running down from his eye to the side of his mouth that only added to his mystique. His table partner, Fat Tony Bonnelli, however, was an obese man with a huge pock-marked face. A black leather cap was plopped on top of his balding head. His jacket was not buttoned since he had apparently outgrown it a long time ago. Rolls of fat hung down over his bloated belly. Around his neck he wore a rusty-looking dog tag on a chain that was almost concealed by his saggy jowls.

Fat Tony and Ray were seemingly unaware of anything else going on around them. Ray began pushing his beer mug back and forth, tracing patterns and indentions that had been made over many years on the well-worn, wooden table top. Fat Tony was rocking back and forth while continually biting his lips.

"I ain't sure I like this," Fat Tony said. "I don't like getting in on something when I don't know everyone involved."

"You know me, Tony. You don't need to know the others," Ray said tersely.

"Says you. You take orders from someone you call *The Man,* who takes his orders from some damn dude called *The Big Cheese.* Sounds like a kid's story. You want me to do a job that you can't do, but you don't let me in on the whole enchilada."

"Have I ever let you down? No. You always got your cut and we came out with our skirts clean. Are you complaining about the money?"

"No. But once I pull the trigger, there's no going back. I like my freedom, boy, and I want to keep it that way. Who the hell do you really take your orders from?" an agitated Tony asked.

"I can't give you a name. But you already had lots of help from him," Ray said adamantly.

"Help? What the fuck do you mean?"

"Who do you think got you out of the cooler last March? Remember? You never heard another word about that mess, did you?"

"No, I just thought…"

"Well, it was him. And he'll be backing you all the way this time, too. So stop with the questions and let's get to the problem on hand."

"Ray, just one more question," said Tony as Ray gave him the eye. "Why do they call him *Big Cheese?*"

"Tony, so help me I'm ready to walk out. This will be a big pay day for you. You should be happy about that. How the top guy got that name I don't know and I don't care. All I know is that he's powerful and rich. What more can we ask?"

The two sat quietly for a few minutes, sipping on their drinks. Ray reached into his jacket pocket and pulled out a photo that he tossed to Tony.

"Her name's Florence Gibble," Ray said.

Fat Tony looked at the photo for some time. "She ain't what I was expecting."

"What do you mean?" Ray said, shifting restlessly on his seat.

"Well, first of all this is a graduation picture—probably all of eighteen. Oh, she's a looker, but boney. I guess skinny or fat doesn't mean anything to you. I bet you stick your dick in more broads than a porcupine has needles," Fat Tony said with a boisterous snort.

Ray rolled his eyes.

"Oh, don't get like that now. We might as well get some fun out of this. She had to leave a trail of some kind. What about her family?" Tony said as he took another gulp of beer.

"The old man's dead and her old lady's in some kind of old folks home where she talks to birds all day long. By now, our target could be anywhere in the country or, even overseas somewhere. I do know that she was born and raised in Burlington, Vermont, on a tree farm."

"A tree farm—what the fuck is a tree farm?"

"A Christmas tree farm."

"That aint farming to me," Tony said. "What do they do all day—sit around and watch trees grow?" Tony laughed so loud that several patrons at the bar turned around for a few seconds. "Farming's when you plant stuff—corn, tobacco, like that there—or raise cattle. Trees sound dumb to me. Do you know where the fucking tree farm is? He gives us a picture but not much else. This could take a long time. That's what I mean, Ray. We usually get a name, a place, and a time—quick and easy. We're in. We're out. We get our dough and that's that."

"But think of the money, Tony. That alone should make you feel good. I'm not certain but I think this babe used to be Big Cheese's goomah and, apparently, one day about two years ago, she took off with a suitcase full of green and some documents that he wants back. Seems like Big Cheese is still pissed off, but I think there could be a lot more involved here so we need to be alert. We just might find out some stuff about Big Cheese and then we'll have a bigger bargaining chip for future jobs. Right now, Tony, we have a job to do, but we can't act like dumb asses."

Fat Tony scowled. "Okay, I'll give you that much. Are we supposed to find the money, too?"

"That's another thing—The Man said if we could locate the cash we could keep it. But he thinks it's gone by now. He didn't say how much she took and I was smart enough not to ask. He said Big Cheese wants the documents though. I asked him what the documents were but he wouldn't tell me. He did say that they were in a heavy, yellow plastic binder. And, if we can't find them, our orders are to torch the place. Finding those papers will be a much harder task than getting rid of the chick."

"Hell, let's hope that the babe still has some of the dough left stuffed under the mattress. That will only sweeten the pot. Are you sure Big Cheese is good for that kind of moola?"

"Christ, Tony, our man said that Big Cheese apparently has money up to his ass. But the documents intrigue me. How the hell will we recognize them if we do locate any paperwork? But I've been giving that some thought. What do you think about us keeping the binder—that is if we really find it? Let's hope that the chick tells us where the papers are—and she just might do that after I romance her a bit. No telling who we might be able to shakedown with the documents; it depends on what they are. First, however, we must find her."

"Oh, and when we do, I won't hesitate telling her the different ways she could die. I love that part," Fat Tony said, with a black smile, revealing teeth that probably had never been seen by a dentist.

"Look, Tony, I'll do my part but I won't stick around for that. Besides, he said **neat and clean.** But I'm telling you that I want no part of setting anything on fire."

"Pussy! You can't take much, can you, Ray? You run the fucking **finding** part of this job and let the **how** part up to me. I ain't gonna miss out on an opportunity to enjoy myself while I'm offing her. Get it?"

"Never mind, now let's get down to business," Ray said as he tossed a small tablet on the table. "I have a few ideas on where to start. I'm going to Burlington and hit the night life there; if there is such a thing in the middle of all those damned mountains. Damned place is the capital of Vermont." Ray made a few notes in the tablet. "I'll go online tonight and do a little research on Burlington—sort of get the lay of the city. I still believe that my best bet is to find one person who knew her, and I'll be able to figure out where she went. Maybe I can even discover just why she left. You never know—such info might prove valuable in future dealings with The Man, or even better, with Big Cheese."

"You sound awfully sure of your talent, pal. Are you really that damned good?"

"I have my ways—you have yours—and then we both can have some fun before all this is over. Let's concentrate on our payday." Then picking up the photo and examining it carefully, Ray said, "She's pretty though—but me I like 'em more filled out. Know what I mean?"

"You sure as hell ain't gonna marry the bitch; just fuck her good, so she's totally relaxed when I enter the picture. Now, do you know what I mean?"

As Fat Tony waddled out of the bar, Ray suddenly had another idea. If he found the binder, he would keep it for himself. Besides, Fat Tony was too dumb to understand what the impact might be if the papers held any incriminating information about Big Cheese. Ray's future was getting brighter by the minute—he would find the girl and the documents. As he stood up, he said softly, "Vermont, here I come."

***

One week later, as Ray walked down the East Shore pathway along Lake Champlain, he pulled his jacket closer to his body. The citizens were not only celebrating the holiday season, but many of them were getting ready for a party designed to welcome in 2011. But after hearing the long-range weather forecast, Ray had doubts that it would really take place. According to the uptight weatherlady on TV this morning, Burlington should prepare for what could be its largest snow storm ever.

Yesterday, Ray had visited the tree farm where Florence had grown up. The new owners, the Ballards, claimed that they had no idea where Florence was. When they purchased the old Gibble Tree Farm, the transaction was completed by Mr. Gibble's younger brother, who had Power of Attorney. When Ray suggested that perhaps he could speak with the uncle about Florence, he was told that the man was a nature photographer, who traveled the world completing assignments for several publications. He would only return to Burlington when he was on hiatus. They stated that while they had never met Florence, their neighbors told them that she was a lovely girl, who had gone to New York City to become a dancer. Ray had to listen to a long, drawn-out story about how Florence's dad had died and how much he suffered before he finally closed his eyes. Ray managed to get the conversation shifted to Florence's mother, and, once again, the talkative couple went on for some time about how sad it was that she was in the final stages of dementia.

Ray surprised himself when he decided to visit the nursing home to see if he could speak to Florence's mother. The pretty young woman sitting at the reception desk gave him a smile that at any other time would have started a romantic pursuit. He asked the girl if Florence ever visited her mother. The receptionist just shook her head back and forth. When he asked about the financial aspect of caring for Florence's mother, the young thing whispered, "Someone faithfully makes an electronic transfer of funds into Mrs. Gibble's account each month. I don't know who does this, but I'd like to think that it's Florence."

As Ray walked down the hall to Florence's mother's room, he began thinking about the electronic transfers. Perhaps Florence was using Big Cheese's money to take care of her mother. But then there also was the money that Florence had probably received from the sale of her parent's tree farm—or did someone else get that money?

The pleasant surroundings surprised him. He had always thought that retirement homes were dark and dreary—smelly and disgusting. The hallway was well-lit and the tiled floors were bright and shiny. As a lady in a wheelchair passed him and smiled at him, he returned the smile. Each individual room had a large window on one wall that looked out over the snow-covered lawn and a television on top of a dresser. A lounge chair, with little pillows propped against each arm, was positioned alongside the window, giving each resident a view of the outside world.

When he found the room, Ray entered cautiously. There, by the window was a little gray-headed lady leaning on the window sill. Ray cleared his throat and the old woman turned around.

"Oh, hello there. Is it too cold for my little birds to come visit me? I really miss them."

"Well, I don't know anything about birds, but it's very cold today. Perhaps they'll come tomorrow."

"Okay, tomorrow," the old lady replied. "Do you know where my little opal ring is?"

"No, I'm sorry. I don't," Ray said.

"Maybe Florence does," the woman said.

And that was it. No matter what Ray said or did, the old lady simply stared out the window, but she did not speak again. It spooked him somewhat. With a sweet smile on her face, and occasionally nodding her head as if she was hearing something way off in the distance, the old woman totally ignored Ray. Unlike anything he had seen or experienced, the old woman surprisingly seemed content in her aloneness. Ray didn't like to be alone.

As he hurried down the hallway, Ray felt a chill go over him. He took this as an ominous sign. He knew that he had to get the picture of that old woman out of his mind. He began to concentrate on his date with a waitress, who claimed that she knew everything about everyone in Burlington. Tonight, Ray might get his first good lead on his target. And, if all went well, not only would he have a night of pleasure, but, more importantly, he'd be able to get out of Vermont before that damned snowstorm arrived.

But, by morning, he decided not to go back to the nursing home. It was too depressing and the old lady was off her rocker. He had had enough of Burlington. The waitress had been a disappointment in all ways. He regretted spending any time with her. He tossed his bag in his car and headed out of town. He hadn't learned much. However, the fact that someone was paying the bills for Mrs. Gibble, reassured him that Florence was somewhere, probably cleverly hidden, for now. With a little luck, Ray was certain that he would find her before too long. He had given his card to Mrs. Ballard and if she heard anything about Florence, Ray was certain that she would call him. She was an easy one to charm. He was unaware that just as he was crossing the state line, Florence's mother had stood up, waved goodbye to her birds, and dropped over dead.

CHAPTER 2

It happened again—that dream—or rather that nightmare. There he was, pinning her against the cold metal table, all the while whispering obscenities. Amanda sat upright in bed while reaching for the light. It had been some time since this had happened and she had begun to think that at last--at long last--those memories had died just like he did. She swung her legs over the side of the bed and felt the plush carpet beneath her feet. Once more, she knelt on the floor and reached under the bed for the battered box. Lifting the lid with great trepidation, Amanda wanted to be certain that in fact he was dead. She inched the top of the old dress box up and let it slide into her lap. There, on the top was the headline—*Ayden Ash, convicted child molester dead from fall.*

She should go no further into the newspaper clippings. She knew perfectly well what would happen—the fear, the shame would return and she would once again be a victim. Quickly, she closed the box and pushed it with her bare feet under the bed. Perhaps it was time to get rid of it—well, not just yet. Here she was 40 years old, running a profitable business that was all her own, and she was still unable to get Ayden Ash out of her mind. She needed to let go of the fear—and the hatred—she had harbored so long.

Shivering from the cold, Amanda got into her chenille robe and fuzzy slippers. She walked to the window and looked out on the property she loved so much—Amanda's Tree Farm. It had stopped snowing during the night and the scene before her was breathtaking. All the little pine needles seemed to have been meticulously painted silver and they shone like candlelight in the early morning sun. If she stood on her tip-toes, she could see the east side of her property that led down to the highway. While all types of fir trees completely encircled the cottage, her favorite view was the west side where there was no intrusion of anything but trees. *This is my own special haven.* Here was Mother Nature in all her finery. Amanda loved the look of the trees, the smell of the trees—the total essence of each and every one. She even loved the work that came with owning a tree farm. The growth process always fascinated her. Each year, the process of planting the seedlings and anticipating their growth, always reaffirmed her belief that she was put here, in this heavenly place, in order to heal her soul. Maybe she would just push that box under her bed all the way to the back where she just might forget its existence.

Glancing to the left, she could barely see the rooftop of the old mansion sitting on top of the little hill—The Haven, she named it long ago. Amanda could see every column, every window, and each architectural detail of the house in her mind. The winding driveway that led visitors to The Haven ended in a surprisingly large parking area. Six wide cement steps, flanked on either side by ornate wrought-iron railings, led to a flag-stone walkway, followed by another series of steps leading to a wrap-around porch. Four tall massive columns, reaching from the floor of the porch to the top of the second-floor windows, appeared to be guarding the home from any unwanted trespassers. A heavy oak door, framed in stained glass, added to the elegance of the entryway. A large reception area was dominated by a six-foot tall bronze of an Art Deco maiden. Her arms were out stretched—one held her skirt, while the other grasped a frosted, glass lamp that served as a night light. Mrs. Nesbit, the previous owner of the tree farm, as well as Amanda's benefactor, was curiously superstitious about the statue. She had often reminded her that Fifi was extremely important to all who entered the manor. Not only was she the muse of The Manor, Mrs. Nesbit claimed that Fifi wielded special powers over all who entered. Amanda closed her eyes for a moment. And, almost as if Mrs. Nesbit were standing beside her, Amanda recalled her words, "Remember, my dear, always respect Fifi. Take good care of her and she will do the same for you."

To the right of Fifi was a large cloakroom where, in the 20s and 30s, when dinner/dance parties were all the rage, the ladies could pause to hand their wraps and boots to the butler. While Fifi got the lion's share of attention from visitors as they entered the reception area, some were swept away by the elegance of a grand staircase that led to seven bedrooms on the second floor, some of which had been converted into classrooms.

To the left of Fifi was a ballroom with an old-fashioned fresco ceiling and a small raised platform that was now used as a classroom for students of the ballet. The last room on the left was also unique. It boasted windows that rose from the floor to the ceiling, providing a spectacular view of the mountains that seemed to roll on endlessly. It begged to be used as a studio for those interested in putting brush to canvas and Amanda was pleased that there were always students clamoring to take art lessons. Tucked in the corner at the end of the hallway was a small store where the products created at The Haven could be purchased.

To Fifi's right was a formal dining room that could comfortably seat twenty-six guests. Two crystal chandeliers hung from the ceiling and, when lit, cast an almost heavenly glow from one end of the room to the other. The next room was a large working kitchen with cupboards that still housed the original dishes and glasses. A sunroom, filled with wicker furniture and brightly-colored cushions, ran along the back of The Haven, providing an excellent view of the evergreen trees that seemed to go on endlessly.

The Haven was the center of Amanda's universe. It was her sanctuary—her retreat, her refuge from the cold, harsh world. And, she gave much of the credit to Fifi. It was only natural that she wanted to provide the same shelter to others and, as a result, she had decided a year or so ago to invite various artists to come to The Haven to teach their crafts and to sell their wares in the small gift shop. She wanted to fill The Haven with talented people who would create things to add to the beauty of the property that Fifi guarded so well. Amanda felt that The Haven would reward the artists by providing a safe place for them to create beauty on a daily basis. About a year ago, Amanda had created and distributed brochures that included registration forms for classes being offered at The Haven, as well as gift shop hours. She made a mental note that it was probably time to develop a new and exciting brochure that would catch the eyes of even more students and customers.

Remarkably, her first teacher had come to her through an email from a woman she had met several years before when she had gone to an arborculture conference. Florence Gibble, whose parents had owned a tree farm in Vermont, was much younger than Amanda, but the two of them seemed to have a common bond beyond Christmas trees. While the email had been somewhat vague, Florence was seeking asylum, but from what she did not say. Since Amanda knew that Florence was a ballerina, it had popped into her mind that this lovely woman could be a teacher. Amanda had been enchanted with the idea, and, more importantly, Florence had agreed immediately. However, the dancer had changed her name and now wanted to be known as Phoebe Snowden. Amanda asked no questions about the name change for she understood the feeling of wanting to get away—away—where one could get lost in a new identity—for, after all, hadn't Amanda done the same thing?

My Haven, she thought. And, apparently, it has also become Phoebe's haven. Amanda remembered how long she herself had looked for a place to belong—where no one would call her a slut or a whore. After the trial, when she had faced Ayden Ash for the last time, she continued to make some extremely bad decisions. First, she had run away with a boy who immediately left her when she had become pregnant. Then, tragically, she had lost her child. Had it not been for her stepfather, who had she wouldn't be the owner of the tree farm today.

From then on, her staff had grown rapidly. She now had teachers for art, jewelry making, needle-working, and dancing. But, in order to be ready for the upcoming semester, she still needed a writing instructor. Previously, that course had been taught by two friends, who had resigned to go in a different direction with their talents. But the writer she had hired last week over the phone should be arriving today and, if all went well, by late afternoon he will have moved his things into a classroom on the second floor of The Haven.

Shaking off thoughts of the Ayden Ash nightmare, Amanda grabbed her back brush and stepped into the shower. Laying the brush aside, she shampooed her short wavy blonde hair. Letting the water run down her face and over her body, she started feeling much better. She delayed getting out from under the water as long as she could. Stepping onto the bath mat, she had already begun to lay out her schedule for the day. Needing one more look at the scenic beauty of her yard, she walked back to the window. Just then, she spied a rabbit hopping across the back lawn. She smiled. Suddenly, she noticed footprints in the snow leading from the embankment and stopping at her back door. But, by the time she had dressed, all thoughts of the footprints had left the recesses of her mind. Instead, a feeling of contentment and happiness came over her. This was indeed her haven. Fifi will see to that.

CHAPTER 3

The Artists: The Writer (January, 2012)

Wearing a checkered leather jacket and faded blue jeans, Barclay Henderson certainly didn't look like a writer. With a cigarette hanging out of the corner of his mouth, and a coffee mug clutched in his right hand, he was steering his old truck on Interstate 80 West in Pennsylvania. His beard and side burns showed traces of gray, but his piercing blue eyes, and his ready smile made him appear younger than forty-five. He was looking forward to beginning a new life—one that was not cluttered with anything connected to Victoria. While he was grateful that she was out of his life, she had taken just about everything that he had owned—the house—the car—and even the dog. Luckily he still had his computer and his electronic gadgets. Barclay was now free to write whatever he wanted. He only had to please himself, and, hopefully, a publisher or two. The only other possession that he had been able to keep was a necklace that had belonged to his grandmother. An Australian crystal opal, set in rose gold and hanging on a rather modest chain, was nestled in a blue velvet box inside his backpack. He had no idea of its intrinsic worth, but fortunately, neither did Victoria so she didn't want anything to do with it.

The writer wanted to get as far away from New York as possible and lose himself in a new and inspiring environment. He no longer wanted to participate in readings or attend social functions, aimed at promoting the arts among the upper crust. That's how he had met Victoria—a meeting that he later regretted. At first she seemed to encourage him in his efforts, but that didn't last too long. She kept nagging him about writing something that would produce nice royalty checks so that she could meet what she referred to as *the right people*. Well, now she would have to find them on her own.

Avoiding agents, he had published his latest book himself—twenty copies were riding in a carton in the bed of his truck. He loved to write. He couldn't picture himself doing anything else. He had to admit that he was a failure in the many jobs that he had tried during the last twenty or so years, and, if Victoria was right, he was also no good as a writer. But now, an opportunity had fallen into his lap and this could be the turning point, or as Oprah put it, *'the aha moment'*. While browsing channels just two weeks ago, he had been fascinated with a piece about a woman who had established a place she called *The Haven* that was located on the grounds of a Christmas tree farm in Pennsylvania—intriguing. Amanda Murray, the owner of The Haven, had explained that she provided studios where different artists could practice their trades, sell their wares and teach their skills to others. She was especially proud that The Haven offered courses in painting, jewelry making, ballet, needlework, and writing. She also stated that through the generosity of a local philanthropist she could also award a few scholarships each semester. But when she said that she was looking for a writing teacher, Barclay immediately made the decision to get in touch with her even though he didn't have any credentials other than the few books he had published. Miss Murray was not only a beautiful woman, she had displayed such enthusiasm about the teaching of creative skills that it was catching. When he had finally tracked her down by phone, Amanda told him that the writing classroom was already equipped with a whiteboard, plenty of outlets for computers, a podium, and a pull-down screen. He immediately faxed her his resume and, much to his surprise, she had responded quickly with an offer—he accepted.

Just a few hours later, Barclay had started to feel nervous. He began to doubt his ability to teach fledging writers anything. But when an image of a sneering Victoria entered his thoughts, he suddenly experienced a renewal of faith in his own abilities. In spite of Victoria's success in getting her hands on most of his possessions, she had not been able to get any part of his trust fund. So, even if he would not attract many students, thanks to the generosity of his beloved grandfather, he could live on those modest semi-annual checks for some time. While his truck was not in the best condition, Barclay was handy enough to keep it running until royalties for his book would come rolling in. He had to laugh at this thought—rolling in—maybe, but not probably. But he had high hopes for his newest creation *After the Divorce:Now What?* Barclay wasn't sure whether he had written this book for the public or as a cathartic exercise. Either way, he felt good about all the research that he had done and was proud of the end product.

As far as the future was concerned, Barclay knew that as soon as he was settled in at The Haven, he would have time to focus on one of the four manuscripts he was working on. They were tucked away in his computer—all in various stages of completion. He could hear his old professor in his ear, saying, *"Focus, boy, focus. You cannot write every book in the world, so focus."* But that had always been difficult for Barclay. Every time that he was around several people he would begin writing in his head—giving everyone an imaginary background and plotting out ways they could interact with one another.

Grateful that the roads were cleared of snow, he was making better time than he thought he would. Of course, he couldn't be sure that as soon as he turned off the interstate that the roads would be as clean. Sweetbriar had been described on the internet as a well-kept, sleepy-looking, little town nestled between two mountains. According to his GPS, The Haven, was just a five minute drive from this point. He passed a sign that indicated the population of Sweetbriar was less than five thousand—contentment at last. He drove past several grocery stores, a barber shop, three churches, a public library, and the local fire company. He spied a bakery shop that had pink and white metal awnings, loaded with snow. He immediately pulled his truck into the only available parking space. Little wrought-ironed tables and chairs, also covered with piles of snow, were reminders that winter was still around. Barclay could get along without fine dining establishments, but freshly baked cookies and cakes, right out of the oven, brought out the child in him. He was going to like this town.

The Dancer

Phoebe parted the drapes just a bit. She had heard someone pulling into the parking area, and knowing that a new tenant would be arriving today, she was curious to get a glimpse of the man who would be occupying the empty studio upstairs. She was feeling a bit melancholy and had been hoping that the former writing teachers would change their minds about retiring and come back to The Haven. As she spied heavy work boots sticking out of the door of a truck, she was appalled. When Barclay was fully out of the truck, he stood up and began to examine the lovely white building. Phoebe pursed her lips when she spotted his rugged leather jacket and blue jeans. But what shocked her more was the sight of a cigarette hanging out of the corner of his mouth. She hoped that Amanda would stand firm on her policy of no smoking in The Haven and put that scruffy-looking man in his place. Phoebe jumped when she realized that the man had spotted her at the window and was waving to her. She shocked herself when she timidly waved back.

Phoebe walked over to her white wicker desk and sat down to review her schedule for the upcoming week. She was a study in grace with her every movement. Her raven black hair was pulled back in a chignon that was encircled with a gold comb. Coffee brown eyes were offset with high cheek bones. Her skin had a natural glow that didn't need any make-up. She was dressed in a knee-length skirt and an embroidered white peasant blouse that was tied with a simple little white cord. Phoebe had always been blessed with a slender figure, so she had never experienced the problem of weight that so many dancers had to face. She did, however, envy those who were unencumbered with a checkered past. Looking down at her hands, she realized that she needed to rub a little mineral oil on the opal ring that she always wore on her pinky finger. Every time she did this, she would smile as she remembered how proud her mother had been when she had given it to her so many years ago for her birthday one beautiful October morning. In her heart, was a special place that only her beloved mother could fill.

While she didn't have as many ballet students as she had had before the economy went downhill, she would be able to survive—at least financially. As her thoughts began to revolve around money, Phoebe looked at the small cedar chest tucked in the corner of the room. She couldn't decide where she should place the money that she had received a few months ago from the sale of her parents' tree farm, so she had placed the cash in the chest under some costumes—perhaps not the safest place for such a sum, but, she was hesitant to open a bank account since she had no identification to account for her assumed name. Maybe she should get a safe deposit box and then she could stop worrying about money.

Soon it would be time to begin planning for the next recital— something that she relished. She would be working closely with the needlework teacher to design outfits for the girls. This year she wanted her students dressed in pink and lilac skirts, and she planned on asking the jeweler to make little tiaras for each one. Phoebe was dedicated to her students. She loved them all—the younger ones were between seven and ten, and the older girls ranged from eleven to fourteen. She wanted them to develop confidence, self-esteem, and self-discipline in order to be well-rounded young ladies—so rare these days. She always started her students with classical training, teaching them in a methodical way. While they may not become professional dancers, their disciplined bodies would always allow them to be graceful in whatever they did.

Phoebe loved her studio, the former ballroom of the house. Opposite a wall of mirrors was a fixed barre, mounted below a row of windows, where her little ones began each session. They had to learn the five basic positions that were set down by the dancing masters, Lully and Beauchamp, in the late 17th century. Phoebe always enjoyed watching her students as they moved from awkwardness—trying hard not to pull on, or not to rely too long on, the barre—to performing positions with a fair amount of grace. She especially loved observing them as they executed plies, bending their knees, while maintaining turn-out at the joints that allowed their thighs and knees to be directly above the line of the toes. And, when the students had realized that they had mastered this movement, their joy was evident by the smiles on their faces. The wooden floor seemed waiting, waiting, to feel the toes of the little dancers.

Glancing at the bulletin board near her doorway, her eyes lingered on the advertisement for a ballet to be performed in Pittsburgh in April. She wished that she could be on that stage and participate in her favorite ballet, *Swan Lake,* but she didn't dare to be seen in such a public venue. She longed to be Odette, queen of the swans, who had caught the eye of the handsome prince, Siegfried—after regaining a human form at night. If only she had made different decisions she could have avoided so much heartache. But she had only herself to blame. Here, at The Haven, she had been successful in avoiding any publicity that could reveal her whereabouts and she wanted to keep it that way. As thoughts about her past began creeping into her mind once again, she closed her eyes—that usually pushed the ugly memories back into their own hiding places. Some day she may have to face her past head-on, but not now, not until she was certain that *he* could no longer harm her. However, whenever she thought about turning twenty-six this year, it became difficult for her to accept the possibility of her never being able to dance on a professional stage again. Her only solace was that she could come back to The Haven at night and become the crown-wearing swan when no one else was around.

Suddenly Phoebe's thoughts were interrupted when Amanda entered the studio with the man whom she had seen earlier getting out of that ugly truck.

"Phoebe, I would like to introduce you to Barclay Henderson—our new author in residence. Barclay, this lovely lady is Phoebe Snowden. As you can see by her studio she teaches dance."

"Hello there," Barclay said, "It's nice to meet you."

"Hello, Mr. Henderson," Phoebe said as she blushed openly.

"Please, call me Barclay. I hope that I didn't scare you when I waved to you at the window. But you were such a lovely image that I just couldn't help myself."

Phoebe bowed her head a bit, trying to avoid his genuine smile. "Okay, Barclay. I hope you will like it here as much as I do."

"Isn't it nice that all our studios are filled with artists again?" Amanda said as she put her arm around Phoebe. "Barclay, as soon as possible, I'll introduce you to the other three wonderful craft persons that make up our faculty here at The Haven. They are such talented people.

We will be having a meeting on Friday so perhaps you can share your background with them at that time. You will find that we're like family here, won't he, Phoebe?"

"Certainly," Phoebe responded.

As Amanda guided Barclay out of Phoebe's studio, he turned, took hold of Phoebe's hand and said, "Little lady, if you need help at any time, please feel free to call on me."

Phoebe found herself smiling. She wasn't sure why. Could it be that that man, that guy in his flannel shirt, hit a special chord? Or was it the blue eyes? She decided to run a few errands and thought she might stop at home and have a bite to eat. However, once she was home, the longing to dance returned again. She had to go back to The Haven—back to her studio. As she opened her studio door, she began to breathe much easier. The gnawing need to dance was like a drug. She loved coming back to her studio when no one was around so she could lose herself in the music and the dance. She could pretend that she was on the stage—as she was a few years ago—and let her spirits soar. It was then that she had no qualms—no fear of the past. Her only focus was to become one with the music. All by herself, she could become Odette, who, with her lover, became united in love for all eternity. Or, she could assume the role of the Black Swan. She just wanted to dance. She put on her leg-warmers and began her warm-up. Her body was ready—her mind was ready. When the routine was completed, she walked over to the bench, took off her leg-warmers, and pictured the stage in her mind. After lowering the lights, and turning the music on, she took her place in the center of her studio. In her favorite chiffon skirt and pink tights, she could once again become a dancer. As the music began to increase in intensity, Phoebe's dancing became even more aggressive. She had reached that pinnacle—the one that only dancers know and understand. Every movement was perfectly timed—she was pleased with her efforts. As she created the impetus necessary to spin one turn, she was able to stay in place while continuing one turn after another, recreating—to the best of her ability—the bravura performance of the Black Swan that expressed the strength and triumph of the character. This was her reward. She knew that it had to be enough for she may never be able to dance for an audience again. She could improvise all she wanted. She didn't have to please anyone but herself.

Just then, Barclay was coming down the stairway. When he heard the music, he realized that it was coming from Phoebe's studio. He moved quietly toward the door and peered around the door frame, entranced at the sight. In all his life he had never seen such beauty. Her long neck held her head high and her posture was perfect. The way she moved her fingers, her hands, her arms—movements that seemed effortless, smooth, and graceful were captivating. He knew that he would never be capable of expressing in mere words what he was witnessing. How could words ever capture such undeniable, heaven-sent beauty? Softly, so as not to disturb her, he left the building. As he drove away, he was smiling. He tucked the sight of Phoebe away in his heart. In just a few seconds, the lovely dancer had touched his psyche as no one ever had. How lucky he was that he had decided to come to The Haven. If nothing else happened to him like that again, he would always treasure Phoebe's poignant image. *Careful old boy, she's definitely out of your reach.*

The Artist

Darcy Hamilton was wandering around her apartment aimlessly looking for something to occupy her mind until it was time to get dressed for her date. She began flipping through the many paintings that were stacked against the wall. While she did most of her work at The Haven, she also had a small area in her bedroom where she kept water colors and pastels handy so that she could create whenever the mood struck. Her studio was the beautiful solarium that was next to Phoebe's dance studio. It was ideal for painting with the large windows facing north with drapes that could be opened when the sun was in the correct position. And, she loved that, from time to time, she could hear the lovely music coming from Phoebe's studio. Just imaging the dancers, gliding across the wooden floor, ever so gracefully often gave her motivation to keep on painting.

Darcy sat down at her vanity and picked up her hairbrush. As she examined herself in the mirror, she thought that perhaps it was time to get her hair cut. She pulled the chestnut tresses away from her neck, trying to see how she would look with one of those perky short cuts that so many of the women were sporting nowadays. Darcy was a slave to taking care of her skin. Her face showed little signs of aging, and she attributed this to her nightly skin routine that involved several different products that had been advertised as revolutionary. Of all her facial features, she was most satisfied with her lips—full and needing hardly any lipstick at all. She felt that her cheeks were a bit too full, but then there was nothing she could do about that. She only hoped that her date would find her appealing.

While Darcy was a big-city girl, she hadn't been sure that she would like living in the middle of nowhere. But, much to her amazement, getting used to a quieter lifestyle had been easier than she had expected. And, to her complete surprise, she always had a backlog of students waiting to get into her art classes. To satisfy her longing for urban life, Darcy would occasionally drive into Pittsburgh for a day or two so she could shop till she dropped—never missing a good shoe sale. And, of course, she could party until dawn in the many after-hours clubs. Although she had invited Amanda to go with her countless times, Amanda always had one excuse or another so she eventually stopped asking her. One time, however, Amanda had agreed to go along on one of Darcy's trips to several art galleries. Amanda was eager to learn more about the art world and Darcy was flattered to be her teacher.

Still, Darcy longed for male company—so she had turned to the Internet. Tonight she was going to meet her first contact—Kevin. She hadn't said a word to Amanda because she didn't want to hear a lecture from her about the terrible things that could happen by going out with someone she had never met in person. Darcy could handle herself. While she was the first to agree that she wasn't a beauty like Amanda, Darcy felt that she was just a cut above average. But admittedly she was nervous. Suppose Kevin didn't look anything like the picture he had posted on Facebook? Perhaps he was just too good-looking for her. Maybe she was setting her hopes too high—just maybe.

Stretching her arm out, she pulled her class roster off her dresser and onto her lap. She would be doing quite well this semester—four full classes and one small group involved in painting nudes. She really enjoyed teaching art. She found great joy in encouraging fledging students to appreciate their talents and their techniques. Someone once told her that she was a genius at criticism since students seemed very willing to take the time to understand a certain method before they applied it. Teaching students how to handle and apply different brush strokes was always a pleasure. It never took her long to discover intricate details about each student and she used that knowledge to gain their trust. Lively discussions about shape, form, color, value and line often took place as teacher and students squatted on the floor examining prints of famous paintings. And, once a semester, the group would travel to one or more art museums where these discussions sometimes involved some heavy but friendly arguments.

Once more she checked the clock—now it was time to get ready. Slipping into her best little black dress, she began turning around and around in front of her full-length mirror. *Not bad for a woman of thirty.* The shoes—which shoes should she wear? She had no idea how tall Kevin was and she certainly didn't want to tower over him. Checking her vast supply of dress shoes, she tossed aside the ones with four-inch heels, finally settling on the sexy, black patent leather three-inch heels that were fairly comfortable. Since Kevin was meeting her at the *Diamond Club,* a few miles north of Pittsburgh, she wanted to be able to dance the night away with her handsome stranger. Or, perhaps she should wear boots. She finally decided on the boots but she would take her heels along to change.

As she was rummaging through her jewelry boxes, looking for just the right pair of earrings, the phone rang. Stretching across her bed to the nightstand she picked up the phone. "Hello."

"Darcy, this is Kevin."

Flustered, Darcy said, "Oh, oh, Kevin, hello."

"I hate to tell you this, but I can't make it tonight. Something has come up. I would have called you sooner, but I was trying to rearrange things so that I could at least meet you."

Darcy thought her heart had stopped beating. She didn't know what to say.

"Darcy—Darcy—are you there? I'm really sorry but I'll make it up to you later. But not now, I must run. I'll call you over the weekend." And, with that, Kevin hung up.

Darcy sat for some time with the phone still clutched in her hand. She was barely breathing. Then gently, as if she didn't want to hurt Kevin, she laid the phone down. Her mind was telling her that Kevin probably had some type of emergency, but that didn't ease the pain she felt in her heart. She had to face it—she had been stood up once again. Slowly, she began to undress.

Stark naked, she stood in front of her mirror. She felt as if she did not know the woman looking back at her. All she saw was a pathetic loser who couldn't even get a date. She just knew that she would never hear from Kevin again. Suddenly, she slumped to the floor and began weeping.

Darcy was startled when she heard the door bell ringing. Throwing her old satin robe over her body, she staggered to the door and looked through the peep-hole. She spied a familiar face but she didn't want any company—not tonight—maybe not ever. She simply ignored the bell and crawled into bed.

The Jeweler

Russell Weber was rearranging the supplies in his studio in order to accommodate an influx of students for the upcoming semester. He wanted to offer his students a more functional space to create their jewelry. When he had first begun teaching jewelry-making at The Haven, he had considered himself lucky if there were at least six students in each of his three classes. Now, apparently in response to Amanda's latest brochure, there would be twelve students in each class.

While hand-crafted jewelry had been made with the same tools for decades, Russ also wanted to introduce some new implements to his students that would improve the professional look of their finished products. The finer institutions teaching jewelry-making, such as GEA (Gemology Institute of America, were now making very expensive equipment available to their students; so Russ wanted to provide his students at The Haven with an opportunity to develop the skills needed to be competitive in the jewel-making profession. Russ' students were becoming quite proficient in making jewelry using sterling silver or brass. Since these materials were more economical than gold, they could experiment not only with the materials, but also with their artistic designs.

Russ then turned his attention to checking the engraving tools and the riveting and soldering systems. Since his first class would start their jewelry-making career making birth-stone pendants, he doubled-checked his supply of beading wire and stamped blanks. While Russ wanted to allow his students to strive for the best, he had to keep his eye on the budget. So, to add a little excitement for his students, he was going to allow them to choose a birth-stone to design and create a pendant to be submitted in a contest. His good friend Julia Matthews, a retired teacher of jewelry making from the *Arts Institute,* would be the judge. And, the winning piece would be showcased in the reception area of The Haven. After the contest, the students could either keep their creations or put them on consignment in The Haven's gift shop.

Russ was a stickler for making sure that his students could not only create their own pieces, but develop the appropriate skills needed to repair all types of jewelry. He also believed that there was no better way to teach neophytes how to make lasting jewelry than to have them examine broken pieces. Every time a student repaired an item, they had to determine whether the repair was necessary because of faulty construction or careless handling by the owner—creating some interesting dialogs among the students.

Russ was experienced with creating pieces in gold filled but he worked primarily in 18-carat gold. Over a dozen shops on the east coast were only too happy to feature his very expensive pieces. In fact, the monies he made from these sales, along with his monthly retirement checks, allowed him to live quite comfortably. Julia had often reminded him that when he could no longer teach, he could apply for social security—something he vowed that he would never do. He just didn't need a lot of money and what was the use of banking it—who would he leave it to?

A confirmed bachelor, sixty-two-year-old Russ seldom dated. One time, however, he had taken Darcy to the county fair. While it had been fun, Darcy had made it quite clear that he was not her type—whatever that meant. But, from that time on, the two had developed a friendship that he treasured very much. He felt that Darcy was a bit quirky, but he delighted in her company. Surprisingly, he really never wanted more. He never had a sister to look after, so perhaps Darcy was filling that role for him. Whenever Julia would question him about Darcy, and asked if there were any romantic attachments, Russ would change the direction of their conversation. He loved the idea of having Julia wonder about Darcy and him. He was still in good health, and, if anyone asked him, quite good-looking, with two gregarious women in his life—one was definitely just a friend, the other was a friend with benefits. From time to time, Russ tried to analyze why these two ladies liked him so much. Perhaps it was his dapper silver moustache and beard that appealed to them. Or, possibly it was his surprisingly strong frame—no aches or pains in his joints like some of his buddies were experiencing. Or, as his mother had always insisted, perchance he was simply just irresistible. With this fleeting thought, Russ laughed and said out loud, *"Maybe Mom. Maybe I am."*

After he was satisfied that all was in place in his studio, he realized that he really didn't want to go home. Since it was early yet, maybe he would zip by Darcy's place and take her out for a drink. Darcy had seemed a bit depressed the past few days and this would give him an opportunity to make certain that she was alright.

The Needleworker
(The next day)

As Hannah made her way up the steps that led to the front door of The Haven, she had to tread carefully since her view was partially blocked by the height of the bundles that she was carrying. Placing her right arm over her prized possessions, she was trying to find the door handle by moving her left arm around in circles.

"Here, little lady, let me help you with that," Barclay said as he tried to take the woman's arm.

Startled, Hannah jumped. "Sir, I can handle these things if you get the front door for me," Hannah replied, not trying to hide her annoyance.

"Certainly, madam," Barclay responded as he held the door open.

"Thank you, sir. Now, if you move out of the way, I might be able to get to my classroom."

"Oh, are you one of our students?" Barclay asked.

"Heavens no—I'm the needlework instructor, Hannah King—and you are?" Hannah asked as she peered over the top of her glasses.

"I'm Barclay Henderson, the writing instructor. I just arrived yesterday. Really Miss King, I would be pleased to carry your items to your classroom. It's the least I can do for a lady."

Hannah blushed openly. "Well, if you insist," Hannah said as she handed her cumbersome load to Barclay. Hannah was a bit off kilter. She was usually uneasy around men and this one was no exception. Her auburn-colored hair was pulled back into a bun that was held in place by a tortoise-shell comb. It was obvious that she wasn't wearing any makeup, but her flawless skin provided a beautiful setting for dark brown eyes. While her nails were nicely manicured, they were minus any type of polish. She held her head erect and kept her back straight. As she lifted her flowered cotton skirt a bit to mount the staircase to the second floor, short leather boots were visible.

As they entered Hannah's classroom, she said, "Just put those things on the center table please." Hannah paused for a second and then turned to face Barclay, "Mr. Henderson, please accept my apology for being so short with you earlier. I was a bit flustered since I didn't see you coming down the steps. I usually have better manners than that."

"It was my fault. I shouldn't have frightened you the way I did. I apologize for that. I must admit that I'm a bit rough at times, but I'm completely harmless—especially to lovely women." Barclay said as he smiled at Hannah.

They both jumped when one of Hannah's packages slid off the table. Several pieces of her crocheted work spilled out onto the wooden floor.

"Oh, Miss King, I'm so sorry. I'm just a clumsy ox," Barclay said as he hurried to pick up the items. "Wow, I haven't seen these for a long time. My grandma used to make doilies like these. She would put them on the arms of her parlor chairs so we little ones wouldn't get her beautiful furniture dirty. She also crocheted baskets that she would starch real, real stiff and then she would use them to hold flowers from her garden. You know what I mean?"

Hannah, now completely relaxed, said, "My, yes, I still have some of those baskets in my china closet at home. I used to weave colored ribbons through the openings on the lip of the baskets to add a bit of color."

"Miss King, did you make the quilt draped on that stand over there?"

"I surely did," Hannah said proudly. "My mother, bless her soul, taught me how to quilt when I was just a young girl. That pattern is called a star-crossed nine patch and I love it since it's so colorful. Next week I'll begin my first class on quilting. I'm anxious to pass my knowledge on to my young students. Maybe, Barclay, you could join the class," Hannah teased.

"You wouldn't want me in your class. I'm all thumbs and I have no patience at all," Barclay said as he headed toward the door. "Nice meeting you, Miss King. I'm glad to be your neighbor."

"Mr. Henderson," Hannah said softly. "Please call me Hannah."

Barclay stopped in his tracks. "I will, Hannah, if you agree to call me Barclay."

"That's a deal, Barclay." As Hannah watched the door close quietly behind Barclay, she was disturbed to feel so flustered. After all, a plain-looking fifty-year-old woman should be beyond such a state. But his blue eyes were fascinating. Heavens, what would her neighbors at home say?

CHAPTER 4

Amanda arrived at The Haven well ahead of her scheduled meeting to discuss the upcoming spring semester with the artists. As she unlocked the heavy oak front door, her eyes, once again, took in the beauty of the stained glass above the doorway that depicted the rising of the sun. Whenever she saw that lovely work of art, it always made her grateful to have another day to enjoy her most precious possession. Pushing the door open with her foot, Amanda put her briefcase down on the parquet floor and took a few moments to drink in all the beauty of the lovely reception area.

"Good morning, Fifi," Amanda said to the large bronze statue. Fifi represented the glamorous age when the reception area and the salon had been designed by the famous architect and furniture designer, Le Corbusier, in the 1920s. One could sense the presence of the heyday of interior design and the influence that the silver screen had had on the planning and the creating that went into choosing the pieces of furniture that were placed strategically around the Grand Salon. No sets of furniture for this treasured room; only single pieces—each seemingly making a statement of its own. The sun was peeping through the windows and little beams of sunshine seemed to be fighting for a place to rest on the huge geometric-patterned circular rug that served as the centerpiece of the Grand Salon.

In the far corner, where an inglenook fireplace had once stood, was a shiny silver cocktail cabinet that now held the tea set that the previous owner of the home, Mrs. Nesbit, had given to Amanda so many years ago. Amanda smiled broadly as she remembered how Mrs. Nesbit had taught her how a lady should hold a tea cup, all the while keeping her little finger crooked at just the right angle.

One wall of the Grand Salon was paneled in oak. However, several ornate mirrors had been interspersed between the panels, giving off an unexpected glow throughout the expansive room. The walls on either side of the doorway were tiled, offsetting the darkness of the wood perfectly. Art deco pieces were featured on the tables, enhancing a feeling of sophistication. Some people might think the room was over-the-top. Amanda, however, cherished and treasured each item as she allowed her eyes to travel from one piece to another—loving each one more than ever before.

Mrs. Nesbit had once told Amanda that the salon had been a gift from her beloved husband, Marvin. He had been a wealthy land baron who had owned many properties all over Pennsylvania. While her husband had lost a great deal of his fortune when the stock market crashed in the late 20s, he had been able to hang on to the Christmas tree farm and the surrounding hillside. And now, with the money Amanda had received from a lawsuit regarding the tragic death of her mother who had been killed by a drunk driver, she was the rightful owner of the place she had come to love. *I might not be a land baron, but I certainly feel like one.* However, there were still times when her mind would slip back—to that time of darkness—and that bastard who had used her and took her innocence away. She shivered. Opening her eyes, she said softly, "No, Ayden Ash, I will not let you in my mind again. You took enough away from me."

The sounds of car doors slamming shut startled Amanda and she hurried to the front door to greet her staff. Darcy, Phoebe, Russ, and Hannah all came trudging up the steps, each carrying packages and bags.

"Well, it certainly looks like all of you are ready for your students. May I help you with anything?" Amanda asked.

"Nah," Russ said. "I offered to be the donkey, but these women are too independent."

"Oh, Russ, you know you're too old to carry all of these things," Darcy teased.

"Look here, you Mona Lisa painter, I'm in better shape than all of you put together," Russ responded. "Why women all over the world would be happy to have me carry their things."

"Morning, Fifi," Hannah said as she passed by the bronze figurine.

"How about that," Russ said. "She pays more attention to that statue than she does to a handsome, debonair man like myself."

Just then Barclay stepped into the salon. "Barclay, welcome," Amanda said.

After all the introductions were made, Amanda said, "Folks, let's go into the sunroom to hold our meeting. It's such an unusually warm, winter day and I'd like to take advantage of it by basking in the sunlight."

"Mr. Henderson, I mean Barclay," Hannah said, "the other day I picked up a copy of one of your books at the library—a bit racy for me but I really loved the plot."

"Why, thank you, Hannah," Barclay replied.

"Barclay, why don't you share some of your background with these folks?" Amanda encouraged.

"Not too much to tell. I worked at various things—and that's putting it loosely—but I always wanted to write. Took some classes here and there. I was married. No longer though. Now divorced. No children. And, as far as books are concerned, I have published just a few, but I hope to add to that number shortly."

"Barclay, would you put copies of your books in the library case in the salon? That way we could take turns reading them and that could probably lead to some lively discussions," Amanda asked.

"I'd be honored to do that. No guarantees though on whether or not you will like them," Barclay chuckled as he winked at Hannah.

"Ok, folks, let's get down to business," Amanda said. "Before I forget, I must remind all of you that smoking is not permitted on the grounds of The Haven. This may be a hardship for you, Barclay, but we are concerned about the possibility of fire in such an old house. Now for some exciting news—there is a possibility that we will host some weddings on our grounds. I spoke with Liz Becker—by the way, Barclay, she operates a bridal shop downtown—and she thinks that it's a great idea and has agreed to help. However, I don't think we could do anything like that until at least early May or June since there will be some additional work needed on the front terrace. What do you think?"

Darcy was the first to respond. "Good idea, Amanda, But in the meantime we could do smaller weddings right in the salon. I'm certain the atmosphere would really attract the younger more hip couples."

"Why didn't we think of that sooner?" Phoebe asked. "Any bride would be pleased to be married in The Haven no matter what time of year."

"All right then. I'll get busy with that but I'll keep you updated and I certainly encourage your ideas and suggestions. Now, I want to develop a new brochure about our classes and this time I would like to include your pictures. In addition, I want to include a registration form. I think it could help us increase our enrollment. Since a brochure goes in every shopping bag in the gift shop, we may also want to include a questionnaire regarding classes that customers would like us to offer."

"Hey, when the ladies see a picture of me you may be swamped with applications," Russ, said as he laughed loudly. "But, seriously, Amanda, that's a splendid idea."

"They just might run the other way," Darcy said.

"It's also important that you check your classrooms and work areas carefully for anything that may need repair. I looked around your classrooms, but only briefly. I didn't disturb your closets and cabinets. Yesterday, I hired a new handyman to do odd jobs around the buildings and grounds—Homer Hoover is his name. Homer will also be working with Jason to take care of the Christmas trees. I need to warn you, Barclay, things get fairly noisy around here when Jason begins to prepare the trees for the holiday season. When the trucks begin to arrive, you'll need to be careful coming up the driveway."

"I love it when I hear those saws because I know that Santa is just around the corner," Russ said.

"You still believe in Santa, Russ?" Hannah teased.

"I sure do. And, I also believe in the tooth fairy. They make my world a much happier place."

"Homer would like each of you to make a list of any repairs that your classrooms may need, but please give them to me first so I can be sure that our budget can accommodate the updates or changes you would like."

"How did you find this Homer guy, Amanda?" Russ asked.

"Well, he just came trudging up the path in the snow looking for work one day. We had a long discussion and he told me that he was planning on renting a room and would be buying a truck before too long."

"You really should have checked his background first," Hannah said. "A single woman like you can't be too careful these days."

"Oh, I think he's fine. He doesn't have any family so I hope that you'll make him feel welcome. I really believe that he'll be one of us before too long," Amanda said.

"Maybe he's one of those secret millionaires from that television show. They seem to be popping up all over the place," Darcy added.

"Well, that's one thing that can't be said about me," Barclay said as he laughed. "Amanda, you mentioned a Jason. Who is he?"

"Oh, I'm sorry, Barclay. Jason is the overseer of the tree farm. He and his family run a carpentry shop just outside of town. Jason is a loner—he simply doesn't like to mingle with others. He is kind, considerate and knows all about trees. And, even though he is a part-time worker, he's very protective of the farm. He doesn't put up with any nonsense when it comes to the trees. Any more questions? No? I guess that's all for now," Amanda said. "If you need me for anything I'll be at my cottage."

"Wait," Russ said. "Since you now have a full time handyman, Amanda, don't you think it would be a good time to take that closet in the reception area and convert it into an office for you? After all, with the ever-increasing enrollment, you really should have a formal place where you can meet with people. At the rate that we're growing, you need to move your files out of your cottage and look ahead to when you will probably need a secretary."

"Secretary? I haven't given that a thought but an office is a great idea. I'll talk with Homer about that today. Thanks, Russ. Okay, everyone, I'll see all of you later."

Phoebe hung back as the others scurried to their classrooms. "Amanda, I need to talk to you about your idea of taking our pictures for the brochure," she said very quietly.

"Would that be a problem for you, Phoebe?"

Phoebe paced a bit and then turned to Amanda. "Yes. I need to keep my location a secret. I have reasons, Amanda. I'm not a wanted criminal, or anything like that, but there is someone who could harm me if he knew where I am."

Amanda put her arms around the trembling woman. "Phoebe, you needn't tell me more. I know what it's like to be afraid of someone. I won't take your picture. I promise."

"You could take a picture of me in one of my costumes—just so it isn't a full frontal of my face. I could have my head bent down. What do you think?"

"That's a great idea. Now don't you worry any more about it," Amanda said as she kissed the lovely dancer on her cheek.

Phoebe gave Amanda a hug and hurried down the hall.

As Amanda passed Fifi on her way out the door, she said, "What do you think, Fifi? I actually saw terror in her eyes. We must make certain that we protect her."

CHAPTER 5

Around dawn the skies grew darker than Amanda had ever seen them. Just a little while ago, when she had first looked out the window, it had been snowing but now heavy rain, accompanied by thunder and lightning, was pounding on the roof of her little cottage. Trying to ease her apprehension, Amanda, still dressed in her pajamas and robe, was curled up on the sofa with her nose in a detective novel. After a few minutes, she decided that she needed a snack, so she made herself a cup of hot chocolate and popped two pieces of bread in the toaster. Hannah had given her some home-made strawberry jam that was scrumptious and she thought that would be the perfect topping. She was lonely. Quentin was on a business trip and, like a silly schoolgirl, she missed her steady date. Is that what he was, a date? No, he had come to mean much more to her. She had finally accepted the fact that for the first time in many years, she was in love.

Just then the thunder grew louder, and when the lightning lit up her kitchen, she ran into the living room and pulled the drapes open. She went through this all the time during bad storms—terrified that her tree farm could be in danger. It seemed as though the lightning was everywhere at once. She hung on to the side of the drapes as though they could provide a shield between her and the violence of the storm. As the noise dissipated, her heartbeat returned to normal. But when the doorbell chimed, she almost jumped through the ceiling. Trembling, she neared the door, unsure whether or not she should open it. But then she realized that whoever it was needed a haven from the storm and that's what she must provide. She opened the door to find a small-statured woman, holding a toddler in her arms, standing there drenched and silent. The look on the woman's face seemed to say it all—complete and utter terror. Amanda felt that she should know this woman—but was at a loss to identify the rain-soaked woman and child.

"Come in—come in, my dear," Amanda said. "Here, let me take the child."

When the woman handed the child to Amanda, she dropped a small valise near the fireplace.

"I'm sorry. I'm sorry," the woman kept saying, as she watched the water run down her trench coat and onto the floor.

"Wait right here while I get some dry clothes and a blanket," Amanda said as she scurried to the closet. "I'll get the child undressed while you take your things off. Just put that bathrobe on and, oh, here are slippers, too. My Lord, child, you're soaked through and through." Amanda said. "Precious—look the baby fell asleep. How did you get here?"

"I got off a bus and the lady at the bake shop got one of her customers to bring me here."

"I feel that I should know you, but child, what can I do for you?" Amanda asked.

"When you know who I am, you may not want me here," the frightened woman said. "I'm Ana, the wife of Adam Ash, Ayden Ash's son."

As she heard his name spoken out loud, the past came flooding back as if it had just happened yesterday. Amanda could almost feel his touch. She could even see the sneer on his face when he violated her, all in the name of the Lord. Amanda drew her breath in. She put her hands over her mouth, not wanting to believe what she had just heard. She was trying to regain her composure when Ana fell in a heap onto the floor crying uncontrollably. Amanda jumped into action. Knelling beside the woman, Amanda said gently, "Ana, how can I help you?" as she cradled the sobbing woman in her arms. "Now, now, no need to cry. You have indeed found a haven."

Amanda rocked Ana back and forth, trying to comfort her by giving her a sense that she was safe. Amanda knew a great deal about the gnawing feeling of not being safe—not having anyone to love her.

When Ana was calm, she looked at Amanda and said, "I had to get away. I tried to be a good wife, but when the molestation began—when I became aware that he was doing the things that my dad had warned me about—I could no longer stay and let the same thing happen to my little Jennie. I didn't know where to go."

"What about your parents, Ana? I know your dad, and he's a fine man," Amanda said.

"They're both gone. My mom died three years ago of an aneurysm. My dad was never the same after that. He was covering the annual harvest festival for the newspaper when he had a massive heart attack. I honestly believe that he really died of a broken heart."

"Oh, my poor child. How terrible," Amanda said as she managed to get Ana off the floor and beside the sleeping child. "How did you ever manage to find me?"

"One day, when I was rummaging through Adams' desk, I found an old address book that had belonged to Ayden, his father. Your name was circled and it was marked *Our Haven*. Ayden also had a letter attached that you sent to him stating that he and his flock could come to live at The Haven. I quickly memorized the address when I heard Adam coming up the stairs."

"I wrote that letter trying to get Ayden to come to The Haven. I hate to admit this Ana, but at that time my stepfather and I had planned to do away with him. But, it was your father who brought us back to our senses."

"My husband has no idea where I am. You see, before I ran away with Jennie, I left a receipt for a bus ticket to Chicago lying on the floor. I'll understand if you want me to leave your home. I put myself in this position by not listening to my parents' advice. I thought that I was in love with Adam—but I was only in love with love. I don't have any money. Adam diverted my inheritance money, telling me that I was too scattered-brained to understand finances."

"Ana, dear Ana, of course I want you to stay. It appears that we were both victims of Ayden. So, we can use that connection in a positive way. Let's see where this goes—you, Jennie, and me."

CHAPTER 6

As Barclay entered the small brightly-lit Sweetbriar Public Library, he was pleased to see a row of computers lined up on the far wall. He spotted reproductions of famous paintings, all in matching black wooden frames, positioned neatly above the computer work stations. A small conversation area, in the center of the room, held several over-stuffed, olive green chairs that circled a bronze statue. He wasn't surprised when he saw that the statue was in honor of Frank Lloyd Wright since one of his most famous designs, Fallingwater, was just a fifteen minute drive from the center of town. While Barclay knew little about the famous architect, he was aware that Wright had been dedicated to producing buildings that would blend in with the natural environment. He made a mental note to put a visit to Fallingwater on his list of things to do.

Just then, a woman approached him. "Hello," she said in a voice as soft as velvet.

When Barclay looked up, he found himself looking into the most beautiful lilac eyes and longest eyelashes he had ever seen. She appeared to be in her late fifties or early sixties and her smile was warm and friendly.

"I don't believe that we've ever met. I'm Priscilla Davis, the librarian. Is this your first visit to our library?"

"Yes, it is," Barclay said as he shook Priscilla's hand. "My name is Barclay Henderson. I was just admiring the statue of Wright. Was it done by a local artist?"

"No. Our library angel, Quentin Toth, commissioned a gentleman from New York to create the statue. We're extremely proud of it. We have an extensive collection on Wright. In fact, the small room to the left is dedicated entirely to him. You'll also find several of his important blue prints on display there, including the ones for Fallingwater."

Barclay chuckled. "You have a library angel? How nice."

"Indeed, we do. Quentin was an executive with MGM in Hollywood for many years before he retired. He's been living in Sweetbriar for, oh, maybe two or three years, and he has been very good to us. He also provides scholarships for people who want to take classes at The Haven. He's such a giving person. Mr. Henderson, are you just passing through?"

"No, I've just moved here. I'll be teaching at The Haven."

"How nice. Amanda is such a lovely woman, don't you think? And, Quentin and Amanda are very good friends," she said with a little nod of her head. "You'll love The Haven; it has done such wonders for Sweetbriar. And, may I ask, what is your craft?"

"I'll be teaching creative writing."

"Wonderful—have you been published?"

"Yes, but my body of work is small. My most recent book, *After the Divorce: Now What?* is a self-published book. But, before that, I published two novels through Anderson Press. I must confess, however, that they didn't hit the best sellers list."

"Henderson? Why I think we may have your books here," Priscilla said excitedly, as she hurried to one of the computers. After tapping a few keys, she said, "I was right—here you are—*Danger in the Dark* and *A Touch of Murder.*"

"I'm impressed, Miss Davis," Barclay said. "You have good taste in purchasing books," Barclay teased.

"I have a great idea—I'd love to feature your books on the marble table by the front door. Oh, and perhaps, if you would agree, we could have you here for a reading and signing. Would you want to do that? Please say that you will," Priscilla begged.

That soft velvety voice of Priscilla pierced Barclay's heart and, although he had promised himself that he would never do another reading, he found himself unable to refuse her request. "I'm not too sure that anyone will show up, but I'll be happy to do that for you," he replied. Her smile was all the payment he needed to let him know that he had done the right thing.

Priscilla jumped up and grabbed Barclay's hand and shook it again. "Oh, that's wonderful and so gracious of you, Mr. Henderson. Our literary club will be delighted to know that you're living here in our little town,"

Priscilla said as she nervously paged through her appointment book. "How about the first Saturday next month—let's say at two?"

Barclay pulled his phone out of his shirt pocket and turned to his calendar. "Yes, that will be fine. I am free that day." He knew perfectly well that he would be available almost any day, but he didn't want to burst Priscilla's balloon.

"I'll get on the phone and order some extra copies of your books and then we can have a signing. Oh, I'm so excited about this—I can't wait until I tell the library board that you'll be making a presentation. Oh, my, I forgot, Mr. Henderson, I didn't ask you what your fee will be," Priscilla said as she tried to regain her composure.

Barclay chuckled again. "No fee—not for neighbors."

"How generous of you—what about your self-published book? How can I get copies of that one?" Priscilla asked as she grabbed a pad and pen to take the information down.

"I'll bring some of them along with me. But, are you sure that your patrons would be interested in a book about the aftermath of divorce?" Barclay teased.

"Mr. Henderson…"

"Please call me Barclay."

"Alright. Barclay, we may be a small town, but believe me, we have some of the same social problems that exist in big cities. Personally, I know of at least four people who have divorced recently."

"Well, that might mean we may have at least four customers," Barclay replied, smiling ear-to-ear. "Now, I would like to become a member of your library, Priscilla," Barclay said as he leaned against the check-out counter.

"Oh, dear, I've become so flustered that I forgot one of my most important duties," Priscilla said as she handed him a small index card. "Just fill this out and I'll process your card immediately. All of our work is now computerized—just like our big city neighbors.'

After Barclay completed the form, he handed it back to Priscilla. Barclay was impressed with the gregarious librarian. While Barclay had not met the library angel, he knew that Pricilla's presence probably had charmed him, too.

"Now," Priscilla said a she handed him a small yellow card, "you're formally one of us."

As Barclay left the library with his new library card clutched in his hand, he began to have regrets about agreeing to do a book signing. He hated these kind of things in the big city, but surely, here in Sweetbriar, things would be more laid-back. Besides, who could ever say no to someone as charismatic as Priscilla?

CHAPTER 7

Amanda and Ana were seated at the breakfast table having a great time with little Jennie who was propped up in a high chair. They giggled as the child stuffed Cheerios in her mouth. It had only been two weeks since Amanda had found two people who looked like drowned rats at her front door, but now it seemed so natural having them in the spare bedroom.

"I can't wait until Quentin meets the two of you. He'll love you as much as I do," Amanda said as she put a few more Cheerios on Jennie's tray.

"Is he your sweetheart?" Ana asked.

"Well, he's my only beau so perhaps he is," Amanda said. "But I need to caution you about one thing, Ana. You might know the whole story involving your father-in-law, Ayden Ash, but I haven't told Quentin yet. I just haven't found the right time and I really don't know why. Perhaps it's fear—fear that he may think less of me then."

"Amanda, you were only a young girl when that all happened. No one blames you at all. But I too was blind. So blind that I didn't see that my husband was turning into a carbon copy of his father. You need to have faith in your Quentin. You're a marvelous, kind woman with a heart of gold. What more could anyone ask for?"

"Thank you, Ana. You and I are two wounded souls. Perhaps we can help heal one another. Now I must run over to The Haven. I want to spread the word about Barclay's reading at the library. I want you to come, too. The Ladies Library Society will have a nursery for little ones so Jennie will be well taken care of. I'll see the two of you by lunch time," Amanda said as she kissed Jennie on the cheek.

As Amanda was approaching The Haven, Homer was coming out the front door, carrying a tool box in one hand and a short ladder in the other. His baseball cap was pulled down over his forehead, and he almost bumped into Amanda as he came trudging down the steps, leading to the circular walkway.

"Oh, excuse me, Miss Amanda, I didn't see you a-coming. Sorry," Homer said as he pushed his cap up a little higher on his forehead. "I finished the work in Mr. Russ's room and tomorrow, since it's Sunday, and no one will be here, I'll do the closet in Miss Phoebe's dance studio, if that's okay with you."

"Certainly Homer. You're so prompt. We all appreciate your attention to details. I'm so glad I bumped into you. I want to invite you to go along with the rest of us to the library down town next month," she said as she began rummaging through her purse. "Here's your invitation."

"The liberry, ma'am? Why would you want me to go there? I ain't much of a reader. I'm a little slow in that area," Homer said rather sheepishly.

"It's going to be an exciting day, Homer. You see, Barclay will be doing a reading of some of his books. You'll enjoy it, Homer. It will give you a chance to mingle with the teachers in a different setting. The library is right on the main street—just a few steps away from the bakery. The staff will be so pleased to see you there."

"Oh, I don't know, Miss Amanda—I'm not educated like the rest of you. Will Jason be going, too?"

"No, Jason's very busy in his carpentry shop. But we'd really like to see you there. Homer, you have a gift that many people wish that they had. We haven't given you anything that you couldn't repair and make it look like new. Please, we all would like to have you there—please say that you will," Amanda coaxed.

"Well, for you, Miss Amanda, I'll be there. Should I wear a shirt and a tie?"

"No, that won't be necessary. Just a nice shirt and trousers will be fine. Oh, thank you, Homer. Barclay will also be pleased to see you there," Amanda said as she hurried up the steps. Turning around, Amanda shouted to Homer, "Thank you again, Homer. Oh, don't wear your work boots. The boots you wore the day we met will be fine."

As Amanda entered Phoebe's studio, she was surprised to see Barclay watching Phoebe dancing with her students. She moved closer to a red-faced Barclay and whispered in his ear, "I just want to tell you that all of us will be at your reading—even Homer."

With a surprised look on his face, Barclay turned to Amanda and smiled. "That's nice of them. I hope they won't be disappointed in me."

The two of them watched the dancers in silence. Phoebe finished her instruction and dismissed her students. Even in plain tights and a knit top, Phoebe reminded Amanda of a runway model—sleek, slim, and amazingly beautiful.

Phoebe gave Barclay a big smile and asked, "How did you interpret that little dance?"

"First, let me say that your students are very lucky to have you as their teacher. You are like a feather, gliding over the floor. I'm not sure, but I think some of the little girls were flowers, while one was the sun, and a few others represented rain."

Phoebe clapped her hands. "You got it—you got it, Barclay," she said, not bothering to hide her enthusiasm.

"You see, Amanda, I'm working on a book, and, I have a scene where this little girl goes to her dancing class so I asked Phoebe if I could look in on her practice today. For such young ones, her students are extremely graceful. I sometimes find it hard to put womanly motions into words, so, Phoebe, thanks so much," Barclay said as he stood up and began walking toward the door. Over his shoulder, he said, "Perhaps, Phoebe, later on you could help to critique my work."

Amanda became aware that Phoebe's eyes followed Barclay as he left the dance studio. "I'm glad to see that the two of you are getting along so well," Amanda said.

A flustered Phoebe sat down beside Amanda and seemed at a loss for words.

"Here's an invitation to Barclay's reading. I thought it would be nice if we all demonstrated our support for him."

After Phoebe read the invitation, she said, "You're always so thoughtful. You do so many nice things for us." As Phoebe ran her hands over the invitation she said, "I'll save my invitation for Barclay so he has a little memento from the event."

"I really encourage staff members to interact with the community since it strengthens the bond we already have. But I also wanted Barclay to know that we appreciate his talent and that we are here to support him in all his efforts. But, apparently, he already has your support," Amanda teased as she winked at the red-faced dancer.

As Amanda walked away, Phoebe began playing with the ring on her little finger. Touching it always brought back memories of her childhood. But, at the same time, it caused her to think about the lie she was living.

CHAPTER 8

Ray felt that he had exhausted all his leads in his efforts to find Florence. While he had had a few jobs--well-paying ones—during the past weeks, he was eager to get on with finding the ballerina and getting a very big pay day. It made him extremely nervous since he had no idea what Fat Tony might be up to. That dumb son-of-a-bitch could get himself involved in a heap of trouble that might bring unwanted attention to Ray. It wasn't often that Ray felt frustrated, but he certainly was now. He had searched the internet for hours on end, hoping that he would find the dancer. Once again he sat down at his computer and renewed his search. He was trying to broaden his digital search by casting a wider net since Florence could be anywhere by now. Turning his attention to what he could find outside the borders of the US, he was deeply involved in reading the screen when his phone rang. Annoyed that he was disturbed, he picked up the receiver and angrily said, "What do you want?"

"This is Abigail Ballard."

"Who?"

"Oh, I'm sorry, you probably have forgotten me by now. Abigail Ballard from the tree farm in Burlington, Vermont."

With that, Ray sat straight up in his chair as he clicked on his tape recorder. "Excuse me, Mrs. Ballard, I was deep in thought. I truly apologize for my gruff response to your call," Ray said, using all the charm he could muster over the wires.

"Don't you worry about that, young man, and it's me who owes you an apology," Mrs. Ballard said sweetly.

"An apology. For what, Mrs. Ballard? You were so very gracious to me when I visited you at your beautiful tree farm."

"You're such a polite young man. I have sad news and somewhat good news for you. Let's get the sad out of the way first. Well, it was right after you visited us that Florence's mother passed away. In fact, it was New Year's Eve. Later, Florence called me and asked if I would help her uncle make the arrangements for her mother. Of course, I agreed. You know, the good Lord put us here to take care of one another and that was the least I could do, don't you think?"

Ray rolled his eyes. "How like you, Mrs. Ballard. Kind and thoughtful. I know now that angels are among us," Ray replied.

"How nice of you to say that. Well, anyway, I did my best. I thought of you and I remembered that you told me that Florence was your sweetheart in college so I looked for the card you gave me. I just couldn't find it. I felt terrible. I looked and looked. You know how it is when you know you have something but you just can't find it. Then, yesterday I decided to re-read a favorite book of mine and there it was. I had used it for a bookmark."

Ray was wishing she would get to the heart of her message. "I lose things all the time, Mrs. Ballard. But you did find my name card. Now how can I help you?" Ray wished that the old bag would get to the point.

"Oh, I can help you. I know where Florence is."

Ray swore his heart skipped a beat. "Marvelous! I have had her on my mind all the time. You know how it is, Mrs. Ballard, when you are in love, that is, true love, that person is always with you no matter where you go."

"Ray, I wish there were more young men in the world like you. So many young people don't know what love truly is but you understand."

"You said you know where Florence is?" Ray asked as he anxiously awaited her reply.

"I sure do. She lives in a little town in Pennsylvania called Sweetbriar, and she teaches dance at a private school."

"Mrs. Ballard, I'm so grateful for this information. How can I ever repay you?"

"Just invite me to the wedding."

Ray leaned back in his chair with his hands behind his head. He couldn't believe that he was about to end his quest to find Florence. Quickly, he entered *Sweetbriar* into his computer and, in no time at all, found just what he needed. When he clicked on the home page for a school called *The Haven,* he was excited when he saw that one of the classes offered was dance specializing in ballet for children but the teacher's name was Phoebe Snowden. The pictures that accompanied the home page were impressive, but they all were of the buildings and the classrooms. There were no pictures of the teachers. Now he needed to develop a plan to get into the school to see if Florence was really there.

As he read a bit further, an idea struck him. He certainly couldn't sign up to take a children's ballet class, but he could register for an art class. While Ray had never tried his hand at painting or sketching, when he saw that the class was being taught by a woman, he knew that it would be the right course for him. Next, he had to choose an ID from the many he had created over the years. He decided on Roberto Pellagrino.

He got out his cell phone and contacted the school.

"The Haven, Amanda Murray speaking."

"Hello, Miss Murray. My name is Roberto Pellagrino. I currently live in Harrisburg, but I am planning on moving to the Sweetbriar area shortly. When I did some research on your little town, I discovered that your school is offering classes in art. Now, I must warn you, I have never tried to paint, but I have always longed to try my hand at something creative. I may not be able to attend every class since my government job keeps me on the road sometimes. Do you think I could benefit from taking lessons at your school?"

"Certainly. Our art instructor, Darcy Hamilton, is used to handling students who are on different ability levels. She would be happy to have you in one of her classes. I can fax you a registration form if you would like," Amanda offered. "Do you have any idea when you will be arriving in Sweetbriar?"

"Not for certain, but I'm aiming for this coming weekend. Tell you what—I'll email my personal information to you—phone-fax-email."

"Fine. Darcy and I will be looking forward to meeting you."

When Ray hung up, he said, "Sweet, sweet… I'll get into that school and it won't take me long to know if Florence is there or not. Now all I have to do is keep Fat Tony under wraps and out of trouble until I have those documents in my hands."

Now it's time to become Roberto Pellagrino one more time.

CHAPTER 9

Darcy felt the butterflies in her stomach. It happened every time that she thought about her new student, Roberto. He had joined her beginners' class last week and he seemed to have enjoyed the experience so far. She could drown in his eyes. When he smiled at her, she felt weak in the knees—almost as if she were going to faint. She had to get ahold of herself. There were ten other students in the same class who needed her guidance.

One by one, her students were arriving and getting their stations ready to continue their work. Darcy walked from one student to another, critiquing their work, answering questions, and offering suggestions on color and form. Then, out of the corner of her eye, she spotted him. As he removed his jacket, she could see that he was wearing a knitted shirt that fit his form as if it had been molded to his body. Trying to be as casual as possible, Darcy strolled over to Roberto's easel to welcome him.

"I see you're back," she said as she smiled at him. "I'm impressed with what you have accomplished so far. I like the way you positioned the objects in your painting. You have an unusual style—one that I really like."

"Why, thank you, teacher. Coming from you that is definitely a compliment," Ray said as he touched her arm ever so lightly. He looked around the room and then moved his easel over to the far end of the room.

Darcy gave the class a review on brush strokes, showing them how to maneuver the brush to get different effects. "It's all in how you see your painting—where and when you may want to use different strokes. On each of your easels I have placed a piece of canvas board for you to practice brush strokes. Take the time to practice before you try anything on your current art work. As she leaned in toward Roberto to point out a few details, she could feel his warm breath on her neck. Roberto seemed to move in even closer.

Just then Amanda walked into the studio. She greeted the students and spent some time looking at their work. Darcy felt nervous. She wasn't doing anything wrong, but she felt that Amanda might sense the electricity that seemed to flow back and forth between her and Roberto.

"Darcy, will we see you at the reading?" Amanda asked.

"Oh, yes, I wouldn't miss that," Darcy responded.

"Mr. Pellagrino, how are you enjoying your class?" Amanda asked.

"This class is better than I anticipated. Darcy is a terrific teacher. She even makes a terrible art student like me feel good about my work."

"Well, if your current painting is any indication of the type of work you can do, you will not be a beginner much longer. I'm pleased that you like the class, Mr. Pellagrino. I must run now. I'll see you on Saturday, Darcy," Amanda said as she left the studio.

"Something happening on Saturday?" Ray asked.

"Our writing instructor, Barclay Henderson, is giving a reading of some of his books at the local library."

"Sounds interesting, Can anyone attend?"

Darcy hesitated. "Would you like to go along?" Darcy asked hopefully.

"Yes, I would. Could I be your date?" Ray asked.

Darcy couldn't believe her ears. She swallowed hard and then said, "I'd really like that."

When the other students had left the studio, Roberto remained at his easel. Darcy was not sure what she should do next. She had had such bad luck with men the past few years. She was certain that something was wrong with her and, whatever it was, drove them away. She didn't want to make the same mistakes with Roberto.

Ray stood up and walked toward Darcy. "Did I make you feel uncomfortable by asking to go along to the reading?"

Darcy was speechless. Ray took her hand and lifted it to his mouth and kissed it. "Darcy, I'm hoping that you will let me in your life. If I have overstepped my boundaries, just tell me and I will go away." Ray took her other hand and pulled her close to him. "Should I just leave?"

Darcy lifted her head. "No, please don't go away."

Ray put his arms around Darcy and said, "Come here, you beautiful vixen."

As the two stood there, with their arms around one another, music began drifting out of Phoebe's dance studio, filling the air with the heavenly sounds of violins. Darcy could not remember ever feeling this way before. Their lips met.

CHAPTER 10

It was the day before the reading and Quentin Toth was filling time on his enclosed side porch with a crossword puzzle in hand. Every once in a while, he would lay the paper down and take a sip of coffee from his old brown mug—just about the only sentimental thing that he had brought with him from Los Angeles when he moved to Sweetbriar. He had grown to hate that crowded city and its urban problems as well as the rat race that always seemed to envelop the film industry. However, he had to admit that he missed his old friend, Steve Konopecki. The two of them had worked together on several properties and they were almost like twins in their thinking. He looked at Steve as his so-called 'heir-apparent'. But he also knew that Steve could get along very well without him—a little dent in Quentin's armor.

He kept checking his watch. It was much too early to call Amanda. He had gotten home too late last evening to call her. Now, his damned watch seemed not to be moving at all. He couldn't wait to see her. He kept thinking about the necklace he had purchased for her. He was anxious to see the expression on her face when she saw it. If that went well, then he planned to propose—a scary thought—he didn't know what he would do if she said *no*. Maybe the proposal should come first.

While he considered his trip a success, selling four of the buildings he had owned in LA, he begrudged the time that he had to spend away from Amanda. One of the smartest decisions he had ever made was to move to this wonderful part of Pennsylvania. Two years ago, on a trip to Fallingwater with his cousin, Quentin had discovered Sweetbriar, and immediately decided that it would be where he would spend his retirement years. While he was grateful that he had been so successful in a business where many were just one-production wonders, he longed for the peace and quiet that seemed to surround Sweetbriar—especially its little library. Almost as soon as the moving truck was empty, he had hurried downtown to get his library card and become an ordinary citizen.

The more he had learned about his new home town, the more dedicated he had become to helping the library address the literary needs of the community. It was only natural for him to create a special reading room in the library dedicated to Frank Lloyd Wright—a man he truly admired for his creativity. Since Fallingwater was only ten miles from Sweetbriar, he considered that area his home, too. He loved Fallingwater and the way that the stone and concrete home stretch out thirty feet over a waterfall created by Bear Run. Since the home was surrounded by moderately rugged terrain, integrating the home with the natural landscape, only added to the magic of Wright's creation. Quentin visited Fallingwater frequently, spending considerable time just roaming from room to room. But what he loved the most were the sounds of the water spilling over the rocks, generating a feeling that the home had been created by nature and not by man. While it was built in the late 30s, Quentin never tired of the feeling of exhilaration that he felt when he stood at the bottom of the hill and noticed that the heavens above became one with the home. While Fallingwater was located in the rural Laurel Highlands, the area had become an iconic playground for the very wealthy. At one time, elegant tailgating parties were all the rage. Now, there was a guest house on the property and a barn where elegant weddings were sometimes held. But the beauty and ingenious design of Fallingwater remained intact.

After he had commissioned the statue of Wright and had placed it in the library, Quentin began purchasing documents and artifacts related to the famous architect and these too were placed there. As a result, he was appointed to the Frank Lloyd Wright Board, where he met people who were as fascinated with the man as he was. While Quentin received some recognition for doing this, he no longer needed to be acknowledged by others—he had had enough of that in the film business. Now, he could just be himself. He no longer had to compete for stardom.

To make his adopted town even sweeter, he had found Amanda. When the librarian had mentioned that there was a bronze statue at The Haven, he decided to take a look. And, as soon as Amanda opened the door, he was smitten. The two had been dating for almost a year now, and he was ready to take their relationship to the next level. Just thinking about asking Amanda to marry him made him nervous. His friends in LA would laugh at him—the tough, successful director afraid of a woman. Here he was, at the age of sixty-two, financially secure—head over heels in love with a self-directed woman. He knew that Amanda had purchased the tree farm, along with what was now known as The Haven, years ago. But he couldn't shake the feeling that there was something in Amanda's past that she was not willing to share with him. She didn't realize that no matter what had happened, he would love her. If Quentin only knew what it was, perhaps he could help her—he *knew* that he could.

Just a month ago, he had spent significant time at the tree farm, observing the harvesting of trees purchased by a landscaper. He was amazed how Amanda took charge and made certain that the work was being done properly. She knew exactly what had to happen and how each step needed to be completed. As the men were getting the first trees ready to be shipped to New York, Homer was keeping track of the number of bundles being loaded onto the truck bed. Amanda was directing the men, who were harvesting the trees and dragging them to the bailer. While she was dressed in jeans and a plaid jacket, with her blonde waves tucked under a cap, Quentin had never seen Amanda so irresistible. Would he ever be able to lure her away from the tree farm? Would she even want to be Mrs. Quentin Toth? Maybe she would think he was too old for her.

After noticing that he had let his coffee get cold, he got up and entered the house and sat down at his desk. He began shuffling through paperwork. Perhaps the time might go a bit faster. He glanced around the room, trying to picture Amanda here with him. He knew every inch of his home since he had had it built from the ground up, sort of the way Edward Kaufmann did with Fallingwater, but on a more unassuming level. His home might be considered modest using LA standards, but it was big enough for him for it truly reflected his taste—plain, functional, and modest. However, it was not as glamorous as Amanda's Haven. The little cottage where she actually lived was more to his taste and surprisingly void of girly decorations. He wasn't certain that Amanda liked his home enough to leave the tree farm behind her if they married. What he did know was that whatever she wanted, he would give her.

Finally, it was seven. He reached for his cell phone and pressed number one—Amanda's number.

"I have a surprise for you, Amanda," he said as he felt for the necklace box in his jacket pocket.

"That's funny—I have one for you, too," she laughed. "Or, perhaps I should say that I have two surprises for you!"

Quentin wasted no time, running down the steps and getting in his car. He was willing to do anything to please Amanda. The world of dog-eat-dog was far behind him. No more worries over trophies and awards. All of that now seemed unimportant. He had found the one thing that had always been missing in his life—a reason for living—and her name was Amanda.

As Quentin walked up the flagstone pathway, he was surprised when the front door of Amanda's cottage opened to reveal her holding a small child. "Is this the surprise you have for me, Amanda? If it is, she's certainly a cute one."

"Quentin, this is Jennie. Come on in and meet her mother," Amanda replied.

Ana stood behind Amanda, bashfully peering over her shoulder.

"Quentin, this young lady is Ana. Jennie and she will be staying here at the cottage until we can find a more suitable place for them to live."

Just then the doorbell rang. "Oh, that must be Hannah. She's taking my guests to the mall to get a few things for Jennie. Ana, wrap Jennie in this shawl until you get to the store. Her little coat doesn't fit any more," Amanda said as she handed Ana an envelope.

"Amanda, I can't let you do this for us," Ana said.

"The baby needs clothing. Get what she needs. We'll work out the details later," Amanda said as she guided Ana to the door.

As Ana headed out the door, wearing one of Amanda's coats, Amanda pulled Hannah aside and whispered, "Make sure that Ana gets all the things she needs for the baby. Ana needs underwear, too. There should be enough cash in that envelope to cover everything."

"Homer's driving us to the mall since he thinks it may start to snow. That is, if he has your permission to do so," Hannah said with a little smile on her face.

"That's a splendid idea, Hannah."

When they were alone, Amanda said, "Quentin, I spoke with Ana last evening and discovered that both her parents are deceased. I hated to talk to her about money, but I wanted to know whether or not she has support for herself and Jennie. And, it turns out that she does—a hefty sum. She inherited money from both parents. But her husband took control of the funds, and she has no access to any of that money now. Is there any way we can help her without letting her husband know where she is now?"

"Of course. I'm certain my attorney can help. Let me speak with him before we say anything to Ana. While this situation is a bit complex, Ana has every right to that money. I'll call him this afternoon. Now Amanda, I want to talk with you," Quentin said as he took her hand. "While I was away I did some thinking about us."

Amanda hesitated. "Oh, this doesn't sound very good," she said as she sat down on the sofa.

"Look, Amanda, you probably already know this: I love you. I have since the day we met—when I came to The Haven to look at the famous Fifi. I have never felt this way about any woman. I feel like a young man all over again whenever you are around," Quentin said as he slid to the floor, and on bended knee, he said, "Amanda, my darling, will you marry me? Or, am I too old?"

Amanda was quiet. Stillness pierced Quentin's heart and his nervousness grew stronger. As tears began rolling down Amanda's face, Quentin got off the floor and took Amanda in his arms. "I'm sorry if I made you cry. What's wrong, darling? We can fix anything. Does it have anything to do with Ana and the baby?"

Amanda said, "I'll be back. I need to show you something." As she reentered the living room, she said, "I should have shared this with you long ago, Quentin. Please read the clippings in this box and then we'll talk."

Quentin reached for the box. As he did as she had requested, Amanda could not take her eyes off him. A million thoughts were running through her mind. Would he still love her after he knew about her connection with Ayden Ash? It was so long ago. Memories should have faded by now, but the recurring dreams and the arrival of Ana indicated that they still lay underneath the surface. From the time that she began attending that damned church school, through the molestation, and then the death of her baby, she relived the horrors again and again. The silence was deafening. After what seemed to be hours, Quentin snapped the lid back on the box, laid it on the floor, and then turned to Amanda.

"My precious. How sorry I am that you had to experience such an invasion of your childhood."

"Quentin, Quentin, I wanted to tell you so many times but I was afraid and ashamed. There's more."

"We can leave the rest for another time."

"No, I must do this now. After the trial was over, my stepfather took the job as manager of this tree farm. The property belonged to Mrs. Nesbit who was my saving grace. She took me under her wing and taught me how to be a lady. I used to think that she didn't know anything about my past, but she knew all of it and loved me anyway. She even taught me how to hold my tea cup, she taught me how a lady enters a room, but most of all she loved me. I found a haven here. I felt protected. I learned to smile again."

"And how does Ana relate to what happened to you?"

"When Ayden Ash's trial for molestation was taking place, there was a reporter who relentlessly covered the story. His name was Pete Forster. Well, Ayden had assumed that he was a friend, but when Pete wrote damning articles about him, Ayden swore that he would get revenge on him. Ironically, about twenty years later, Ash's son married Pete's daughter—Ana. She was young and in love. It took some time for her to realize that the son was a carbon copy of the father. She's a victim, too. See, Ayden's been dead for a long time, but he's still wielding his power of abuse."

"Amanda, listen to me. No, don't look away. Ayden is dead. He cannot hurt you any longer unless you allow him to control you. I love you with all my heart. Now, I am going to ask you again, will you marry me?"

Amanda smiled. "Yes. I only have one request and that is that we will not tell anyone until we have Ana and Jennie situated. I don't want to put undue pressure on her right now."

"Anything you want, Amanda. As far as Ana and Jennie are concerned, with a little help from us, they'll start a new life—one with people who demonstrate love and respect. Now it's time for you and me. I brought you something from LA that I believe was created just for you."

Quentin fumbled with the box as he opened it with trembling hands. He held the necklace up to the light. Hanging on a lovely chain was a gold evergreen tree that was topped with a diamond.

"Oh, Quentin, how lovely," Amanda said as she clapped her hands together.

"Let me put it on you, darling,"

Amanda bowed her head, and even though he was nervous, Quentin managed to close the clasp. "Amanda, let me love you—let me take care of you. If God gives me ten years with you, I will die a happy man."

CHAPTER 11

It was an unusually warm day for March and Darcy was enormously excited about Barclay's reading today. She was seated beside Roberto in his red sports car, and they were on their way to Barclay's book signing event. As they rode along the highway, she kept stealing glances at her handsome date. His dark, black hair was sleeked back, revealing a high forehead that Darcy felt only made him even more handsome. She loved the way he would occasionally look her way and, each time their eyes met, Darcy's heart beat just a bit faster. She had to pinch herself several times to make certain that this was really happening. Telling herself that she should not read too much into this date, at the same time, she was already thinking about what the future might hold for the two of them. Darcy had not been lucky in love for a long time. Not wanting to believe that the lack of love was all her fault, since her suitors always seemed to run away, Darcy would look for their faults so that she could justify a break-up even before it happened.

"Darcy, so nice to see you," Amanda said as she greeted them at the door. "And Mr. Pellagrino, how nice to see you again. Quentin, this is Mr. Pellagrino…"

"Please, call me Roberto," Ray interrupted.

"Alright, Quentin, meet Roberto. He's one of our art students—and doing very well, I might add," Amanda said.

"Quentin Toth—nice meeting you," Quentin replied. "You're just in time for Barclay's reading. I understand he has chosen a few excerpts from his books. Amanda, I have a seat for you over there," Quentin said as he began to guide Amanda to the front row of folding chairs.

Ray was looking over the crowd. "Are all your fellow teachers here? Could you point them out to me?" he asked as he touched her shoulder.

Darcy felt the warmth of his hand and she was thrilled. "Well, the man sitting to Amanda's left is Russ Weber, our jeweler, and the lady seated next to him is Hannah King, our needlework genius. The beautiful gal at the end of the second row is Phoebe Snowden, our dance instructor. You might have already seen her since her studio is next to mine. The lady next to Phoebe is Ana, Amanda's house guest."

Ray leaned to the side to get a good look at Phoebe—a gesture that didn't go unnoticed by Darcy. A little pang of jealousy swept over her. *Oh, God, here I go again--losing him before I have him.*

"She's lovely, isn't she?" Darcy asked.

"Yes, she is. But you, my dear, you are just what the doctor ordered," Ray replied as he slid his arm around Darcy's shoulder.

As Priscilla walked to the front of the room, the murmur in the room abated. "I'm Priscilla Davis, librarian of our wonderful public library and I would like to welcome all of you. We are so pleased that you're here, and I'm certain that you'll thoroughly enjoy Barclay Henderson's presentation. We have copies of his books in the lobby available for purchase and Mr. Henderson has graciously agreed to sign them. And, the Sweetbriar Ladies Literary Club invites you to join them later in the Frank Lloyd Wright Room, where you'll find tea sandwiches and punch. Please feel free to join us and stay as long as you like. I also encourage you to investigate the rest of our beautiful library and if you have any questions for me, or any or our staff, please do not hesitate to seek us out. And now it is my pleasure to turn the mike over to Barclay Henderson."

"Thank you, Priscilla. I'm pleased to be with you today. As a newcomer to Sweetbriar, I could not have asked for a nicer welcome than to be asked to speak with you today. While I have been a writer for a long time, it's only in the last few years that I have published three books. Today, I plan to present a short overview of each one and then I'll open the floor for questions," Barclay said as he strolled back and forth in front of the small crowd.

Barclay spoke about his books, told a few jokes about writers, and then turned to smile at Priscilla. "Questions?" Barclay asked.

"Mr. Henderson," a gray-haired lady in the rear said as she raised her hand. "You have written two murder novels and one non-fiction. As an author, which genre do you prefer?"

"Well, my non-fiction book was really a cathartic experience for me. I had gone through an acrimonious divorce. Since I had found the end of my marriage a gut-wrenching experience, I began putting my frustrations down on paper. As a result, after many rewrites and baskets filled with rumpled sheets of paper, the book finally emerged—a tiring effort, but one that seemed to make me well again. The mysteries, however, were much more fun to work on since I could do with the characters as I pleased. I truly believe that any author interweaves his or her own characteristics, as well as those people who have had any impact on their lives, into their writings. By the way, I feel that I'm not an author as such, but rather a storyteller. For instance, let's look at the people seated in your row. Perhaps the gentleman seated to your right could be a banker who has just absconded with monies that really belong to his depositors. The lady wearing the straw hat to his right could be an heiress to a vast fortune that she doesn't even know exists, while the lady next to her could be an Olympic champion."

"Just where is my fortune?" asked the lady wearing the straw hat.

"I better hurry and make up that part, too," Barclay laughingly replied as he pointed to another woman who had raised her hand.

"Madam?"

"May I ask, Mr. Henderson, did you have any formal training as a writer?"

"Yes, I took quite a few courses from several colleges, but I consider my real classroom to have been a small newspaper in upper New York where I worked for several years. I had to write all kinds of articles and my boss was a stickler for the truth. But when a writer is working on fiction, much of what is included in the output comes from his heart, or his experiences, or his hopes, or his dreams. And sometimes, a writer simply does not know where a certain idea comes from—it just suddenly appears."

After taking a few more questions, Barclay turned to Priscilla and said "Thank you, Miss Davis, for this opportunity and thank all of you for attending."

Darcy spotted Homer coming her way. "Why, Homer, how nice of you to come to the library today. What did you think of Mr. Henderson?"

"Gosh, Miss Darcy, I'm sure out of my league just being here. But, Miss Amanda—well she was so nice I just couldn't say *no* to her. That there writer seems to be a nice fella. He's so polite to me at The Haven," Homer said as he pulled at the lapel of his frayed jacket nervously. "But then all you teachers are nice."

Ray looked Homer over and then said, "Remember, Homer, I have staked my claim for Miss Darcy."

"Oh, dang, I'm sorry. I didn't mean nuthin disrespectful in what I said, sir. Miss Darcy, Miss Phoebe and Miss Hannah are all nice to me. I think I'll get some goodies and then head home," Homer said as he quickly gathered himself together and headed for the refreshments.

Darcy smiled at Ray. "Your claim to me?"

Ray pulled her a bit closer. "Well, I have to be careful. I need to know who my rivals are so I can keep an eye on them," Ray said, while looking over Darcy's shoulder to watch Phoebe.

Some of the participants strolled through the small library, while others filled small glass plates with tea sandwiches and cookies. Homer looked at the small offerings and decided that they were just too delicate for him. He started walking toward his green truck, when he spotted Hannah walking just a few feet in front of him. "Miss Hannah," he called out, "would you like a ride?"

Hannah turned, and surprisingly, she smiled at the burly man. "Why, Homer, I certainly would appreciate that. How nice of you to offer."

When they neared the truck, Homer rushed to the passenger's side. "Miss Hannah, may I help you?" Homer said as he extended his calloused hand.

Blushing, Hannah graciously reached out and placed her soft hand in his.

"There we go, Miss Hannah. Don't forget to buckle your seatbelt," Homer said as he scurried over to the driver's side. He said, "I think I know where you live, Miss Hannah—over by the ice cream shop—is that right?"

"Yes, it is," Hannah answered. "But, please, call me Hannah."

Hannah felt something at her feet. As she picked it up, she said, "Homer, here's a church bulletin. I didn't mean to step on it. I hope I didn't get it dirty."

"Don't worry about that, Miss Hannah—I mean Hannah. At one time I used to keep all my bulletins, but I don't do that no more. I just started going to that church. It's nice. I think I would like to join the choir, but I don't have no training or nuthin."

"I'm sure they would welcome you with open arms, Homer. If you join, you'll not only get many opportunities to sing, but you'll meet lots of new people. I think that would be good for you," Hannah said. "I see you're wearing a gold cross around your neck. It's a lovely piece."

"It's the only thing I have from my mama. She gave it to me when I joined a church a long time ago. I like it cause it reminds me of her." Homer sad

Homer drove at a slow pace the few blocks to Hannah's little clapboard house. It had been a long time since he had been in the presence of a true lady and he was nervous.

"You sure look pretty today, Hannah—don't want to be too forward though."

"Why, Homer, thank you. I guess you can see that my favorite color is pink."

Just then, they passed a billboard advertising Fallingwater. "Homer, have you ever been to Fallingwater?" Hannah asked.

"No, but I've heard people talking about it. Guess I should get the directions and head up there some time," Homer said a bit sadly as he realized the ride with Hannah by his side was quickly coming to an end.

"I'd be pleased to be your tour guide if you would like, Homer. I love that place. Before I took the job at The Haven, I used to work there as a professional guide. I think you would enjoy not only the home, but the surrounding hillside. It's quite nice."

Homer couldn't believe his ears. Hannah had just offered to go on a date with him! "Wow, I sure would, Hannah," Homer said as his hands began to shake.

As he pulled up in front of Hannah's home, the handyman was smiling from ear to ear. Once again, he rushed to help her out of the truck. "Be careful, Hannah, it's a bit of a high step."

"You're so thoughtful, Homer," Hannah said. She noticed that her hand was still in his and she was delighted when he gave it a little squeeze.

As the two of them stood on the sidewalk, still hand in hand, Homer suddenly realized what he was doing and he tried to look away. "Sorry, Hannah."

"Nothing to be sorry about, Homer. Tell you what—I would love to treat you to some ice cream. Their strawberry banana is the best," she said as she pointed to the quaint, little ice cream shop. "That is, if you can spare the time."

CHAPTER 12

It was early April and Barclay was feeling a sense of renewal. He was running a bit late since his truck hadn't started right away this morning. But, once again, he worked his magic and it began to purr. Running up the walkway to The Haven, he even felt healthier, especially when he spotted a bed of tulips on the slope of the terrace. Taking the steps, leading to his second floor classroom two at a time, he was certain that somehow he had become a few years younger than he had been yesterday.

"Good morning, class," Barclay said cheerfully as he entered his classroom. "Did you remember to bring your laptops?"

"Got mine," George, a lanky, curly-haired young man said as he struggled to wrap a blanket around his shoulders. "Why the blankets, Barclay? Are we gonna go camping?"

"No camping. Today, we're going to try something different— inspirational, I hope—but different. It will involve two writing assignments."

Barclay reached into his back pack and pulled a few books out and stacked them on his desk. He held up one of them. "Anyone ever read this book? It's called *Avoiding Writers' Block.*" Holding up another one, he said, "How about this one? It's entitled *100 Ideas for Writers.*" He waited a few seconds. "No? Well, don't bother. They're pure nonsense."

Barclay walked over to the window and opened it wide. Then he said, "Writers often get one particular question that always seems to generate interesting discussions. *Where do you get your ideas?* Most writers simply respond, *I'm not always sure where they come from or just what sparks their arrival.* A true statement sometimes, but almost anything can trigger an idea for a writer. For instance, it could be a piece of music that brings back memories, either good or bad. It could be a personal experience that has been in the writer's mind for some time. Or, it could be something as magical as turning your computer on to a fresh page and suddenly seeing characters racing across the screen, almost fighting to get onto the page."

George raised his hand. "Barclay, do you think that I'll ever see characters fighting to get on a page in my book?"

"Indeed I do—but you must first pay your dues. And how do you do that? You write, write and then write some more. What do you think is the hardest part of writing? Anyone?"

"I think its grammar and stuff like that," one student said.

"I think it's developing good characters and making them come alive," another one added.

"For me, it's still getting a good idea—one that has not been beaten to death," one lady said. "But Barclay, what do you think?"

"The hardest part of writing is not the idea—it's what happens after the idea germinates. Genuine characters must be created and then you must put your words down—one after the other—creating a new story—one that's never been told before. A wonderful story can come from just asking yourself, *What if?* For example, what if you went home today and your house had vanished? Wouldn't it be interesting if a person had the ability to know the numbers that were going to be in today's lottery drawing?" Then Barclay held up a blank sheet of paper. "Can you see a story here?"

"I wish I could," George sighed. "But all I see is a blank sheet of paper."

Barclay was quiet for a few seconds. "Well, George, a blank piece of paper or a computer screen can sometimes be scary for a writer. But it's what the writer puts down on that paper that makes him a writer. Being a good writer, however, requires much more. It's a rather lonely occupation. While there are instances where two or more writers work on one manuscript—that blows my mind—what I like about writing is that I'm the master of the story—the director, the dictator, of what happens to my characters. In other words, it's a sense of power. Whatever it is for me, I want to be a writer more than anything else. But it's up to me to make it happen."

Barclay stretched out his arms as if he were reaching for something. "Can you feel it? Can you feel your success? It's out there, so let's see if you can capture it. I want you to free your imagination and keep asking yourselves, *What if?* Okay, let's tackle your first writing assignment for today. Here is a list of fifteen words. Using this list of words, I want you to write a one-page story. You must use all the words. Try to draw the reader into your plot as quickly as possible. And, you must provide a plausible ending. I'll give you thirty minutes to complete this task. You will then share your stories with one another—any questions?" Barclay paused as his students looked over the list of words.

"I don't see any relationship between these words," one student said.

"That's right. You'll create the relationship by how you use the words. Okay, you may begin."

While the students began to work on their assignment, Barclay turned his attention to his computer. But his mind wanted to focus on one thing only—Phoebe. He hadn't been able to get her out of his mind no matter what he was doing. He hadn't been ready to have anyone interfere with his new life, nor had he wanted to get tangled up with any woman—or so he had thought. But there she was—even when she was not in sight. Like some silly schoolboy, Barclay kept thinking about that night when he saw her dancing—twirling, and spinning around the candle-lit room. Looking down at his scruffy work boots, he tried to picture Phoebe's small dainty feet next to them—incongruity, that's what it was. Suddenly, he asked himself the same question that he had just posed to this students, *But what if?*

"Okay, folks. Let's see what you've been able to create. Using the list I gave you, make sure that as each student reads his story that they have incorporated all of them into a story that makes sense. Who would like to go first? Alright, George, go ahead."

When the young man finished his presentation, the students applauded. "That was really a funny story—clever, too. Mine is not nearly as good," one student said.

One by one the students shared their writings. Barclay was pleased with their apparent willingness to share and their openness to exchange ideas.

"Now, we'll move on to the next assignment. We'll be going over to the lot next to the trees just beyond the front yard. Find a spot that will allow you to lie down on your back and study the clouds. Put your laptops near your side. As you lie there, empty your minds of all the things you must do after this class. Lose yourself in the beauty that you will behold.

Then ask yourself a question beginning with *'what if'*. If your words make sense, fine. If they don't, well that's fine too. When you feel that you have captured your thoughts, and imprisoned them in your computer, go back to the classroom. Print a copy of your work and put it on my desk before you leave for the day. After I've read your submissions, I'll make an appointment with each of you to discuss what you have created. Let your imagination soar. Don't try to imitate any other author. Be yourself. I really want you to let go of any negative thoughts or inhibitions about writing and just write."

His students practically bounced out of the classroom and nosily clamored down the staircase, all the while dragging their blankets behind them. As the last student ran down the stairs and disappeared out the front door, Barclay followed. However, he stopped on the porch and took a seat on a newly-painted, white wicker rocking-chair. His mind drifted once again to Phoebe. He could hear music coming from her studio as it seemed to float effortlessly down the hallway, escaping the confines of The Haven, and becoming one with the warm spring air. He had no idea what the name of the piece was. He just knew that it was melodious, almost spiritual in a way—charming and captivating. How very much like Phoebe.

***

Darcy was propped against the ornate mailbox in front of her apartment house and seemed almost lost among the packages and bags that surrounded her. But Russ spied her as soon as he turned the corner in his dark blue Malibu. Once again, Darcy had had car trouble, and she had called Russ to get her to The Haven. And, just as any good brother would, he did just that.

"Hey, gorgeous," he said as he got out of the car and approached Darcy. "You asked me for a ride. With all this stuff, it looks as if you're moving. My rates for serving as a mover are high, young lady," he said as he began loading Darcy's things into the back seat.

"Oh, Russ, I have really good news—wait till you hear," Darcy said as she got into the passenger seat.

"What's good news about car trouble?"

"Oh, that's not the news. I sold them—I sold them," she said excitedly. "You know, I told you that I submitted four of my paintings to my artist friend in Philadelphia. Well, he sold them!" she said as she playfully hit Russ on his arm. "He sold them all—can you imagine that?"

"Darcy, that's really good news, indeed. Next thing you know, you'll be leaving The Haven and joining your *artsy* friends in San Francisco or some other such place. Just where do the *artsy* people hang out nowadays?"

"Look who's talking about *artsy* friends. How about your friend in New York who makes jewelry for the really, really rich? Russ, I'm so excited. Now I can begin to look for another car—or maybe a mini-van to give me room for my paintings. At last I'll actually have balances in my checking and savings accounts. And, maybe the teller at my bank will smile at me instead of glaring at me over her wire-rimmed glasses."

"What time will you want a ride back home today? I have a class at three."

"Oh, another piece of good news. You don't have to worry about that. Roberto will be picking me up. I didn't tell him about selling my paintings yet. I thought that would be a great thing to talk about over dinner tonight."

Russ glanced at Darcy and he could see the joy on her face. He asked, "Darcy, how did you meet this guy?"

"He's one of my students. Why do you ask?"

"You didn't meet him online?"

"No, Russ, I didn't."

"What do you know about him?"

"Russ, you're taking this big brother thing a bit too far. I am a grown woman and I can choose who I want to date. He's been a perfect gentleman."

"Perfect gentleman? What's perfect?" Russ asked.

"Now, Russ, that's all I'm telling you. A girl must keep some secrets, you know. What's going on over there?" Darcy asked as she pointed to Barclay's students lying all over the ground.

"Well, since they have computers, I would guess they belong to Barclay. You know how nutty writers are, Darcy. C'mon, I'll help you move your things to your classroom," Russ said. He suddenly placed his hand on Darcy's arm. "I know you trust this guy, Darcy, but I'm telling you that if he ever treats you badly, or if he hurts you in any way, he'll have to deal with me."

CHAPTER 13

Darcy was dressed to the nines and she couldn't have been happier. She was seated across the table from Roberto and he looked more handsome than ever. In her eyes, he was perfect. When he smiled at her, she could feel her knees knocking. Even his name, *Roberto* was sexy.

"Darcy, do you see anything on the menu you like," Ray asked.

"I think I'll have the petite steak," she responded.

"Good choice. They do a good job with their steaks here," Ray said as he reached across the table to take her hand. "Darcy, you look absolutely amazing tonight. The way the candlelight reflects on your hair is picture-perfect."

Darcy couldn't believe her ears. Roberto was the most romantic man that she had ever met. "Thank you, Roberto."

"Darcy, since I believe that you and I really have something here, I'm going to be honest with you about my job."

"Russ thinks you may be an ax-murderer."

Ray chuckled. "Well, if I were, I certainly wouldn't kill someone as beautiful as you. Maybe I'd choose Russ—but surely not you,". Ray said as he moved his chair closer to Darcy. "What I'm about to tell you may seem bizarre, but it's the truth. I have a very special job with the government. I investigate high officials who, for one reason or another, are under scrutiny with law enforcement. Because of the delicate nature of these investigations, everything must be kept secret. I'll have to leave town from time to time, and I cannot tell you where I'm going or what I'm doing. I cannot even tell you my real name, at least not just yet. To you and your friends, I must be Roberto Pellagrino. One day I'll be able to tell you much more. But right now I cannot tell you too much. I must make certain that you are safe. I need to protect you from harm, and the only way I can do that is for you just not to know what is going on in my professional life. You see, Darcy, you have hit a spot in my heart that no one else has. I know that it's early in our relationship, but I need your trust. I hope in time that I will also win your love. I know that I must earn that, Darcy, but will you keep on seeing me?"

Darcy was stunned. "Roberto, certainly I'll keep on seeing you. You're so sweet to be worried about me."

"I will always keep you as Number One in my life, Darcy. No matter who I must investigate or where I must go, you must be shielded from the dark side. I promise, Darcy, I promise that I'll take good care of you," Ray said, as he dropped his head a bit. He then lifted her hand to his lips and kissed it, slowly and gently, all the while gazing steadily into Darcy's eyes.

Darcy had just moved into seventh heaven. She already knew that she was in love with this man—without question. "Roberto, my lips will be sealed—that is, as far your work is concerned."

After they finished their dinner, Roberto ordered another glass of wine. "Look, darling, the wine is the color of your lips." He leaned over the table and kissed her gently. "Oh, your lips are so soft and sweet. I have never seen anyone more desirable than you. How lucky I am that I decided to take your art class. Was it luck, Darcy, or was it destiny?" Ray asked as he stroked Darcy's hand.

Darcy was almost in shock. Here was everything that she had been looking for. She was so proud of Roberto—imagine, a secret government agent. Of course, she would never be able to tell anyone about his work. As she looked into Roberto's eyes, she was certain she saw love looking back at her—true love.

Ray took her hand and brought it to his lips. His smile broadened. He knew for certain that he had reeled her in. She would be helpful—and when she wasn't—well, then he would take care of everything. Meanwhile, he planned to relax and milk the situation for all that it was worth

Darcy glanced at the scar on Ray's face. She had no idea how he got it, but she knew that someday he would tell her. The mark on some people would be considered ugly, but on Roberto, it only added to his overall presence—somehow it made him even more desirable.

She planned on rewarding Roberto tonight and every night that she would have the opportunity. She would plant kisses down that scar to his full lips. Come hell or high water, Roberto was about to become her lover.

CHAPTER 14

Homer was surprised at his boldness when he took Hannah's hand in his to lead her up the path to Fallingwater. A smile came across his face when he realized that she didn't pull it away. In fact, he was certain that she gave his hand a gentle squeeze.

"Homer," Hannah said as she stopped walking, "look at the way the home and the surrounding hillside appear as one. Those masonry walls you see going around the house on all levels were actually made of the sandstone found here on the building site. Frank Lloyd Wright, the architect of this fabulous place, designed hundreds of buildings, but he's best known for Fallingwater, and many consider it one of the greatest architectural triumphs of the 20th century."

As Hannah tugged a bit on Homer's hand, the two began walking once again. "Now, if I talk too much, just let me know, but it's difficult for me not to act as a tour guide."

"Hannah, you talk as much as you want. You're so smart."

Hannah blushed. As they entered the home, she said, "That's nice of you to say, Homer. This was actually the home of the Kaufmann family. They owned a popular, upscale department store in Pittsburgh. It appears that the men, I mean Wright and Kaufmann, had had previous dealings when various organizations had commissioned Wright to design dozens of civic projects, so they had already formed a special bond."

"I can't get over all of this, Hannah. I ain't seen nuthin like this before. You're right. It looks as if it really belongs exactly at this spot," Homer said. "I can see why you really liked being here. Do you miss not being a guide anymore?"

"Well, yes, I kind of miss it. But, I love what I'm doing at The Haven. I enjoy teaching and I have grown attached to the tree farm and all. Besides,

I met you and that was a good thing." Homer sucked in his breath. A beautiful lady like Hannah—a good, sweet person—was still holding on to his hand. Perhaps he had died and this was really heaven.

As they strolled from room to room, Hannah was sharing interesting facts about the furniture—where it came from and who had designed each piece. A small cadre of other visitors, obviously impressed with Hannah's knowledge of Fallingwater, had worked themselves as close to her as they could.

One woman put her hand up and asked, "Is this place open for visitors all year?"

A surprised Hannah turned and smiled. "While Fallingwater is closed during January, February, and much of March, it's quite lovely here when it snows—somehow, regardless of the season, Mother Nature seems at peace with what man created on this spot," she said.

"I apologize for butting in on your conversation," the woman said. "But, I just couldn't help myself. You know so much about this place that I'm beginning to think that you are a tour guide."

Hannah laughed and Homer's chest swelled with pride. "Well," Hannah said, "I used to be. As you can tell, I love this home. I've always felt that Fallingwater, especially now during the lovely spring season, represents a connection between man and a Higher Being. Mr. Wright had an innate ability to place this home as if had grown out of the stone surrounding it rather than something man just built."

When they had completed their visit, the happy couple worked their way down the path toward the parking lot. Homer said, "That there Frank Wright, he was sure a genius."

"You know, Homer, when I first saw a picture of Mr. Wright, I immediately thought of Einstein—they both had a shock of silver hair and a craggy-looking face," Hannah said as she chuckled.

Homer had no idea what Einstein looked like, but if Hannah thought it was funny, he thought so, too. "I have an old craggy face, too, but I sure ain't a genius like those guys," he said.

"Oh, Homer, you're much more handsome than both of those men," she said as she gave Homer's hand another gentle squeeze.

"Hannah, would you like to stop somewhere to eat? Or am I being too forward?"

Hannah stopped in her tracks. "Why, Homer, I would love to have dinner with you. It will give us even more time to get to know one another."

Homer couldn't be certain, but just then he thought that he heard a bell chiming—perhaps from a nearby church or maybe right from his own heart. He glanced again at Hannah. He hadn't felt this happy in a long time. But the reason that he had taken the job at The Haven, even though he had tried hard to forget about it, came to the forefront once again. He had to do something about it. Now that he had found Hannah, he no longer wanted to be involved in his old world. Somehow he had to work it out. Nothing—revenge or retribution—would be worth losing Hannah. As he slid into the front seat, he touched Hannah's hand ever so softly. She smiled at him. *No,* he thought, *I will not fulfill my assignment. I love Hannah and now that's all that counts.*

CHAPTER 15

Phoebe and Barclay were sitting in a restaurant, lingering over coffee. Off in one corner, a pianist was softly playing love songs. Barclay couldn't have asked for anything more. Here he was on a second date with Phoebe, and she was lovelier than ever.

Phoebe smiled at him, and said, "Barclay, that was simply one of the best dinners I have had in a long time. The wine was a nice touch too. I was planning on going back to The Haven tonight since I feel like dancing, but now I'm not too sure about that."

"Look, Phoebe, if you want to do that, I'll take you there. I really don't like you going back to that big old place all by yourself. How about I stay with you—you can dance as long as you like—then I'll drive you home. That way I'll know that you're safe."

"You're a worry wart. I've danced on many nights and nothing bad has happened. I do have my keys with me though. But, Barclay, with my warm-up routine and all, it could take up to two hours."

"I have my laptop in my truck, so I'll just work on my book. But, you know, I'm not too sure that Amanda should have given all of us keys to The Haven. That's a lot of keys flying around," Barclay said.

"Amanda trusts us all. She's absolutely marvelous. The Haven is off the beaten track, and I have always felt that it was truly my haven—the one place where I can feel safe from harm."

As they drove toward The Haven, Barclay kept watching Phoebe out of the corner of his eye. She seemed to be unusually quiet. "Phoebe, is something worrying you? Are you afraid of something?"

Phoebe laughed. "Only snakes and spiders," she teased, hoping to change the topic. Barclay felt that his questions had hit a tender spot so he remained quiet during the rest of the drive.

As Barclay opened the front door of The Haven, he said, "After you, Miss Ballerina."

Barclay flicked the hall lights on and followed Phoebe to her studio.

Phoebe took off her coat and tossed it on the bench. "I have to change into my practice clothes. I'll be back shortly."

Barclay was amazed as he watched Phoebe complete her warm-up routine. He was surprised to see how hard she worked. He had had no idea that dancers had to be in such great physical condition. After some time, she lit the candles, turned the music on, and disappeared into the dressing room. Barclay was astounded when she returned. Her leg warmers were gone. She was a vision in a lilac-colored, knee-length chiffon skirt and she glided across the floor in perfect timing with the music. He watched in awe. Her hands and arms were as graceful as her legs. He knew, from that moment, Phoebe could get him to do anything she wanted. When the music stopped, she was standing directly in front of him. He stood up, took her hands, and pulled her close to him. She didn't pull away—she came into his arms willingly. Without saying another word, the two were lost in time and space that only lovers can find.

Suddenly, Phoebe pulled away and screamed.

"What is it, Phoebe?"

"There, in the window, I saw a man's face."

"Did you recognize him?"

"No, but it was a big face—I have no idea who he was."

"Phoebe, keep your studio door locked. I'll see if I can find him. Don't come out of your studio," he shouted as he rushed to the front door.

Phoebe was trembling. *My God, did he finally find me?*

She went to the far corner of her studio and began to cry. It seemed like forever until Barclay returned. "I couldn't find him. There are no strange cars parked anywhere. But, he could be hiding anywhere in the tree farm. I'll take you home and then I'll get in touch with Amanda. We can't take any chances. He might return. Phoebe, now listen to me, I don't want you to come here at night without me at any time until we discover who it was. Promise me, Phoebe, promise."

"I promise Barclay," she said as Barclay took her in his arms once again. "Barclay, thank you. I don't know what I would have done had you not been here."

"Sweetheart, I'll be with you as long as you want me to."

While Barclay was very concerned about who could be lurking around The Haven, at the same time, he knew nothing else mattered because Phoebe was in his arms. "Come, let me take you home," he said. As soon as he heard Phoebe lock her apartment door behind her, he headed back to his car, pulled his cell phone out of his pocket and called Amanda.

"I hate calling you this late at night, Amanda, but you need to know what happened tonight," Barclay said.

"Is everyone alright?"

"Yes. Phoebe and I were in her studio and we were dancing. She suddenly screamed when she saw a face peering in the window."

"At her studio?"

"Yes. I told her to keep her door locked while I went outside looking for the intruder. I didn't see any strange cars but, the person could have been hiding among the trees. I think Jason and Homer should scour the area in the morning. However, I think you should call Darcy and Hannah and tell them not to go to The Haven alone at night any time until we know for certain who that man was. We need to be make certain that they are safe. Maybe he was just a bum, but we can't take any chances."

"I think you're right. I'll call the ladies. In all the years that I have been here we have never had an intruder. But, I guess times are changing. I cannot bear to lose the sanctity of The Haven."

Amanda called Hannah first. She smiled when Hannah assured her that she would not go to The Haven without informing Homer. After she explained the problem to Darcy, she was surprised that Darcy said that she might have a clue regarding the intruder.

"Let me get back to you, Amanda," Darcy said "Roberto might be able to help us with this problem."

***

"Thanks for letting me know, Darcy," Ray said. "Tell Amanda not to call the police. I'll step in and I'll investigate this incident. You don't want people to begin to be afraid to go to The Haven. I can handle this matter for you. But, remember, don't tell them anything about my job other than I work for the government. In that way, The Haven will avoid any bad publicity. I'll stop by in the morning and speak with Phoebe and then I'll take it from there. And, please, follow Amanda's idea about not going to The Haven alone, especially at night."

"Thank you, Roberto."

"You see, sweetheart, I won't let anyone or anything hurt you. You're my woman."

***

"Amanda, I just spoke with Roberto. He has offered to conduct an investigation so that you won't have to bring in the sheriff. He feels that The Haven can avoid the bad publicity that could follow an open investigation. He has a great deal of experience in this area. We don't want parents feeling apprehensive about sending their children to our classes as well as the many women we currently have enrolled," Darcy explained. "He'll start working on this in the morning by visiting Phoebe."

Although Amanda agreed to the arrangement, after she hung up the phone she was having second thoughts. She didn't know why, but for some reason, she felt uneasy when she was around Roberto. She wanted to like the man, especially since Darcy was obviously in love with him. But that little voice inside her—the one that had guided her for many years—kept whispering in her ear to be careful—very careful of Roberto.

CHAPTER 16

Early the next morning, Ray hurried up the front steps to The Haven, heading for Phoebe's studio. Now, at last, he was getting somewhere with the job he took on for Big Cheese. He felt certain that it had been Fat Tony who Phoebe spotted in the window, and, if it was, he would deal with him. Phoebe was just coming down the hall, carrying some clothing in her arms.

"Hello, Roberto. I don't believe Darcy's here, yet. I know she'll be here a little later since we plan on doing some shopping today," Phoebe said.

"I need to talk with you about last evening. Where can we go to discuss what happened?"

"Let's go in here," Phoebe said, as they neared the salon entrance. "The gift shop won't open for another hour."

Ray made certain that he sat facing the reception area so that he could watch who would come and go. He had to get information out of Phoebe, and he hoped that he could keep others at bay while they talked.

"I understand that you were frightened last night when you spotted a face in the window of your studio. According to Darcy, you did not recognize the man. Is that correct?"

"Right. I have no idea who he was. But I do know that he had a big head."

"Was he wearing a hat of any kind?"

"Not that I remember."

"How tall was he?"

"I just saw a face. He must have been kneeling on the porch, leaning on the windowsill. But as soon as I screamed, he disappeared into the darkness."

"Was he wearing glasses?"

"No."

"I also was told that there were no strange cars parked on the grounds. Is that correct?"

"Yes. Really, I only saw a face. I remember how fat his cheeks were. Barclay went outside but he couldn't find anyone lurking about."

Ray stood up. Now he was certain that it had been Fat Tony. "Thank you, Phoebe. I would like to look around your studio, if you don't mind," Ray said, as he smiled at Phoebe.

"Certainly. Go on over, the door's open. I'll be back in about twenty minutes. I need to take these things over to Amanda. We're participating in a clothing drive for a charity," Phoebe said as she walked out the front door heading for Amanda's cottage.

Ray felt that it could not have gone any better. He knew how he would handle Fat Tony. But, more importantly, he would have some time to look around the studio for the money and the documents. He headed to the back of the studio where he could see a dressing area. One side was lined with small lockers, none of which were locked. But all they held were tutus and other sundry clothing items. He then headed for Phoebe's desk and quickly began opening and closing drawers as quietly as he could. Nothing. Spotting the trunk in the corner closest to the window, he scurried over and knelt down before it. He had to hurry. She would return soon. Slowly, he lifted the lid and almost fell over when he saw the money. He reached down to see how many stacks there were when his fingers sensed some plastic—there it was—the yellow binder! Hot damn! What luck! In one fell swoop he had found the money and the papers Big Cheese was looking for. Wow. Just then he heard the front door closing. He quickly took a seat on the bench and pretended that he was writing in his notebook.

"Sorry, Roberto. That took a bit longer than I thought," Phoebe said. "Is there anything else I can do to help you?"

Ray's smile grew wide. "No, thank you. Please don't worry about that nasty fellow any longer. I'm certain that I'll be able to keep him away from The Haven."

"How nice of you, Roberto. I'm curious though. How can you do that?"

"Oh, Phoebe, I can't tell you that because law enforcement doesn't reveal any investigative techniques. But, rest assured, all you ladies will be safe at The Haven."

"I didn't meant that I don't believe you, Roberto. Please forgive my impertinence."

"Phoebe, here's my card. I want you to call me if you have any further problems. I mean it, Phoebe. You could be dealing with some rough characters. Promise me that you'll keep me in the loop," Roberto said.

"I promise, Roberto. And, thanks for being so thoughtful."

CHAPTER 17

Amanda barely had the car door closed when she said, "Quentin, something wonderful has happened. Ana now has a job and a place to live. I'm so happy for her. When Ana was in the bakery yesterday, she saw a sign for a full-time baker and applied for the job. And, to make things even better, the job comes with an apartment on the upper floor. I have a few things in the warehouse that will be perfect for her—a bed, some living room furniture and even some household goods."

"Wow, sweetie, that sounds perfect for her," Quentin replied.

"Yes, my goodness, yes. I guess you can tell how happy I am that things are working out for Ana. Can you help us move some things tomorrow?"

"I'd move the world for you, my dear," Quentin said.

When Amanda had accepted Quentin's marriage proposal, she had requested that in order not to put pressure on Ana, that they keep it a secret until she could find other arrangements for Ana and her baby. Quentin was pleased that a solution had arisen so quickly.

Just then they arrived at the jewelry store where they had taken Amanda's engagement ring to be sized. As he slipped the ring on her finger, Amanda said, "Oh, Quentin, this is so lovely. Thank you so much."

"Now, are we going to tell everyone that we're getting married?"

"I heard you telling your Hollywood buddy, Steve, on the phone last night," Amanda said as she giggled.

"Well, it just slipped out, sweetie. I can't help it if I want to brag a bit."

"Mr. Toth, here are the matching bands you chose. Please examine them carefully to be certain that everything is satisfactory. They certainly make a stunning set," the clerk said.

"Hello Amanda. Hello, Quentin. Are you two aware that you were featured on *What's Knew in Hollywood* this morning?" Priscilla said as she entered the store. "You're TV stars. My goodness. First, I had a published author make a presentation in my little library, and now, here I am talking with TV stars."

"I guess I owe this fame to Steve. He must have blabbed. Those rags seem to have spies all over the place," Quentin said.

"But it was very complimentary, Quentin. They used a great picture of you, Amanda."

"I wonder where they got that." Amanda said apprehensively. For such a long time, she had lived with a low profile, but now, she might have to get used to people knowing about her past.

"They have ways," Quentin said wryly. "As long as they didn't say anything derogatory. I thought that I would be yesterday's news by now."

"I was going to surprise my staff this afternoon by telling them. By now they may all know," Amanda said, obviously disappointed.

"Tell you what, sweetheart. Let's take them all out for dinner on Saturday. You know, we can have our own celebration in spite of that damned TV," Quentin said.

Later, that day, Amanda arrived at The Haven for a meeting with her staff. As soon as she opened the front door, she could hear her staff talking. "Congratulations, Amanda. How wonderful," Darcy screamed as she jumped out of her chair and rushed toward Amanda. "Let me see—let me see," she said as she grabbed Amanda's left hand.

"Wow, Phoebe, look at that rock! I bet that's at least two carats," Darcy stated.

"Your ring is gorgeous, Amanda. It's so beautiful. Congratulations. Any plans?"

Just then, Hannah burst through the doorway. "Amanda, I just heard it on the news. I am so happy for you," she said as she embraced Amanda. "I was working on a quilt and I had the TV on. You know, that show called *What's Knew in Hollywood* and Quentin's picture popped up and then yours. I almost fell over, I never saw anyone I knew on TV," Hannah laughed. "Homer saw it too. He was waiting for me, he was as surprised as I was. Oh, I wasn't surprised that you were engaged, I kinda thought that would happen. But since Mr. Quentin was an award-winning director in Hollywood, I guess that's why it was on. Oh, I said that all wrong, not that you're not important, Amanda, it's just that—oh well, I was just dumb-founded."

The women had formed a circle around Amanda and everyone was hugging everyone else. They were all firing questions at her--where and when the wedding would take place.

"Well," Russ said. "These women are gushing all over you, Amanda. But I too give you my congratulations. Barclay, don't sit there like a bump on a log, let's get in on this group hug!"

"Okay, if you all sit down, I'll tell you our plans," an excited Amanda said.

"Now hear this, gang—shut up and we'll all hear the good news," Russ ordered.

"Guess who will be having the first wedding at The Haven?"

The women screamed again and began jumping up and down. Darcy said, "Perfect. Absolutely perfect! When, Amanda, when?"

"During your summer break. Quentin and I plan on inviting just a few friends, including all of you as well as Jason and Homer. Of course, Roberto will be invited, too. Russ, if there is someone you would like to bring along, please do. I also plan on asking Liz Becker for advice."

"Amanda, I'd like to offer my assistance in any way. I could make your dress if you would like. Are you having any attendants?" Hannah asked.

"No. Quentin and I will stand for ourselves. After all, we're not kids, you know."

"How about Phoebe and I taking care of the decorations and the seating arrangements. I guess you're planning on an outdoor wedding? But, just in case, we should also have the salon ready. Jason and Homer can help with the chairs and the ladders we might need. Okay with you, Phoebe?" Darcy asked.

"Yes, yes. This will be so much fun," Phoebe said, clapping her hands together.

"Hannah, I would be delighted to have you make my dress. Do you have enough time?" Amanda asked.

"My yes, more than enough. When we are done here, let's go upstairs to look at some bridal books. Whatever style you want—dress—suit or whatever," Hannah said with obvious joy.

"Russ, you and I seem to be left out of this," Barclay said.

"I'll make a tiara for the bride. Barclay, maybe you can write a book for the bride," Russ said as he laughed hard. "That's what you get for not having a craft that fits into a wedding. We'll get all the glory. Can you by chance sing?"

"Heck no. But, Amanda, I would be honored to give the bride away. You have to walk down the aisle with *someone*," Barclay said.

"What a nice idea, Barclay. I'd be pleased to have you as my escort," a happy Amanda said.

When Barclay and Russ headed down the hallway together, Russ said, "Did you hear any more about that guy who scared Phoebe the other night?"

"No, but Darcy assured me that Roberto would take care of it. I only hope she's right."

"What the hell. Is he some kind of superman or something? I don't know what everyone sees in that guy. I think he's a phony," Russ said, not bothering to hide his contempt.

"Well, Darcy claims that he's an investigator for the government. What kind I don't know."

"I'll tell you what kind—a scam artist—that's what he is," Russ said as he stomped away.

***

Homer headed for the tree farm. He found a stump and sat down. He needed to think things through. He knew that he should call Adam Ash to tell him about Amanda, but he didn't want to. He had made a deal with the devil and he didn't know how to get out of it. What would Hannah say if she knew that he had been feeding information to Adam? Miss Amanda was the one who had hired him and he just can't allow Adam to harm her. How could he defend his actions? Homer's mother had belonged to some kooky church, where she would listen to everything Adam, the Primate of the church, would tell her. And, when his mother dropped dead of a heart attack, Adam offered to take care of her burial. He had told Homer that he could repay him by doing a small favor for him—get a job at Amanda's tree farm and keep him informed about any matters going on involving Amanda. It didn't sound terrible at first, but now he realized that he was acting like a traitor. He decided that he would call Adam, let him know about the engagement, and tell him that he was done with everything. He would offer to pay a little each week until his mother's funeral was paid for.

Slowly, he dialed Adam. "Adam, I have news for you. Miss Amanda got engaged and…"

"I know that, you dumb bastard—it was on the news. You have done nothing for me, you ungrateful man. What would your mother say?"

"I'll pay you all that I owe, Adam. I'll send a little each week. I promise. I'm grateful for what you did for me, but I can't do this any longer."

"No, you are *not* finished. You will meet with that rich guy Toth. My father has some pictures of sweet Amanda—the kind that are worth some big bucks. Toth had better make a generous donation to my church or those photos will find their way to the press. Now listen to my instructions and make sure you follow them to the letter. I will meet him at some public place—not at the tree farm. I will be bringing one person with me and he will be allowed to bring only one person—fair is fair. I want fifty grand and he'll get the pictures and the negatives. According to my father's journal, Amanda had invited him and his flock to use the tree farm as a haven, but she never made good on that promise. Now it's pay-back time. Money for the pictures. Simple, clean, and neat. One sign of the law, or if I sense any funny business, my church members will carry my actions forward. Do you understand, you moron?"

"Yes, Adam, I understand. I know of one public place where you could meet."

"And where's that?"

"Fallingwater. It's a famous house that sits on a little hill in the woods. You can see all around and the parking lot is small so you will be able to see who's coming and going. I took a tour there once," Homer said, hoping that he could convince Adam.

"Is it full of tourists?"

"Not during the week—especially on a Monday," Homer said.

"I'll look it up on the Internet. Don't meet with Toth before I get a chance to do some research. Are you clear on this? If you blow this, I'll make your life miserable. Call me in the morning and we may be able to finalize my plans."

The line went dead. Homer felt that he should talk with someone about his predicament, but who? He couldn't tell Hannah, not precious

Hannah. He wasn't important like the teachers and he barely knew Mr. Quentin. But, maybe, that fellow Roberto—the one who was helping to find out who scared Miss Phoebe the other night—maybe he could help. He had to stop Adam from hurting Miss Amanda. But Adam's threat that someone close to him could get hurt made him realize that Adam knew about Hannah and that frightened him. What if Adam would try to hurt Hannah? To protect both women he must confess to Mr. Quentin. He will know what to do. Maybe Mr. Quentin will be so angry that he will fire Homer immediately. But deep in his heart, Homer knew what he had to do. Homer wept.

CHAPTER 18

"What the hell were you thinking, Tony? You almost blew the whole thing. I could break your fucking neck for doing something so damned stupid!" Ray shouted.

"What the fuck did you expect? You didn't get in touch with me for weeks. So I trailed you. By the way, lover boy, you were damned easy to find," Tony replied with a smirk on his face.

"I thought you trusted me. I trust you. And then you go and pull a dumb stunt like peaking in a window and scaring the shit out of our target. Besides, you did it when she was with her boyfriend and now we must watch him too, you dumb sonofabitch."

"Look, boy, watch who you call *dumb*. I ain't dumb. Maybe I ain't the smartest crayon in the box, but I sure as hell ain't dumb," Tony said as he kept pointing his finger at Ray.

"Okay, okay. But, damn it, Tony, I worked hard to get this whole thing set up so that the two of us won't get blamed for anything. I have been amazed at how great things have been going—that is until you shoved your fat face against the window pane."

"Well, tell me then. Just what is your so-called plan? I sure as hell want to know."

"Tony, Tony. You sure know how to get under my skin. Now, shut up and listen carefully. It's important that you do exactly what I tell you. Before you know it, you'll be in Vegas with babes on your arms and lots of money in your pockets."

"You bet your sweet ass I will. You can stay here if you want but not me. I love The Strip and all that goes with it."

"Okay. I made a direct connection with our target by dating the art teacher at The Haven. She's nuts about me. I have met the other teachers and staff as well. They have accepted me with open arms. Well, anyway, there's going to be a wedding there shortly. I have already been invited, and the teachers are used to seeing me coming and going. After the wedding, The Haven will practically be deserted. The first thing I'll get out of there is the folder with the documents Big Cheese wants so badly. The dancer will never know that they are gone. I'll bring them to you for safe keeping. Then, during the summer recess at The Haven, I'll set it up for you to move in and do your thing. You'll never be seen by anyone, except for the dancer. Tony, this is going to go down without any problems at all—I guarantee it."

"It better, Ray. I don't want no more surprises. I'll keep away, but believe me, I'll be checking up on you. This is gonna be a big score and I want my share," Tony said, empathizing each word.

"Tony, this is going to be your biggest payday yet. If I'm right about the documents, Big Cheese will pay anything we ask to get them back. You see, I have an inkling who Big Cheese is—no, don't ask, I won't tell you. You almost ruined everything and I don't want any more mistakes. You'll know when the time's right."

The two sat in silence for a few minutes, listening to the hum of the wheels of cars whizzing by them on the highway. Ray had found this little hide-away when he was looking for a place for his plans to do away with Tony—just off the interstate, practically hidden by all the bushes and trees on both sides of the dirt road. He was enjoying this moment—Tony had no idea what would be happening to him. But then, Ray rationalized, Tony truly was a dumb shit. "Tony, remember this place. This will be where we'll meet whenever it's necessary. I'm thinking that, when I lay my hands on those precious documents, this will be the place where we can transfer them from my car to yours. So, make sure you memorize just how far this is from the exit ramp. Got me?"

"You mean that you're really going to let me hold them? Christ, Ray, why?"

"I want to look like a boy scout to all those damned teachers. I want to look like a hero, not a thief. You see how much faith I have in you, Tony?" said Ray with a smile on his face.

"I'm sorry, Ray. I was so sure that you were going to cut me out of the deal. When I have the papers, where should I keep them?"

"I have a storage locker rented already. We won't have to keep them there long. As soon as Big Cheese knows we have them for certain, he'll fork over whatever I ask."

"When do I do my thing, Ray?"

"During the shutdown of The Haven. I'll have time to slip in, get the documents, and bring them to you at this spot. I want you to put them in a large cardboard box so if anyone does see you it will look like you're storing household stuff. Here are the directions for the locker. It's only two miles down the road. But don't go near there until you have the documents. The locker's on the backside of the place and is hardly noticeable. It's right down the road from here, Family Storage, across the street from the feed store. After the transfer, I'll set up the dancer for you. It'll be early in the morning, before anyone else is around. After you take care of the chick, get the hell out. The two of us will meet right here as soon as I have the money."

"That's a lot to remember, Ray. But I can do it. When it's all done, how long will it take to get our money?" Tony asked eagerly.

"Once I have the documents and transfer them to you, I figure just two to three days. Think of it Tony—in just a few weeks you'll be in money up to your fat ass! But this is your one and only warning—stay away from The Haven and the storage locker—if you go near either one of them before I have everything set up, the deal, the whole deal will be off."

As Ray drove away, he was smiling. Poor, dumb Tony would never know there was no storage locker, nor would he ever get his hands on the documents, but, best of all, he'd never know that Ray would be the one getting all the money. Ray was pleased with himself. Ray owed all his good luck to Darcy—sweet, gullible Darcy.

CHAPTER 19

Amanda was accompanied by Hannah, Darcy, and Phoebe to the Sweetbriar Yard Goods Store. Amanda had found a picture of the gown she wanted to wear for her wedding, and Hannah said that it would not be a problem for her to draft a pattern and make it in plenty of time for the wedding. Shortly, the women were pulling bolts of satin, crepe, silk, brocades, and shantung from the bins and piling them on a large wooden table.

"Amanda, let me tell you a bit about some of these fabrics. This one, of course, is the typical satin that many designers use for their wedding gowns. This one, however, is one of my favorites—embroidered silk, which is fabulous—it drapes beautifully. Here is a semi-sheer taffeta, while this is regular taffeta. If you would like something heavier, this silk velveteen is gorgeous, but it is a bit too heavy for a summer wedding. Some fabrics come in both white and ivory. But I'd like you to concentrate on the fabric itself first. What's your first reaction?" Hannah asked.

"I'm amazed. I never knew this shop carried so many lovely fabrics. I'm so excited about all of this. I think I like the embroidered silk the best," Amanda replied.

"Good choice, Amanda. Your pattern is one that drapes the fabric across the bodice as well as the skirt. Silk lends itself to draping, while the embroidery will add elegance to the gown," Hannah said, excitedly.

"Gosh, I'll enjoy seeing this creation come to life. This is much more fun than picking a dress off a rack," Darcy said. "Hannah, you must be a genius; being able to look at a picture and drafting a pattern for a dress."

"Well, I owe it all to my mom. She taught me everything about making anything that requires a needle. But, Darcy, you have an enviable talent. Every time I see a new work of yours, I am amazed at how you capture form, line, and color with your paintings," Hannah said as she lifted the bolt of embroidered silk off the table.

"This is beginning to sound like a mutual admiration club," Phoebe said as she walked around the table still feeling the various fabrics. "Oh, Amanda, I too love the silk. It is so you. But then you would look good in a burlap bag," Phoebe said.

"No burlap for this one," Darcy said as she pointed to Amanda.

"Do you plan on wearing a veil?" Hannah asked.

"I think not. Russ is making a small tiara for me. I don't think I need a veil," Amanda said.

"When I get married," Darcy said. "I want a mermaid style dress that is tight, tight, and tight."

"Darcy, you know you would have to walk down the aisle. How would you do that if your dress is tight, tight, and tight?" Hannah teased.

"Perhaps I could jump like a bunny," Darcy said.

"Well, come on, little bunny, after we finish here, we have to go to the flower shop." Phoebe said.

"Look, you ladies run along. I'll get the fabric and then I'll head back to The Haven. I know that Homer's working today, so I'll let him know that I'm there," Hannah blushed.

"Roberto said that he took care of that nasty fellow," Darcy said. "But, of course, Hannah, if you need Homer to protect you," she said jokingly, "go right ahead."

"I'll give you my credit card," Amanda said as she began rummaging through her purse.

"Oh no, you don't. Your dress will be my gift to you," Hannah said proudly, totally ignoring Amanda's plea to pay for the fabric. "I'll get everything I'll need and then I can start drafting the pattern. Since I already have your measurements, I should have the muslin model ready by Friday. Then I'll need you to stop by to try it on before I begin cutting. Oh, Amanda, you're going to look fabulous! Quentin is sure one lucky guy."

"Okay, gang," Darcy said, "let's move on down to the flower shop and let Hannah do her thing."

As the other three left the fabric store, Hannah took her cell phone out of her purse and dialed Homer's number. Of course, she needed Homer. That was a given.

***

Homer's hands were shaking. He had to call Adam. He was not looking forward to hearing what Adam wanted him to do. Everyone was so excited about the upcoming wedding that he could not imagine what they would think if they knew that Adam could spoil everything. He picked up the phone and punched in Adam's number, hoping against hope that he would not answer.

"Hello," Adam said.

"It's me."

"It's about time. Okay, here we go. I'll meet Toth this coming Monday at ten. That's the time that Fallingwater opens. But, I'm warning you—if I see more than one person with him, the deal is off. He's not to bring any cameras, recording devices or any other equipment. If anyone moves in, I'll have people standing by who will take care of the situation, and Toth will pay a heavy price for not following my instructions. Homer, do you understand?"

"I got it, Adam."

"Alright, now go and visit Toth and give him his orders. I already have people in place and if they see anything, and I mean anything that looks the least bit suspicious, people will get hurt. Now get your ass moving and do as you've been told. If you disobey me, someone you are very close to will no longer be around."

Homer sat for a few minutes, still holding the phone in his hand. "No, not Hannah," he said softly. He finally put the receiver back on the cradle and was startled when the phone rang again. He decided not to answer. He needed to talk to Mr. Quentin as soon as possible.

CHAPTER 20

Ray used Darcy's key to get into The Haven. The ladies were shopping and Homer and Jason were working at the far end of the tree farm. Now it was time to get a good look at those documents. His hand was shook as he inserted the key. As long as Tony followed his orders, this was going to be an easy caper. As he heard the click of the lock, he quickly slid into the entrance way. He stood still for a few seconds, making sure that no one else was there. He really should have waited another few days before coming back to examine the documents, but he couldn't bear the agony of knowing where they were but not knowing what they would tell him. He hurried down the hall to Phoebe's studio. The door was standing open. It was as if someone was waiting for him to enter. He headed toward the trunk—the trunk that was going to make him a rich man. Phoebe had placed some costumes and plastic bags from the gift shop on the top which he quickly brushed off with one swipe of his hand.

Getting down on his knees. Ray ran his hands over the top of the trunk. Each stroke reminded him of the feeling he got when stroking a beautiful woman. But the trunk meant more to him than any woman he had ever known. Slowly, he lifted the lid. He was startled to see that the pile of money was gone. Damn! But he relaxed when he realized that the yellow binder was still there and it looked like it had not been disturbed. He lifted the binder up, surprised that it was heavier than he had anticipated. As he examined the contents, it didn't take Ray long to realize that he hit pay dirt. He also came to the realization that he would no longer need The Man. He would be dealing with Big Cheese all by himself. He chuckled as he became aware of Big Cheese's identity. It was so silly—so childish—he never would have guessed. Big Cheese was well known in Pennsylvania. Judge Kraft—Kraft—just like the famous cheese!

If Big Cheese had not demanded proof that the girl was dead before he would pay for the documents, Ray would've been a wealthy man right now. He still needed Fat Tony for *that* part. But once the hit was completed, nothing would stand in Ray's way to be the only one getting paid off. He already knew just how he could dispose of good old Fat Tony. But when?

Ray realized that he should have brought a duffel bag or something to conceal the plastic binder on his way out. He grabbed one of the plastic bags from the gift shop and shoved the binder in, ignoring the little brochure that had been tucked in the bottom of the bag. After closing the lid of the trunk, he picked up the garments that he had tossed on the floor and placed them back on the top of the trunk. Suddenly he stopped. He couldn't remember how the garments had been arranged. He decided he would try to fold them neatly. What he didn't do, however, was to sort them by color. A move that would later haunt him.

He glanced out the window, but he failed to notice that another car had just pulled into the parking lot. Ray hurried down the hallway, pleased with himself. He felt as if were walking on air. He stepped out onto the porch, making sure that he closed the front door firmly. Suddenly he became aware that someone was standing just a few feet away.

"Hello, Mr. Pellagrino," Hannah said.

"My God, Hannah, you scared the daylights out of me," Ray said.

"Oh, dear, I didn't mean to do that," Hannah said as she began to stack her bundles in the driveway. Pointing to the gift shop bag, Hannah said, "Looks like you've been shopping."

Ignoring her statement, Ray said, "You know, you shouldn't be here alone, Hannah. I told Darcy that while I believe that I have taken care of the problem from the other night, I cannot guarantee your safety," Ray said, not bothering to hide his displeasure.

"I apologize sir. I did try to reach Homer but I couldn't locate him. I had all these things for Amanda's wedding dress, and I was eager to get back here and start to work on her pattern," Hannah explained.

Ray quickly put the bag in his car and said, "I don't mean to scold you, Hannah, but I can't help worrying about you ladies. Here, let me help you take your parcels to your classroom."

After Hannah's packages were deposited in her room, Ray hurried back down the steps and out to his car. His heart was beating rapidly and he was still angry with Hannah. It irritated him that she was there at all. Stupid-ass broad! After all his planning, she had to show up. If the old hag interfered in any way with his plans, he might have another job for Fat Tony.

CHAPTER 21

Homer was sitting on the edge of the sofa in Quentin's living room biting his nails. His eyes were wide-open and it appeared that he was holding his breath. Quentin was leaning back on a brown leather chair shaking his head in utter disbelief.

"Homer, do you mean to tell me that all the time that you have been working on the tree farm, you were providing this Ash character with information about Amanda?" Quentin asked incredulously.

With his head bowed, Homer nodded his head. When he looked up at Quentin his tears began to fall. "Yes Mr. Quentin. I didn't think nuthin was wrong because I ain't ever said anything bad about Miss Amanda. Now, I'm ashamed. Miss Amanda has always been good to me and I kept telling myself that I was doing nuthin wrong. I'm sorry—so sorry. I knew Adam was a strange man, but I never thought he would think about hurting Miss Amanda."

"Well, Homer, there are cruel people in this world. So let me be certain that I understand this whole shakedown. Ash wants me to meet him at Fallingwater on Monday at ten in the morning. And, he wants to sell me pictures of Amanda for $50,000 or he'll offer them to the press. Do I have this right?"

"Yes, sir. Oh, and he says you can bring one person with you and no techie stuff," Homer said. "Are you gonna call the cops? I don't trust any of those kooks from that damned cult."

"No. I think I can handle this. I have to make a few calls, but I can put this together and we will send this nutcase packing," Quentin responded. "But, I don't want Amanda to know about this just yet. I'll tell her later, but not now. And, Homer, you must not talk to anyone else about this entire incident. Keep it to yourself. I know that you and Hannah are friends, but don't share any of this with her. The women are already concerned over the man whom Phoebe saw at the window the other night and I don't want them to get all stressed out over this."

"Mr. Quentin, there is one other thing I must tell you," Homer said hesitantly.

"And that is…?"

"Well, it's about Miss Ana and her baby."

"Oh, I know about her. I know that she's married to that jerk Adam."

"I didn't tell Adam that she's here. I knew who she was as soon as I saw her, but I didn't tell him."

"That was a smart move, Homer."

"I was afraid that he would come after her and hurt her."

"Homer, you made the right decision. But I'm glad that you reminded me about her."

"I know I might be fired, Mr. Quentin. I wouldn't blame Miss Amanda. But, if I can help you in any way, I'd be mighty pleased to be part of your plan," Homer said with sincerity.

"I'm sure that you won't be fired. But remember, Homer, that bastard might want to take revenge against you. The best way that you can help is to keep all of this to yourself."

"But he wants me to call him back."

"Certainly. Call him and tell him that I'm willing to give him the money, but I'll need another week in order to get that much cash ready."

"You sure are a smart man, Mr. Quentin."

"Well, Homer, let's hope so."

After Homer left, Quentin began to realize that this problem might be more difficult to resolve than he had thought. He knew that he needed help. But, he would also need leverage to deal with Ash. Suddenly, it occurred to him that Ana might be the person who could tell him the most about Ash. And, the perfect person to help put a plan together could be Darcy's friend, Roberto. After all, he seemed to have solved one problem for them already. Perhaps he could help develop a strategy to get rid of Ash once and for all. Just as Quentin was fumbling for his cell phone, it rang.

"Hello."

"Quentin, you old devil, you. What are you up to?"

"Look whose putting the *old* label on someone. I'm doing fine, Steve. Hey, was it you who leaked my engagement to the rags?"

"Well, I might have mentioned it in passing," Steve replied. "Why, was it some kind of secret? Is the bride that ugly?"

"You should be as lucky as I to catch a beauty like my Amanda. I was taken by surprise that the news guys still classified me as news."

"Are you kidding? After your record here in Tinsel Town. You'll always be news."

"So, why are you calling me? I don't have any more surprises to give you," Quentin said cheerfully.

"Nah, I have one for you this time, old buddy. Remember that book you sent me, *A Touch of Murder?*"

"Sure I do. What took you so long to recognize that it would make a hell of a movie?"

"Well, some of us are not retired and we must do something called *work*. Remember?"

"You want the property?"

"I sure do. Does the author have an agent? Please say *no*." Steve said.

"No, he doesn't. But, remember he's a personal friend of mine and I'll scan any contract that you send him, you miser."

"Oh, come on, Quentin, you know that I'm a fair man. How about meeting with him to see if he's interested in selling the rights. It would be a one-year option and then, if I don't make a film by then, he can have the rights back. Of course, if that happens, he keeps whatever monies I paid for the option. Hell, man, you know the routine. Talk with him and then we can have a conference call and sort of wrap things up. Or, if you would like, you two could fly out here and we could negotiate in my office."

"We're sort of in a temporary hold on traveling. We have a situation that we must take care of first."

"Oh, sounds mysterious," Steve replied. "Can I be of any help, Quentin? I owe you a lot for all that you did for me. Just say the word and I'll be there."

"You know what? I think I'll take you up on that offer. You'll need to bring some equipment along. You know, some recording devices and mikes, like the ones we used in *A Foreign Affair.*"

"I see. The kind no one will find even if they do a body search."

"You got it, Steve. I have to meet with someone next Monday. Can you be here in time to get things set up?"

"You bet. Just make sure that you have plenty of bourbon. I'll call you with the details of my arrival and I'll also email a list of the equipment that I'll be bringing."

As soon as Quentin hung up, he rummaged through his desk drawer for the list of phone numbers that Amanda had given him. He got an answering machine. "Barclay, I have great news for you. Give me a call as soon as you can."

Then he dialed Darcy's number. Again, he had to leave a message. "Darcy, this is Quentin. I'm trying to get in touch with Roberto. I would appreciate it if you would tell him that I would like to speak with him. I think I could use some advice about a problem that I'm having. Thanks, Darcy."

He then decided that he would drive to the bakery shop to see if Ana would talk with him. The shop would be closed by now, but he was almost certain that he would find Ana at home with the baby. When he pulled up in front of the shop, he was pleased to see that the lights in her apartment were on. He decided that he would not ring the bell in case the child was asleep so he knocked as gently as he could.

"Who is it?"

"Ana, it's Quentin. I would like to talk with you if that's alright with you."

She opened the door. "Of, course, Mr. Quentin, come right in. I just put Jennie down. I was about to have a cup of tea and some cookies. Would you like to join me?"

"Why, thank you, Ana. Yes, I would like that."

Ana pulled out a kitchen chair for Quentin. "These are such pretty chairs, don't you think? Of course, Amanda gave them to me. She's been my guardian angel. I don't know what I would do without her."

"How's Jennie adjusting to her new home?"

"She's doing fine. I feel very comfortable here. I baked these cookies today, Quentin. It's one of the shop's best sellers." After Ana poured the tea and sat down, she said, "Is something wrong?"

"I'm afraid so. What I'm going to tell you may not be shared with anyone, not even Amanda—I'll tell her when the problem is behind us." Quentin explained what Ash wanted and what he would do if Quentin didn't comply.

"You're not going to pay him, are you?"

"Absolutely not. But I need some leverage against him."

"What does that mean?"

"I need to have something on him. Something that will stop him from using those pictures. Something that I know about him that will make him stop trying to harm Amanda."

Ana's eyes opened wide. "My God, Quentin, I think I can help you. I brought a video with me. One that Adam made with some children. It's disgusting and disturbing. When I took money out of Adam's safe to run away, I saw that video and I took it. I don't know why I took it, maybe it was to get my revenge on him. He has to know by now that I have it." Ana paused. It suddenly became clear to her that Adam could hurt her, or even Jennie. "If Adam finds out that I'm here who knows what he'll do. I've got to protect Jennie," Ana said as tears began to flow.

"We won't let him find you, Ana. I'll be getting my little posse together and our primary goal will be to keep all the women safe. Don't worry about your safety, Ana. We've got to get rid of him one way or another."

Ana placed the tape in Quentin's hands and said, "This should put Adam away for a long time. I never thought that I would be saying that about my husband."

"You are a very brave woman, Ana. I promise to take care of you both. If our plan works out, and this tape is what you say it is, we should have that bastard behind bars before too long."

As Quentin trudged down the steps to the sidewalk with the tape tucked inside his jacket, he remembered that still needed to tell Barclay the good news about his book. He decided to drive by his apartment to see if the writing instructor was there. Amanda had made him aware that she thought a romance was blooming between Barclay and Phoebe, so perhaps Barclay would not want any visitors tonight. But, then again, he knew that Barclay would welcome the news and this could possibly be his big break into the world of writing. So, when he arrived at Barclay's front door, Quentin rapped the brass knocker as hard as he could—fair warning in case Phoebe was there.

"Quentin," said a surprised Barclay when he opened the door. "I wouldn't have guessed it was you in a million years. I had my nose almost inside my computer and was lost in a new novel."

"Well, I'm here about one of your books, my friend," Quentin said as he shook Barclay's hand.

"One of my books?" questioned Barclay.

"Yes, *A Touch of Murder.*"

"I don't understand."

"Well, I sent your books to my friend Steve in LA—by the way he's a movie producer. And, he's interested in submitting an option for one of them," Quentin explained.

Barclay stood there with his mouth opened. He was speechless and looked almost like a statue frozen in time. "You've got to be kidding," was all he could muster.

Quentin chuckled. "Do you understand what that means?"

"My God, no. This has never happened to me," Barclay said in a weak voice.

"The easiest way to understand this process is to look at an option almost in the same way that you would if you were involved in an agreement to rent-to-own a house. An option is an agreement that a production company owns the right to make your work into a movie of the week or a TV show for a specific time period. Most options are usually twelve to eighteen months. They use this time to negotiate for funds to produce the film and to hire a script writer. You see, they seldom use the author of the book since their own writers know HOW to adapt the work into a film."

"But, what happens if they can't secure funding?"

"The rights go right back to you. For you, it's a win-win situation. But, it does require patience on your part," Quentin explained. "I'm surprised you didn't ask me how much they would deposit on your option."

Barclay rubbed his chin and smiled. "Well, how much?"

"That will be up to Steve, but he's a fair man. It's usually between five and ten thousand."

"Sounds good to me," Barclay said.

"Look at it this way—they want something you own. They want it bad enough to lay out some hard cold cash and they want it bad enough that they don't want someone else coming along taking it away from them. If I know Steve, he probably has certain actors in mind for the major roles involved. I told Steve that you don't have an agent, but, if you want one, I have some names I could share with you."

"Do you think I need one?"

"Unless you have someone who is a legal expert in the option arena, I would say *yes*. But it's not too late to get one. In fact, a good agent, knowing that you already have an offer, will jump at the chance at representing you. And, more importantly, the agent will negotiate how much you get percentage wise of the profits of the film. But that's not the only reason I'm here, Barclay."

"I'm still in shock, Quentin. How about I get us each a drink and then you can tell me your second reason for interrupting a famous author when he is working on his next block-buster book."

Later, as Quentin drove home, his mind was racing. He would call Russ tomorrow. He already had a message on Darcy's machine for Roberto, so with Steve, they would have a group of five. *Hell, with that many good men, they could easily put Ash in his place.*

****

Phoebe felt the need to dance once more. Even though she had been unable to reach Barclay to go with her, she decided to go on her own. Besides, Roberto assured her that she would be safe. She loved her little dance studio, and she wanted to turn it into her stage—the arena where she longed to be. As she moved to the dressing area, she stopped by the trunk to check on its contents one more time. She no longer had to worry about the money she had stored there for several months, since she had recently rented a safety deposit box at the local bank. She knew to the penny just how much she had left from the sale of her parents' tree farm. Suddenly, she realized that the costumes that she had folded and placed on the top of the trunk were no longer sorted by color. Startled, she lifted the lid of the trunk. Her heart almost stopped beating. *They're gone, they're gone.* She frantically waved her hands back and forth—to no avail. She sank to the floor. There would be no dancing tonight.

Who could have taken the documents? What does that mean for my safety? Should I tell all to Barclay? Or, should I seek the help of Roberto?

She opened her desk drawer and took out Roberto's card and quickly dialed his number.

CHAPTER 22

Ray could not have been happier. A lot had happened in the last two days. He had been able to convince Phoebe that she was safe. Now, he was on his way to a meeting with Quentin and the other men about that Ash fellow, he had the documents that Big Cheese was so desperate to get, and soon he was going to be the hero of the day in getting rid of Amanda's abuser. He felt that he had Fat Tony under control, so in just a few weeks, he would not only have all the loose ends of this deal tied up, but he would be a wealthy man. He did feel a bit bad about Darcy. After all, she was the reason that things were going so well, but he would be leaving her far behind and on his way to bigger and better things. The only unknown was this Steve guy who would be coming in from California. So, he needed to play the game perfectly.

He pulled his sports car into Quentin's driveway. He looked the home over and was impressed. Obviously this cat had money. Before Ray even got to the front door, it opened and Quentin was waiting to greet him.

"Thanks for coming, Roberto. Come on in—the rest are here," Quentin said as he guided Ray into a spacious living room.

As soon as the greetings were over, Quentin explained what Ash was threatening to do.

"What a horse's ass," Barclay said. "Does he really believe that you'll be paying him off?"

"It appears that way. This guy is so full of himself and he's used to charming everyone around him," Quentin remarked.

"When is all of this going down? Do we have time to get our act together?" Russ asked.

"We'll be meeting with him on Monday. By the way, that's a good day since the women are having some kind of party for Amanda at the country club. But, to be safe, we need to have them protected without them knowing what's going on."

"That's right up my alley. I can get my cousins to go with me to the club to make certain Ash or his lackeys can't get near the women. We all have permits to carry—just in case," Russ said.

"Alright, Russ. Sounds good. Now for my meeting with Ash—I may only take one person with me."

"Quentin, I'd like to volunteer to be that person." Ray said. "You know, I've been involved in other situations such as this."

"Quentin has told me a bit about your background, Roberto," Steve said, "I think your suggestion is a good one. Quentin and I drove to Fallingwater yesterday, and I think Barclay and I could be there dressed as tree trimmers or landscapers. That way we too can be close by," Steve suggested.

"Let's go over this. Roberto and I will met with Ash," Quentin said as he stood up and waited until he had their attention. "By the way, Roberto, we have some great listening and recording devices that Steve brought with him. Steve and Barclay will be the tree trimmers, and Russ and his cousins will guard the ladies at the country club. I'll ask Homer to drive the ladies to the club in our van, and I'll have him stay there so he can bring them back, along with the gifts that Amanda will be getting. I think he'll like that since he feels that Ash made a veiled threat against Hannah. And we know how he feels about her," Quentin said.

"I'd like to know more about the electronic devices," Ray said. "In my line of work, I've used quite a few of them."

"I can tell you about those," Steve said. "One item is embedded in the visor of a ball cap—totally invisible to the eye. Since you've had experience with hidden devices, Roberto, you should wear the cap. Of course, I'll give you a preliminary rundown on how to position your head to capture Adam's every move. The other little gem is a recorder that will be placed in Quentin's jacket. It is so thin that even a seamstress couldn't detect its whereabouts."

"Sounds like you guys know your stuff," Ray said.

"Timing. What about the timing, Quentin?" Steve asked.

"Ash wants me there at ten. You tree trimmers should get there about nine or so," Quentin said.

"Quentin, you haven't told us how you plan to handle the negotiations with Ash. Don't you think he'll want to see the money?" Steve asked.

"Well, here's where I need Roberto's advice," Quentin said.

Ray thought for a few moments. "I suggest that I carry the money just in case anyone tries to grab it. Quentin, you will do the talking. You'll need to get the cash no later than tomorrow so we can get the bag ready. I'm certain that Ash will want to look inside the bag, so we need to have a nice thick layer of bills. Will that be a problem?"

"No. How much should I get?"

"Can you get twenty thousand? We can make that look real good," Roberto said.

"Sure. How about you going to the bank with me?"

"No problem, Quentin. I'm more than willing to do anything to help you solve this problem," Ray said. "But, Quentin, after Ash looks at the cash, how do you want to handle it? How do you plan on getting him out of the area without the money?"

"Oh, I want him to think he's going to win. I want him to take the money and head for his car. That's when the whole thing will blow up in his face," Quentin said, gleefully.

"I don't get it," Steve said.

"I saved this for last. His wife, Ana, gave me the answer. Not only are we going to get rid of him for a long time, but he'll be in for a big surprise right after he believes that he won."

"Why you old movie director. What's up your sleeve?" Steve asked.

"Boys, we have a video tape. A tape of Ash with some children. I could have given it to Sheriff Wagner right away, but I wanted to run this show myself. The last person Ash will see on Monday will be the sheriff. Think of it, boys. What a way to get even—Ash thinks he has the money, he's ready to drive away, but guess who'll be in the back seat of the squad car? Oh, I'll be standing nearby to wave goodbye as Wagner cuffs him. Won't that be a good ending to the story?"

"Well, you made it work in hundreds of films, Quentin, but this is real life. Suppose Ash has a surprise for you, too?"

"No matter what he has, we'll be ahead of that dumb bastard," Quentin said.

"How did you get the sheriff to go along with all of this?" Ray asked.

"That's between Sheriff Wagner and me. It's good to have friends in high places," Quentin said. "And, I also know another powerful man I can call on if necessary and that's Judge Kraft."

Ray took a deep breath. *Kraft? My God, this cannot be real.*

CHAPTER 23

Amanda's weekly staff meeting was scheduled for nine and Darcy was running late, again. She just couldn't seem to keep her thoughts together ever since Roberto told her that he was in love with her. On one hand, she had been down this road many times before only to be crushed like a bug. But, this time, she told herself, was different. Roberto, even with his secret life, was the real thing. As she pulled into the driveway, she felt better when she saw that Phoebe was just getting out of her car. Darcy gave her friend a thumbs up sign and they both laughed. Phoebe was her usual beautiful self—hair pulled back in a smooth chignon, alabaster skin glowing in the early morning sun. While Darcy was dressed in jeans and a knit top, Phoebe was wearing a silk blouse and an ankle-length, print skirt.

"Woman, no wonder Barclay's nuts about you," Darcy said.

Phoebe smiled. "What makes you say that?"

"Girl, you look like you could dance off in the sunlight right now. It's just not fair for one woman to look that good."

"Oh, Darcy, look who's talking about someone being nuts about someone—you surely don't fall short with Roberto constantly being at your side. You two make a great couple."

"Phoebe, I'm so in love with that guy that I can't stand it. Suppose it doesn't work out? Suppose he finds someone else? Suppose…"

"Darcy, will you stop with the *'suppose this', 'suppose that'*. You're taking all the joy out of your romance. Now, relax and enjoy what you have—no matter how long it lasts. You'll still be *supposing* when you and Roberto are sitting side by side in rocking chairs when you're ninety."

"Come on, we better get to our meeting," Darcy said. Then Darcy stopped, took Phoebe's hand, and said, "Be there for me, Phoebe, just be there for me if this is not real."

As the two of them entered the salon, Russ said, "It's time you two got here. I was just going to dial 911."

"Sorry, Amanda, we got caught up in conversation. We were trying to figure out why we put up with Russ and his grumpiness. But then, we decided he's just too cute to get rid of," Darcy said as she took a seat beside Russ.

"Cute? I sure am," Russ said as he tapped Darcy's arm. "See Darcy, your Roberto isn't the only one around here with charm."

"By the way, Darcy, your Roberto helped me carry in my packages yesterday. He's not only a handsome man, but he certainly has good manners," Hannah said.

"Roberto was here yesterday?" Darcy asked surprised.

"Only a short time. He said he had an appointment. I told him that I didn't think you would be coming in until later, so he left. I think I got a scolding, though?" Hannah said as she smiled.

"Roberto scolded you?" Darcy asked.

"Well, he was just concerned that I was here all by myself. He's a dear to be so concerned about all of us. You're a lucky girl, Darcy."

"That's what I just told her," Phoebe said.

"When I spoke with Roberto the other day, he seemed to think that the problem with that man had been solved. But when you ladies come here at night alone, you could still be putting yourselves in harm's way," Barclay said.

"Thank you, Barclay, I couldn't agree with you more. I spoke with Roberto last evening and he feels that we have nothing to fear from the intruder. But let's be careful, anyway," Amanda said as she referred to her clipboard. "I won't be keeping you very long. I only have a few items to discuss. First, I want to thank all of you for your work during our spring semester. I have heard nothing but glowing comments from our students. You know the routine for closing out a semester as well as preparing for the next one. Homer also needs to know if you have any maintenance needs for your classrooms. Phoebe, I've told him about your special summer class, so he'll be available to you if you need anything. Darcy, I think the time between the summer and fall semesters would be a good time to have your studio windows adjusted the way you would like them. And, Darcy, a piece of good news—the easels you requested will be here in two weeks," Amanda said as she stood up.

Hannah began heading down the hall when Darcy called out to her.

"Did Roberto say why he was here yesterday?" Darcy asked, trying to sound casual.

"No, why?"

"Oh, just curious," Darcy said weakly.

She hurried down the hall to her studio. Pushing the jealous thoughts out of her mind, Darcy walked to the windows and adjusted the blinds so the sunlight would not be on any of the students' easels. She couldn't get her mind off Roberto. If anything would happen to their relationship, she didn't think she would survive. Night after night, she would give herself a lecture that if it was love, really true love, that it would indeed last. But she couldn't understand why Roberto hadn't mentioned that he had been at The Haven. But she knew what was really bothering her—Phoebe. Perhaps he wanted to see Phoebe, and not her. After all, Phoebe was a gorgeous woman, while Darcy considered herself only average.

"Hey, Mona Lisa," Russ called from the doorway.

"Oh, not you, Russ. Now, what do you want?" teased Darcy.

"I just wanted to get your opinion of the tiara I made for Amanda," he said as he held out a little red velvet pillow.

Darcy responded "My God, Russ, it's beautiful! She will be thrilled." Darcy held the tiara up in the sunlight and turned it around and around. "It's beautiful from all sides, Russ. This is a lovely piece."

"Hey, you two, not so close there," Ray said as he entered the studio.

Darcy's eyes lit up. "Roberto, how nice!"

"Well, I guess I better be running along. Nice seeing you again," Russ said as he passed Ray and headed out the door. "See you later, Darcy."

Roberto placed his hands on Darcy' face and held her there while he kissed her lips tenderly.

"Must I be worried about that guy?" Ray asked.

"Russ? My goodness *no*, sweetie," Darcy said as she laughed.

"Does he come in your studio often?"

"Hardly ever," Darcy responded.

"Well, let's keep it that way. You're my girl, Darcy. I don't particularly trust that old guy, and I surely don't want him around you," Ray said sweetly.

"Hannah told me that you were here the other day. I didn't know…"

"Darcy, I thought you understood that there would be days, or even weeks, that I would not be able to tell you where I was going and what I was doing. You know that I must keep my work secret. I thought you trusted me. I'm really disappointed," Ray said sharply as he took a few steps back.

Darcy was stunned to hear anger in his voice. She didn't mean to upset him. "I do trust you. I have to apologize."

Ray came toward her once again. "Come here, you vixen," he said as he pulled her to his chest. "Now, I want you to remember this. There may be times that you will feel neglected, but you will never be forgotten. There will be times that I'll be called away without any advanced notice. When I know ahead of time that I must travel, I'll tell you. I want to be your lover, Darcy. But I need your loyalty, no matter what."

CHAPTER 24

It was early Monday morning when Quentin was awakened from a deep sleep with the chiming of the doorbell. When he glanced at the alarm clock, he saw that is was four o'clock—way too early for any of the men to come for a planning session before meeting with Ash. Just as he was heading for the front door, Steve came out of the guest room, looking confused.

"What the hell's going on?" Steve asked.

"I haven't the foggiest idea, but I won't know until I answer the door."

"Wait, it couldn't be him, could it?" Steve said as he put his hand on Quentin's arm.

"Who? You mean Ash?"

"Yeah, unless you have something else planned for this morning. I always knew you were a bit strange, Quentin," Steve replied. "But, I'll be right behind you when that door opens."

Quentin peered through the peephole and said, "Not to worry. It's Homer."

Before Quentin even had the door fully opened, Homer said, "I'm so sorry to bother you but this is very important. I have a message from Ash."

"He isn't coming?" questioned Quentin.

"Oh, he's a-coming alright, but not to Fallingwater."

"Come in, Homer, come on in," Quentin encouraged.

After they were seated, Quentin said, "Now, why did he change the meeting place and where does he want us to go?"

"He called me and he said that Fallingwater was "out". He wants to meet at the Little League ball field, two miles east of Fallingwater. You know where that is, Mr. Quentin?"

"I do, Homer. Did he say why he changed his mind?"

"He said that you had too much time and you probably have booby-trapped the area. He told me to tell you that he has someone watching the ball field and that, if they see any monkey business, he will email the photos immediately to the scandal sheets. Oh, Mr. Quentin, I'm so sorry," Homer said as he wrung his hands together.

"Nonsense, Homer. This isn't your fault and we'll handle it. All you must do is drive the ladies to the country club for their brunch today and say absolutely nothing about what we're doing. Do you understand, Homer?

"Yes, sir. I won't say anything to the ladies and I didn't tell Hannah nuthin—just like you said."

"You're a good man, Homer. Now get home and perhaps you can get a couple hours of sleep."

After Homer left, Quentin was quiet for a while. "You know, it really doesn't matter where we meet. He's not getting the money anyway," Quentin said.

"Well, we all figured that. But it seems that you're going to a lot of trouble to catch this no-account when Sheriff Wagner would pick him up in a heartbeat," Steve said.

"Maybe it's the Hollywood influence in me, but I want him to believe that he has won. I want him to think that he's getting the money. I want to see the arrogance in his eyes when he thinks that he's proven that he's smarter than anyone else. Think of it, Steve—there it is, a bag of money, all for him. Much more money than this father ever had. He'll already be entertaining thoughts of what he can do with the money, but even more important than that, he wants to be more powerful than his dad was. The dumb sonofabitch will have years and years, sitting in a cell, remembering my face. He'll be serving time among those who will know that he's one of the lowest of the low. Kids. He was abusing kids and he thought Amanda would be his key to victory."

"You need to call Sheriff Wagner, Quentin. He needs to know of this. And, we need to let the others know of the change in plans. How you ever got Wagner to go along with this I don't know. I always said that you could sell eggs to chickens."

"We definitely need the sheriff there."

110

"We have no idea how many followers Ash might have stationed around the ball field. The tree trimming idea won't work."

"You're right." Quentin thought for a minute. "I've got it! There's an old truck parked behind the barn at the tree farm. They use it to haul trash. It's old and rusty, but I think it'll work,"

Steve looked perplexed. "How is an old truck going to help us?"

"You and Barclay, dressed in old clothes, can be in that truck. As soon as you get near the front of the ballpark, you feign motor problems. You get out and start tinkering with the engine. Start arguing with one another. Make it look real. Do some swearing and name calling. One of you stomps away but then works his way back to the park through the woods. In case anyone is hiding around there somewhere, they won't connect you with me. But, then there will be four of us to face the two of them."

"Quentin, you sure haven't left Hollywood too far behind. You're really getting a kick out of this, aren't you?" Steve asked.

"Of course, I am. Amanda and Ana will both be out of sight so he can't harm either one—they will be safe. And, I'll have my fun with this bastard before Wagner carts him off to jail. Just think, after today, peace and quiet will return to Amanda's haven. Now, as long as we're up, let's have some breakfast."

Heading toward the kitchen, Steve said, "I'll be the chef. You make the calls. You better protect your ass or you may find yourself in the cell next to Ash."

CHAPTER 25

Homer had picked up Hannah first. His hands were shaking. He knew something involving Ash was coming down. The handyman was terrified that it would fail and, then, Ash would find him and, maybe strike out at his beloved Hannah. One by one, he picked up the women and they were all excited about the party for Amanda. Homer had to help the ladies into the van and he neatly stored all their brightly-colored packages in the back. He could hardly hear himself think with all the laughing and chattering going on in the van. It pleased him to see Hannah so happy. He thought she was even more beautiful today than ever. He planned to be close by to make sure that Hannah stayed happy all day.

"Isn't this exciting?" Amanda said. "I love that this was not a surprise and that we could all go together to the country club. Darcy, how many others are you expecting?"

"A total of thirty-five," Darcy said proudly. "I really wanted to hold it on a Saturday or Sunday, but they were booked."

"My goodness," Amanda replied. "How nice of you to arrange this."

"Homer," Hannah said, "When the brunch is over, will you be able to drive the van around to the backdoor of the party room? You're going to have to load all her gifts into the van, but we'll help you," Hannah said as she patted Homer's hand. "Homer, you are shaking. Are you feeling ill?"

"Ah, no Hannah, I'm okay. I'm just not used to being with so many beautiful women," Homer replied, trying hard to sound strong.

"Why, Homer, you old Romeo," Darcy teased. "I just want to tell you that you too are invited to join us for brunch."

"Oh, Miss Darcy, I couldn't do that," Homer said as he blushed.

"Yes, you can," Darcy said. "How about it, ladies? Isn't Homer our escort today? You're the only man who hasn't deserted us. The others are chickens. They can't handle all this beauty at one time. We're depending on you, Homer."

"Thank you, ladies. But I'm certain that the others just couldn't come along today," Homer said nervously.

When Homer pulled into the driveway of the country club, he recognized Russ's car in the parking lot. He made the assumption that his presence was pre-planned and that made him feel better since he would not be the only man protecting the ladies.

As the women got out of the van, they took their gifts and headed into the building. Six white columns were lined up across the wide wrap-around porch. As soon as one entered the building, an imposing crystal chandelier almost took their breath away. The walls of the reception area were dark red and the hardwood floors seemed to act as a showcase for the lights streaming down from the chandelier. In the party room, large round tables, covered with pale pink cloths, were decorated with pink and white flowers, and little paper baskets filled with candies were neatly placed beside each plate. The gifts were all piled on a side table that was beside a window that looked out onto the garden.

"Darcy, this is beautiful!" Amanda said.

"I'm glad you like it. But, I must confess, I had help putting this together. It was Roberto's suggestion to put the gift table by the window," Darcy said proudly.

Soon the room was filled with ladies and lots of chatter. As Amanda greeted each one of her guests, there were also lots of kisses and hugs. Homer, who was peeking around the doorway, was pleased to see that Hannah was right in the midst of the women. Maybe one day, he could have such a party for her.

The ladies never noticed that Russ and his cousins were wandering around the garden and the reception area, looking right and left. They would be surprised to know that each of the men had a revolver concealed underneath his jacket.

CHAPTER 26

Steve and Barclay had been successful in getting the old truck from the tree farm started. The two were hardly recognizable. Steve had on bib overalls that were streaked with dirt and grease, while Barclay had a checked bandana wrapped around his head and blue jeans that were slung low over his hips. They both took on a new persona as they drove toward the ball field.

"Say there, partner. How's the trash business today?" Barclay deadpanned.

"Well buddy, if we have it planned right, we'll have a big load of trashy trash captured before its even lunch time," Steve answered back.

As they neared the meeting place, Barclay was scouring the roadside for signs of possible spots that could be used by someone planning an ambush. "So far, I don't see a thing, but someone could be hiding in the underbrush. Get ready for your acting debut. I'm going to pull the truck over."

Steve jumped out first, "Damn it, not again. This damn truck ain't worth the room it takes up."

Barclay tumbled out of the passenger's seat and shouted, "Well, if you wouldn't be so damn cheap, you'd buy a new one. I told you this thing wasn't gonna hold up. Now what? Here we are in the middle of nowhere. You'd better be able to fix it or I'm done."

Steve popped the hood, looked over the engine, pulled on this and that, and said forlornly, "I don't know. It worked yesterday."

"Oh, great, it worked yesterday. Well, buddy, this ain't yesterday in case you didn't notice. Look, this is your truck and it's your problem. See you around, pal," Barclay said as he began walking away.

"Where the hell do you think you're going? Are you gonna let me here all by myself?" Steve yelled at the top of his voice.

Barclay didn't answer—he headed down the road, waving goodbye over his shoulder.

Steve got out a box of tools, put it down along the berm, and began tinkering with the engine. When he heard a car pull up, he merely glanced over but turned immediately back to the engine.

Now is was time for Quentin and Ray to do their part. When they arrived at the ball field, Ray jumped out of the driver's seat and ran around to open the door for Quentin. The plan was to make Quentin look frail and unimposing. He helped Quentin get out. Quentin grabbed Ray's arm and leaned heavily on him as they headed to the ball field. In less than five minutes, another car pulled up and two men got out and headed in the same direction. In the meantime, Steve walked to the other side of the truck so that he could get a good look at the ball field. He had to be ready, if and when he was needed.

Ray and Quentin were seated on one of the spectators' benches when the two men approached them. "I assume you are Toth. I'm Adam Ash and this is Darrell Windsor."

"I am Quentin Toth and this is Roberto Pellagrino. Now let's get down to business. And, I warn you, Ash, I have had just about enough of this nonsense. I'm here to negotiate in good faith and I expect the same from you," Quentin said firmly.

"Before we begin, gentlemen, Darrell will be checking you for any electronic devices or weapons of any kind. That is, unless of course you have an objection to that," Ash said.

"Examine all you want. You won't find anything. Do you think that we're that stupid?" Ray said angrily.

Darrell took some time to examine Quentin and Ray. "They're clean, Adam."

"You have the money?" Ash asked.

Quentin nodded his head. "You have the photos and the negatives?"

"Of course," Ash said. "But I want to see the money."

Ray stood up. "As you can see, Mr. Toth is a bit frail so I'm here to insure that no harm will come to him and that you will, indeed, negotiate in good faith. I'll let you see into this duffel bag, but I will not give it to you until you produce the negatives."

Both Ash and Windsor were unaware that at this moment, Barclay had worked his way to the woods beside the ball field and that Steve was poised to move at a moments' notice. Meanwhile, everything that Ash and his buddy said and did were being recorded in the well-concealed devices that were hidden on Quentin and Ray.

"Ash, look into this bag and you'll see that we have the cash ready for you. I didn't want Mr. Toth to pay you, but he's a gentleman's gentleman. As you can see, I have this bag handcuffed to my arm. As soon as Mr. Toth has the negatives, I'll tell you where the key is and you can then unlock the cuffs, and take the bag," Ray said convincingly.

Ash took a deep breath and walked over to Ray. When the bag was snapped open, his eyes grew large. "I want to feel the money. I need to make sure that it's real."

"Go right ahead, feel away," Ray said.

Ash slid his hand slowly into the duffel bag. He breathed deeply as he ran his fingers up and down the stacks of money. Then, he ran his hand around the sides of the bag to make sure that it was indeed full of money, narrowly missing the video tape.

"Ash, I'm warning you that Mr. Toth will not tolerate your coming back at any time in the future for more money. You get one bite of the apple, not two or three. Have you ever heard of the *Gray Ghosts?*" Ray asked.

Ash pulled his eyebrows together, "You mean the motorcycle gang?"

"Right," Ray said. "If you ever try to blackmail Mr. Toth again, that group will pay you a visit. And, you will not like what they will do to you. Do you understand?"

"Yeah, I understand," a surprised Ash responded. "But I don't consider this blackmail. I'm doing the work of our church—sacred work."

"Oh, sure. I know how sacred your work is," Quentin said angrily.

"Okay," Ray said, "Let me examine the negatives."

"Darrell, let him chose two negatives to examine. Don't let him have them all. Two should be enough to assure you that they are all of Amanda."

After Ray picked out the negatives, he held them up to the light. While he couldn't be certain that they were of Amanda, they appeared to be shots of a very young girl. At that moment Quentin took his cap off and wiped his forehead.

That was Steve's signal to summon the sheriff in an unmarked car. Quentin was watching Ash with a great deal of pleasure. He could see the excitement in his face and he could almost hear his heartbeat. Quentin thought to himself, *Go ahead, you bastard, enjoy yourself, so you will be all the more devastated when it is all taken away from you.*

"Give them the negatives, Darrell. Are you satisfied?" Ash asked.

Ray looked them over, and nodded his head.

"Okay," Windsor said, "Where's the key to unlock the satchel?"

Ray smiled. "Why don't you ask that fellow who's now standing right behind you? Darrell, Ash, meet Sheriff Wagner."

"I thought we were dealing in good faith?" Ash screamed with a sneer on his face.

"Does this look familiar, pal?" Ray said as he fished the tape from the bottom of the duffel bag.

"Why…how…" was all Ash could muster.

"All you have to know is that it's now the property of the sheriff," Quentin said as he handed the tape over to Wagner.

"Ash, I'm certain that you would like to know the fate of the two men from your church who we found hiding in the underbrush. Well, they're sitting in the back of our squad car," Wagner said as he cuffed both Ash and Darrell.

"I'm being arrested? For what?" Ash asked.

"For starters, how about the fact that you threatened this man unless he paid you a handsome amount of money. We don't take kindly to extortion. And you can look forward to other charges before we get through with you. And, after I view this tape, how about child endangerment, child molestation and on and on. We'll have enough on you to keep you locked up for a long time." As the sheriff waved at the officers standing on the berm, he said, "Okay, boys, take em' back to the station and lock em' up."

As the deputies escorted the two men up the embankment, Quentin couldn't help but smile.

"Quentin, I need to talk with you privately," Wagner said as he motioned for Quentin to move to the side.

Quentin said, "Am I in trouble?"

"Quentin, you came close with this one. When we found those guys who were hiding, they were both carrying weapons. This could have been a tragic situation. If anyone finds out that I endorsed your shenanigans, I could lose my job. You better be right about that damned tape. That is my ace in the hole to get out of the mess you put me in. No more Hollywood stunts. Do you hear me, Quentin?"

"Look, I appreciate what you've done. I also appreciate the fact that you trusted me enough to let me play with this bastard for a while."

"Are you prepared for what will be happening next?" Wagner asked.

"You mean a trial?"

"No. That won't be for a long time. I mean the press. They're gonna be all over this. I usually don't stick my nose in press stuff, but I think you should consider making a statement, or giving an interview and lay it out. Now, I don't mean what you guys pulled off here today. I mean let the press know about what happened to Amanda when she was only fourteen and what Ash's plan was. Keep the others out of it. Hell, Quentin, she was only fourteen. The press will be careful how they handle that. Take control, Quentin, take control."

"She's kept all of this to herself for so long that it will be difficult for her to see it all over the news again," Quentin responded.

"But, if you don't lay it out for them, it could get much worse. You never know how they will interpret something or slant something just to capture their audience. Face it. Let Amanda know that she too must face it. Tell your cohorts to keep their mouths shut. Now, as for our conversation just now, I never said a word," Wagner said as he turned and walked to his squad car.

Quentin stood silently until Wagner was out of sight. Then he signaled for the others to come to him. At first, they just looked at one another. Suddenly, the smiles broke out and the hooping and hollering began.

"We did it," Quentin said. "Damn that was really a rush!"

"I was sweating bullets there for a while," Steve said. "I almost passed out when the first patrol car pulled up and they had two guys in the back seat."

"I loved the look on Ash's face as they cuffed him. I thought for a minute that he might pee his pants—he looked so damned scared. This was better than any movie I ever made," Quentin said as he continued to dance around.

"I was clinging to a tree, trying to hear what was going on. I stepped on a twig and, when it snapped, I thought my cover was blown," Barclay said.

"Guys, thanks so much. I couldn't have done this without you. And you, Roberto, you were like a proven movie star. How the hell did you come up with the *Grey Ghosts?*"

"I'm just a frustrated actor, I guess. But I agree, Quentin, this was fun. When can we do it again?" Ray asked as he chuckled.

They all broke out laughing.

"Wagner gave me my marching orders—no more Hollywood stuff. Barclay, will you drive the truck back to The Haven and put it back behind the barn. We'll go to my place and I can call Russ on the cell phone and tell him to have Homer bring the ladies to my place. They must be told what happened, and it'll be better if they all hear it at one time. I'll need to speak to Amanda alone about how we'll handle the press. Before too long, we can go back to just being a quiet haven and watching the trees grow."

CHAPTER 27

Homer had backed the van into the driveway behind the country club. When he saw the pile of gifts that Amanda had received, he wondered how he was going to fit all of them in along with the ladies. His mind was racing since he knew that the men were up to something involving Ash, but he had no idea what they had planned to do. He still felt that all this trouble was his fault. He never should have agreed to spy on Amanda in the first place. But Monday morning quarterbacking would not solve anything. He trusted Quentin and the others to do the right thing. Suppose, however, that Ash didn't show up—all of them would still be in harm's way. The ladies were carrying the packages out and standing in line waiting to hand them to Homer. While he had never had so many pretty women to himself, the only one he wanted was Hannah.

"This is the last one," Hannah said as she handed Homer a heavy box. "Be careful with this one, Homer. It is a set of ceramic bookends that will look amazing in Amanda's living room."

"I'll be careful, Hannah. By the way, I heard you singing," Homer said as he blushed.

"I usually only sing in church, but Phoebe asked me to sing a few romantic songs in honor of Amanda and Quentin. Don't they make a beautiful couple?" Hannah asked.

"Amanda is pretty, but not as pretty as you," Homer said.

Now it was Hannah's turn to blush. "Oh, Homer you must be blind," Hannah said as she tapped Homer on his arm.

"Hannah, do we make a nice couple?" Homer asked.

"My goodness, Homer, are you serious? If you are, the answer is *yes*." Hannah said just loud enough for Homer, and no one else, to hear.

Just then Russ came around the corner and waved to the ladies.

"Russ, what are *you* doing here?" Darcy asked.

"Oh, I was trying to crash your party hoping to get something to eat."

"You should have come in, Russ, we had plenty of food," Amanda said.

"Homer, I got a call from Quentin and he wants you to drive everyone to his place."

"Maybe he wants to continue the party there," Darcy said happily.

As the ladies piled into the van, Homer had never felt this special, but he couldn't forget Ash's threat. He was now *a couple* with Hannah and he must take good care of her.

When the van headed down the highway, Darcy said, "Look, there's the sheriff's car and he's got someone in the back. And there's another police car. I wonder what happened. We seldom have any excitement like that around here. It's usually deathly quiet and perhaps even a bit boring."

"Well, we surely had a good time at the brunch, Amanda. And, you received so many lovely gifts. That's plenty of excitement for me," Hannah said.

"I hope nothing is wrong," Phoebe said.

"We'll know soon enough," Hannah said.

The chatter in Quentin's living room had reached a high pitch. The ladies were trying to guess why they were there, while the men seemed to be enjoying peaking their curiosity even higher.

"Okay, folks, gather round," Quentin said as he joined Amanda on the sofa. "We had a situation today that you need to know about. Let me tell you the entire story. This may take a while so be patient."

As the details of the takedown of Ash came to light, all faces were on Quentin. When Quentin first mentioned Ash's name, Amanda drew her breath in and tightened her grip on Quentin's hand. From time to time, Hannah would glance at Homer in disbelief. Darcy, however, was smiling broadly, as she heard about Roberto's outstanding performance in the well-planned sting. She was obviously proud of his participation.

"I'm pleased to see that you took Ana and the baby home. I'll make sure that I meet with Ana later to express our gratitude for her help. She's the one who gave us what we needed to put Ash away for a long time," Quentin said as he put his arm around Amanda.

"Roberto, you're amazing. I wish I could have been there. How did you ever think about the *Grey Ghosts?*" Darcy asked.

"It just popped out," Ray replied. "But I must say, it's been a long time since I had such a blast though. Quentin, thanks for letting me be a part of this. When are we going to do this again?"

"Never, I hope," Amanda said. "All of you could have been hurt—you know that, don't you?"

"Now I have to go back to boring Hollywood," Steve said. "Here I had a taste of the real thing. Quentin, I thank you for the opportunity. I kinda like these overalls." Steve said as he tugged on the straps. "Not to change the subject, but does everyone know about Barclay's offer?"

"Steve has made an offer for one of Barclay's books," Quentin said proudly.

"Does that mean that he'll be making a movie of the story?" Hannah asked.

"In all probability. But it's an option," Steve explained. "First, I must get the funding. And funders make their decisions based on who we can get as the script writer, what actors are interested, and whether or not they think they can make oodles of money off the project. All of that takes time. But I have high hopes."

"How exciting!" Darcy said. "This Ash thing and now we hear about a movie. I thought this place was dull."

"Steve, you ought to consider using Roberto in the film. He was an outstanding actor today. He even had me convinced that the *Grey Ghosts* were going after Ash," Quentin said.

Ray was taking all this in. Perhaps he could be a good actor. After all, he was acting for several years now—going into and out of one persona after another. But he surely didn't want or need such notoriety.

After the others had gone, Quentin knew that he had to talk with Amanda about the press. He was not looking forward to having to tell her what they must do. "Amanda, darling, Sheriff Wagner gave me some advice today. You know, the press will find out about Ash's arrest and they'll want to know more. Wagner believes that we should be upfront with them."

"Oh, Quentin, I didn't think of that," Amanda said.

"You don't have to tell them everything. You were fourteen, he abused you, and took photographs. Wagner's certain that, because of your age at the time, the press will be respectful. You were not responsible for what happened to you. You were an innocent child."

"In my heart I know you're right, but I'll have to live it all over again."

"No, darling, you won't. You are a woman who has been able to heal herself. You are well thought of by everyone who knows you. You are loved. I will be by your side. The article will come out, and in a few days, it will no longer be news. What will happen in a few weeks is that you will become Mrs. Quentin Toth."

To Quentin's displeasure, someone was knocking on his front door. He heard Homer's voice, "Quentin, Quentin, come quick."

"What's wrong, Homer?"

"It's Ana and Jennie—they're gone." Homer said through his tears.

"Gone? What?"

"Hannah wanted to drop off the baby's car seat that I had in the van. When I tried to return it, there was no answer when I rang the bell. The door was unlocked so we went in. The place was a mess. Things were tossed all over and the two of them are gone!"

CHAPTER 28

Darcy was happier than she had been in a long time. Most of her friends liked Roberto—in fact, they considered him the star of the sting the men pulled off today. She knew that Russ wasn't pleased that she was dating Roberto, but he would just have to get used to it. She brushed her hair and let it fall slightly over her face. Her new lilac satin teddy fit her form perfectly. Picking up the matching short robe, she slipped her arms into the sleeves and tied the sash around her waist, forming a small bow in the front.

"Darcy," Ray called out.

Darcy stuck her head around the corner and said invitingly, "You rang, sir?"

"Babe, come here," he said as he crooked his finger. "My God, you're a vision."

Darcy practically flew across the living room floor.

"Yes, master, I'm your slave," she said as she cuddled up against him.

Ray smiled. "Well, if I'm your master then you must do anything I ask of you."

"Oh, that sounds questionable," Darcy said.

"No, babe, I need to have a serious talk with you. This involves my job and our future."

When Darcy heard the word *future* her heart almost stopped beating.

Ray turned to face Darcy. "I'll be involved in two cases very shortly. One will be about a week or so, but the other might, and I emphasize *might*, take quite some time. While I won't be happy being separated from you, I'm obligated. The good news, however, is that I plan to leave my government job as soon as these cases are over. That will leave us free to plan our own future. We can go wherever we want to and do anything we want. Darcy, how do you feel about this?"

"Roberto, darling, I'll endure any separation now that I know we'll have a future. You have made me the happiest woman ever!"

"I must explain how the government works to protect my identity. They establish paper trails for several different backgrounds for me. One time they may plot out a scenario for a professional man, another time they may make me out as a no-account scoundrel. And, if anyone tries to tell you terrible things about me, you must understand that they are untrue. Act as normal as possible if this happens, but know in your heart that I'm none of those things that you may see on the Internet. And, if I don't show up at Amanda's wedding, you'll need to just say that I am on an urgent business trip." He took her in his arms and kissed her tenderly. "Darcy, Darcy, you're my woman. I'll need you to help me with something involving this case. I won't be able to explain the entire caper that will come down. You will need to trust me. And what I ask you to do absolutely must be kept between the two of us. Do I have your complete commitment to me?"

"Darling, yes, yes, yes."

"If you remember nothing else, remember this—I may be away for a long time, but I will come back for you. As long as I know that you'll wait for me, Darcy, I'll be able to hang on and complete my assignment." Once again, he took her in his arms, and the two were locked in a long, passionate embrace.

Darcy lay in his arms, enveloped in complete contentment. "What is it you want me to do?"

"I have some papers—vitally important papers—that must be kept in a safe place. I trust you enough to turn them over to you. However, no one—and I really mean no one, must know that you have them or that you even know about them. And, if I contact you to bring the documents to me, you must not tell anyone. You must come to me no matter where I am. Remember, Darcy, we are now a team. Now, this part is hard, this case is a bad one and could involve one of your friends."

"Here, at The Haven?"

"Yes."

"Who?"

"I can't tell you, sweetheart. You'll know later, but I can't jeopardize your safety by revealing the name. So, later, when something goes down, even if it goes down at The Haven, you must act as though you're as baffled as anyone else. This case could turn tragic, Darcy, and if it does, it may be hard for you to maintain your silence. But you'll be protecting me, and, most importantly, you must protect that package I give you. No one, Darcy—absolutely no one—must know anything about it." Ray dropped his head and covered his eyes with his hands. "Maybe you would rather I get out of your life right now. I don't want you to be sorry that you ever met me."

Darcy fell to her knees. "Roberto, I love you. I'll do anything you ask of me. You are the most important person in my life. I promise you that I'll do as you ask. I'll wait for you forever. You must know that by now," Darcy said as she wrapped her arms around Ray.

The two of them stretched out on the carpet. Ray took a small pillow from the sofa and placed it under Darcy's head. Slowly, very slowly, he gently pulled on the sash of her robe.

CHAPTER 29

Quentin was seated in front of Sheriff Wagner who was visibly upset. Wagner was drumming his fingers on the desk while muttering, "I knew that yesterday wouldn't be the end of this, Quentin. I never should have agreed to go along with your stunt. Now, we have an even bigger problem that may bring the Feds into all of it."

"The way I look at it…"

"Yeah, the Hollywood way. Shit, this is real life. Now, I've got a missing woman and her baby. By now they could be anywhere. You should have seen this coming, Quentin."

"Now let me finish. Look, if Ash's followers took her, then they want to use her for a bargaining chip. I would venture that either you or I will be contacted before too long."

"I can't bargain with anyone, Quentin, you know that. This is no movie. When are you going to accept that as a fact?"

"I don't think they will harm her. She is, after all, their leader's wife. They want to get Ash out on bail. Then they can whisk him away to God-knows-where. They will threaten to harm Ana, no doubt about that."

"But, Quentin, suppose they do harm her? Are you ready for that?"

Quentin was silent. "If they do, I couldn't live with that. But I really don't believe they would do that."

"Well, sir, you better hope that you're right." Wagner paced back and forth in his office. "I will put someone on this. We can't make an official report until she's been gone forty-eight hours. I hope we can solve this before that time comes. Meanwhile, keep this out of the papers. We have Homer and Hannah in the next room and they're being interviewed. The poor woman is as white as a ghost. You need to reassure them that all will be well and to keep what they know to themselves. Can you do that?"

"Of course. They are good people. They'll do as I ask," Quentin said. "You better hope so."

"If I'm asked to arrange bail for Ash and Darrell, should I do that?"

"You bet. We'll have someone on their tails at all times," Wagner responded. "I used to think that my job was a lifetime thing. Lately, I am no longer that certain. But this time, we could have someone's life hanging in the balance. And, that's more important than any job."

CHAPTER 30

Fat Tony was pumped. Ray had contacted him to arrange to give him the documents. While Ray had told him that he was going to do this, Tony wasn't sure that it would ever happen. Now it was getting closer to the big pay day from Big Cheese. He was making all kinds of plans. First, he knew that he had a hit to do—but this would be an easy one. The dumb dame was an easy mark, especially with all those windows around her dance studio. He wasn't sure yet when Ray wanted the job completed, but then, any day was okay with him. He knew that Ray needed him to complete the job since Ray didn't have the guts to do it himself. It was good to be needed. Tony began to think about the good time that he was going to have in Vegas as soon as the money was in his hands. Later on, Ray would probably need him again and then there would be another pay day.

Ray insisted that Tony steal a car to drive to their meeting place. That seemed a bit odd but then that kooky Ray had all kinds of dumb ideas. Taking a car was the easy part. The hard part was to be patient enough to wait until it was dark when the exchange would take place. Tony had already violated one of Ray's demands, though; he had driven over to the storage place just to make certain that there was one in the back like Ray said—sure enough it was there. And, it looked like there was a brand new lock hanging in the slot.

After what seemed like an eternity, it was time to move to the meeting place. Fat Tony already felt like a rich man. He began to imagine that he was in Vegas, in a rented sports car, with two women in the car with him. He could hardly wait. He hoped that Ray wanted the babe offed immediately. He dimmed the lights and pulled into the dirt lane to make certain that the car would be completely hidden by the tree limbs. He cursed when he spotted an old van parked right where he wanted to be.

He couldn't be certain if there was anyone in the van, but he knew that he had to check it out. He opened the glove compartment and, remarkably, found a flashlight. Tony opened the car door as quietly as he could. Feeling his way along the rusty old van, he lifted the flashlight up and put it on high beam. Caught in the glare of the light, two half-dressed, frightened teenagers were looking back at him.

"What the hell are you two doing?" Tony shouted. "This is private property. I ought to shoot the both of you dumb asses."

"I'm sorry," was all the young boy could get out.

"You turn this fucking rusty bucket around and get the hell out of here, or I swear I'll blow you to kingdom come," Tony said, all the while waving the flashlight up and down.

The young boy looked frantic. He scraped a few trees in his attempt to move the van, but he was finally successful in turning it around in such a small space. Tony stood with his hands on his hips until the van pulled out onto the highway. Then, he walked back to his car, pulled it in a bit farther, and tried to relax until Ray arrived. As he waited, he kept looking into the rearview mirror. Ray also had instructed him not to get out of his car, but to unlock the trunk of his car only when he spotted Ray walking toward him. Suddenly, there were lights behind him. Tony watched intently. Ray got out of his car, carrying several packages. Tony hit the button to unlock the trunk. After a minute or two, Tony heard Ray closing the trunk. Ray walked to the driver's side of Tony's car.

"There, the documents are in your trunk—plus a few other items I want you to put in the storage locker. Here's the key. I don't want you to get out of your car to examine what I put in your trunk. Do you hear that, Tony?"

"Yeah, yeah. When the hell are you gonna stop ordering me around?" Tony said angrily.

"Are you gonna bitch when you get your money for all of this?" Ray snapped.

"No, but...."

"Tony, the hit is scheduled for tomorrow night. The dancer will be in her studio after nine. No funny business, though. Just shoot her and get the hell out."

"That's not the way I usually work," Tony snapped back.

"You want to get your ass caught? You want to go to jail?"

"Course not."

"Then follow my directions. I have it all set up for you. Get there after dark. Do it. Get out. It's as simple as that. Have I ever let you down on anything that I set up?" Ray asked.

"No. How long will it take to get paid?"

"I wasn't gonna tell you this, but I put a surprise in the trunk. Since you'll be done with your part tomorrow night, I put some cash in there to ease things for you until we get paid. So, as soon as I leave, drive to the storage locker, unload, and then be certain that you lock it up tight. Do your thing tomorrow and by next Friday, you'll have all your money. Is that clear enough?"

"Okay, okay," Tony replied. As Ray walked away, Tony realized that he had forgotten to tell him about the teenagers. Well, it's for the better that he doesn't know that. He's such a nervous Nellie about things like that.

Ray backed his car out onto the highway and took off. He was smiling all the way, knowing that Tony was going to be anxious to see how much money Ray had given him. Tony sat still for a few minutes, but he could no longer stand not knowing what was in that damned trunk. He once again popped the trunk open. He wiggled his fat belly from under the wheel and stepped out. His heart starting beating rapidly as he stood there with great anticipation. Slowly, as if Ray might be able to see what he was doing, he pushed the lid of the trunk up. Tony moved his hands around in the dark to feel for the bag with the money. He hadn't thought about taking the flashlight with him. "Come on, where are you?" were his last words. He never saw the wire. But Ray, who was getting off the highway at the same time, chuckled when he heard the loud explosion.

"Arrivederci, Tony," he said to the night air.

CHAPTER 31

"I'm telling you, Wagner, I don't know anything about that car exploding. It has no connection to our little sting with Ash," Quentin said firmly. "Are you going to accuse me every time something strange happens around here? You just had me in here yesterday."

"Let's look at the score board. You pull off your little sting, then a woman and her child disappear, and then a man is blown to kingdom come. Now what does that look like to you? If this keeps up, I'm going to have to hire more deputies. Damn, now I've got a headache," Wagner said as he reached for a pill bottle.

"You forgot one incident, Wagner. How about the man who was peeping in the windows at The Haven?"

"You, it's you who's responsible for my headache. Now get the hell out of here and pray that nothing else happens like this."

"If you hear anything…"

"Get going, Quentin."

As Quentin walked to his car, he thought about what Wagner had said. He had no idea if the car bombing was connected to Ana's disappearance. But somehow he couldn't picture that skinny little Ash being involved with dynamite. Just as he was getting in his car, he heard someone calling out his name. He stood up and spotted Homer running across the parking lot, waving his arms frantically.

"Mr. Quentin, oh, Mr. Quentin, wait, please wait," Homer shouted.

Homer, who was breathing very hard, appeared to be in distress.

"Homer, calm down," Quentin said. As Homer tried valiantly to speak, Quentin put his hand on Homer's shoulder and said, "Okay, Homer, okay. Now just be quiet a minute. That's it. When you catch your breath, then you can tell me what's so important."

"I think I know where she is."

"Ana? You know where Ana is?" Quentin said with a surprised look on his face.

"She tried calling you, but your line was busy so she called Hannah-- she called Hannah," Homer said frantically.

"What?"

"She called Hannah. She said she couldn't speak long. She was in a shower. She asked Hannah to come and get her at the Blue Bell Motel. Amanda told me where you were. I came just as fast as I could."

Quentin turned on his heels and ran back into Wagner's office. "Wagner, get your boys over to the Blue Bell Motel. Ana's there. She called."

"Are you telling me the truth?" Wagner asked in disbelief.

"Don't ask any more questions. Get your men over there now," Quentin shouted.

Quentin wanted to follow the deputies, but he decided that would make Wagner even angrier. It seemed like an eternity until they returned to the sheriff's office with Ana and Jennie. He couldn't help but breathe easier when he saw them. There was a man and a woman, huddled together, in the back seat of the deputy's car. Wagner got out of his car and motioned to Quentin to follow him inside.

"You are one lucky sonofabitch, Quentin. Ana had a cell phone in the bottom of Jennie's diaper bag. She's one smart woman. The woman and the man we picked up are church members." Wagner shook his head from side to side. "Now, will you promise to stay out of trouble and let me get on with just keeping the peace?" Wagner asked.

"Please let me listen in on your interrogation, Wagner. Please. I promise that I won't cause any more problems and I will keep whatever I hear to myself. I may be able to help you in some way. I owe you," Quentin pleaded.

"You are one pushy fellow. Do you know that? Okay, you may listen from the side room. But, so help me God, if you cause any more problems for me, I will personally ship you to China!"

Quentin took a seat where he could look through the one way mirror. He saw Wagner entering the room with just the woman. She was a pathetic-looking creature. Plain ugly brown dress, no makeup and stringy, dirty-blonde hair. A deputy, carrying a tape recorder, joined the group.

"Do you know why you are here?" Wagner asked the woman.

"No, I don't. We did nothing wrong," she said defiantly.

"Well, the last time I looked at the law books, kidnapping is illegal," Wagner said.

"It was not kidnapping. We rescued Ana and her child from the clutches of evil-doers. We wanted an opportunity to speak with her—to bring her to her senses," the woman said.

"The evil-doers are?" Wagner asked.

"Those of you who have not reached the pinnacle of understanding."

"Oh, I see. And you? Have you reached that pinnacle?"

"Of course. And, I feel so sorry for you that you do not understand," she replied.

"You're not here to give a sermon. You're here because you and your husband took a woman and her child out of their home and tried to hide them in a motel."

"Not true. She just needed time to realize that she must remain faithful, not only to Adam, but to her church as well. Is that too difficult for you to grasp?"

"How did you get into her apartment?"

"We are soldiers of our church. We were sent there and told to wait for an opportunity to speak with her. And, when someone dropped her and the child off, we simply followed her into the apartment."

"And, did she want to go with you?" Wagner asked.

"Not at first. But Joshua got her to change her mind?"

"I assume that Joshua is your husband?"

"Yes. Adam married us last year."

Quentin could hardly stay in his chair. He felt as if he were looking in on something that happened many years ago. The woman explained that they had been kind to Ana and the child. They saw to it that they bathed and were fed. She maintained that at no time did they threaten Ana with any physical abuse. Wagner then posed some questions that seemed to focus on the car bombing, but the woman steadfastly denied any connection.

"Do you realize what the penalty for kidnapping is in the Commonwealth?" Wagner asked.

"I am not afraid of that. We did not kidnap her. We are her friends."

Wagner turned to his deputy. "I'm finished questioning her. Now bring her husband in!"

CHAPTER 32

The parking lot at The Haven was filling up rapidly. Homer was busy directing traffic and helping some of the little ones whose arms were filled with fluffy pink and lilac costumes. It was a very important day for the children, who had completed the semester with Phoebe as their dance instructor. The studio had been transformed into a storybook land with large colorful butterflies and fuzzy little bunnies peeping out from behind papier-mâché rocks. Excitement filled the air. The youngest group, representing little ones from nine to ten, would present their recital first. Barclay had seen their presentation several times, so he knew what to expect while he was video-taping the group. He had no idea what the older ones would be doing, but he hoped that he would do a good job for Phoebe.

Barclay was pleased that Phoebe had agreed to go with him to a party that his students were throwing tonight to celebrate his movie option. While he appreciated their efforts, he only hoped that the next party would be one to celebrate a film of his book.

Phoebe was a vision of loveliness as she moved from student to student, making sure that all was well with their costumes and providing the girls with words of encouragement to build their self-confidence. Hannah was not too far behind her, lending a helping hand as yards and yards of chiffon and tulle seemed to be everywhere.

Meanwhile, among the spectators there was a lot of discussion about the explosion on the interstate the night before.

"Maybe it was a meth lab somewhere in the woods," one lady said.

"I saw Sheriff Wagner this morning at the bakery, and he said that the Feds were on their way to investigate and that he has no idea what happened and whether anyone was hurt," another lady said emphatically.

Hannah had a table set up in the back of the room with plates of little cupcakes and several bowls of punch for everyone to enjoy after the performance was over. Russ and Darcy were there, too, helping wherever they were needed.

"What do you think about the explosion?" Russ asked Barclay.

"I haven't the foggiest," Barclay responded.

"Could it be connected to, you know, the thing we did last week?"

Barclay looked surprised. "Russ, it never crossed my mind. I doubt it, though. I think Ash and his crew were strictly amateurs. But, now that you mention it, perhaps we need to talk with Quentin about this. I would hate to think that The Haven is still in jeopardy."

As the music began, Barclay knew what the big finale for the first presentation would be—he had seen it many times. The littlest girls, who were dressed in pink, were the seeds in the garden, while the older girls, in lilac, represented the sun and the rain. It was such a delight to see the little ones suddenly stand up and dance away on their toes. Of course, he found anything that Phoebe did fascinating. Barclay found the second offering just as lovely. The older girls were definitely more poised than the younger ones. When the recital was over, the audience demonstrated their pleasure with a long, rousing round of applause. Phoebe came to the front and was presented with a bouquet of flowers from one of the dancers. Of course, she cried.

When the applause ended, Phoebe said, "Ladies and gentlemen, I have a wonderful announcement to make. As you know, we have a special dance troupe of six girls who have made several appearances at local events. Because of Mr. Quentin Toth's generosity, the troupe will be participating in a contest that will be held in Pittsburgh next month. Mr. Toth has taken care of the entrance fees, overnight lodging costs, and transportation to and from the event. Needless to say, the girls and I are excited and we will be working diligently during the next four weeks, preparing for this very special occasion. The girls already have started practicing some of the routines, and they are eagerly looking forward to their participation. Miss Hannah King, our needlework instructor, will be making our costumes. Regardless where we finish in the contest, this will be a marvelous experience for the girls. They will have an opportunity to meet and greet girls from all over Pennsylvania, who are also interested in ballet. So keep us in mind and wish us luck," Phoebe said almost breathlessly.

As the parents moved forward to congratulate her, Phoebe was delighted. Nothing pleased her more than when she saw others enjoying the art of ballet. She moved effortlessly from one group to another.

"Great job, Phoebe," Hannah said.

"I so appreciated what you did, Hannah. How nice of you to bake so many cupcakes. My little ones are now more in love with you," Phoebe said, laughingly.

"But we have an even bigger event coming," Hannah reminded the other teachers. "Not only must we prepare for the contest, but we must also get ready for the wedding."

"Just think," Darcy said. "The wedding's only two weeks away. "Ladies, we've got to get cracking with our decorations. I have some of them in my studio—I'll go get them."

"Wait until you see the arbor that Homer made. It's beautiful. Now, we must all pray for a sunny day," Hannah said.

When everyone had gone, Barclay sat down on the bench to wait for Phoebe to change her clothes. Just then Russ came back into the studio.

"I had to show you this, Barclay. It's today's paper. Look, they have an artist's sketch of a man they claim was in the car that exploded."

"How'd they manage to get that?"

"It seems there were a couple of teenagers making out in the same lane where the explosion occurred. The boy walked into the police station and told them that he and his girl were parked in that lane when they were chased away by a man who had threatened to kill them. He described the man, and the artist made this sketch. Does he look familiar to you?"

"What's going on," Phoebe asked as she came out of the dressing room.

"Is something going on?" Darcy asked as she appeared with an armful of crepe paper.

"They have a sketch of a man they think died in that explosion," Barclay said as he held up the paper for Phoebe and Darcy to see.

"My God, Barclay, it's him—the man in the window," Phoebe said in a whisper.

"Who? Do you mean the guy you saw when we were dancing?"

Phoebe just stared ahead. Then, softly, she said, "Yes, it's him."

"Darcy, can you reach Roberto?" Barclay asked. "He was certain that we had seen the last of this guy."

"Well," Russ said, "if it was him that got blown up in that car, Roberto was right. We sure as hell won't see him again."

Darcy knew this would be her first test. She wanted to protect Roberto. What's the right thing to say? "Well, he left two days ago for an assignment. I can't call him but he does call me. Yesterday, he was in Hobbs, New Mexico. I think there's some kind of government building there. He probably doesn't even know that there was an explosion near here."

"If he calls, tell him about this. Ask him if he thinks any of us are in any kind of danger. The guy still doesn't have a name, at least according to the papers," Barclay said. "Meanwhile, I think we need to tell the sheriff."

"I'll do what I can," Darcy said. She turned around and quickly walked away.

Russ watched her leave. "You can call me *stubborn*—well maybe I am. But there's something I still don't like about Roberto. I know you think he was great during our little sting, but I still don't like him," Russ said strongly.

"I hear you, Russ," Barclay said. "But, hopefully, he'll know whether we need to be concerned about safety here at The Haven."

"I'm not afraid to say this, Barclay. If that guy does anything to hurt Darcy, I'll be the first in line with a shotgun," Russ said.

As Russ left her studio, Phoebe said, "I feel for him, Barclay. He puts up a good front, but I have known for some time that Darcy is special to him. He's just like a big brother to her. He wants so badly to protect her. But after all, Darcy is a grown woman and, if she wants to be with Roberto, there isn't too much Russ can do."

Phoebe's head was spinning. It seemed as if her whole world was out of control. She needed to get herself together. The fear that she felt when she spied that man looking into the window was retuning—but why? Supposedly, he was killed in the car explosion. She should be relieved that he was no longer a threat to her. Perhaps it was the apprehension she felt ever since she filled out the application for the dance contest. She had to provide information about where she studied ballet, particulars on her current employment, and any stage presentations in which she appeared as a dancer. The documentation identified her as Florence Gibble—not

Phoebe Snowden. She also had to agree that any of this information could be used on the programs for the contest. She realized it was time for her to tell Barclay about her past.

Without a doubt, she must move out of the darkness and into the light. She could not blind-side her lover. He needed to know. As Phoebe Snowden she had become so relaxed—comfortable and secure—surrounded by the aura of The Haven. She didn't want to lose what she had found. But maybe it would all disappear.

CHAPTER 33

Flannigan's patrons were ready to have a good time. The bar was normally busy on a Saturday night but tonight, since Barclay's students were holding a party to celebrate his option, the place was bursting at the seams with happy patrons. The party was in the back room that the students had decorated with life-size posters of Barclay and huge pictures of the book *A Touch of Murder*. When Barclay and Phoebe came through the doorway, the students shouted, *"Author... Author"*. One student quickly pulled out chairs for Phoebe and Barclay. "Please," he said, as he bowed.

"Thanks, Mark," the guest of honor said.

"Barclay, do you know any more about the explosion?" one student asked.

"You know as much as I do," Barclay said. "I haven't heard a thing."

"Well, I happen to know the boy who had been parked in the lane that night. Wow, he's in a heap of trouble with his parents. He had been grounded but he snuck out," Mark said. "They read the riot act to him when they found out that he had taken the van, and was parked in lover's lane."

"Hey, Mark, how do you know that it was a lover's lane?" another student joked.

"I have my ways," Mark replied.

"Barclay, we would like to drink a toast to you. First, I have a few words to say," one woman said as she stood up. "Even before you got an option on your book, we all knew that you were someone special. You made learning the elements of good writing fun. You always pointed out something good in anything that we wrote. But, more importantly, you always led us to discover how to make our own writing even better. While I may never achieve stardom in the writing world, you made me learn to love the art of writing—of listening to the words that I put down on paper to fully understand their meaning. Just hearing the words, words that I write—words that almost sound like music, is magic for me. I will always love you for that. So, raise your glasses one and all. We toast the best writing teacher in the world, Barclay Henderson."

And, with glasses clinking around the table, Barclay knew that, whether or not his book would ever turn into a film, he was already a winner.

"Barclay," one tall lanky student said, "I would like to volunteer to play the part of Jonathan in your movie. I'm tall, good with the ladies, and my mom thinks I'm handsome."

"You've got to be kidding, Harry. I'm much more the romantic type. Don't you think so, Miss Snowden?" another student said playfully.

Phoebe laughed.

"Hey, we aren't even sure yet whether or not there will be a film. But, I'll tell you what, if and when there is, I will give your names to the casting director," Barclay said.

The evening went fast. Everyone had stories to tell Phoebe about Barclay and she was enjoying every minute. The students were circulating around the bar, selling copies of Barclay's book and having a great time telling everyone that he was their teacher. Each student shook Barclay's hand and promised to register for the fall semester.

On the way home, Barclay said, "You know what, Phoebe? How could I be any luckier? With such good friends, and the most beautiful woman I have ever seen by my side, my world could end right now and I wouldn't have any complaints."

"That's nice. But, Barclay, I really hope you and I have a lot more time."

Phoebe laid her head on Barclay's shoulder. "You know what?" She leaned closer to his ear and softly whispered, "I love you."

Barclay's eyes opened wide. He hurriedly pulled the car over to the side of the road.

"Say that again, Phoebe."

"I love you."

He turned toward her and took her in his arms. "Phoebe, Phoebe. I love you, too." They kissed passionately. Phoebe nestled in Barclay's shoulder and he began stroking her hair. When one of the students drove past Barclay's parked car and honked his horn loudly, the lovers laughed long and hard.

"I guess I better get you home," Barclay said as he pulled out onto the road.

The two rode in silence, but Barclay still had Phoebe's hand in his.

When they finally closed the door to Phoebe's apartment, she said, "Remember when I told you that I had something to share with you—well it's time." Phoebe sank down onto the sofa and Barclay followed suit.

"Phoebe, are you sure you want to do this? I really don't...."

She smiled broadly. "Yes. You have taken control of my heart, Barclay, and if I want this relationship to move forward—and I do—then in all fairness you must know about my background." Phoebe began playing with the fringe on the pillow she had placed in her lap. "But, you must promise me that if what I'm going to tell you is something you cannot handle, that you'll be honest with me and let me know. I just realized that I used the word *honest* when I have not been honest with you. Okay, here goes. I grew up on a tree farm in Vermont, much like The Haven. Oh, we didn't hold classes like Amanda does, but it was a tree farm and our major business was selling Christmas trees and other types of evergreens to landscapers and such. My real name is Florence Gibble. Funny, though, I much prefer the name Phoebe. From the time I was a toddler, I wanted to be a dancer. My parents made great sacrifices that enabled me to take classes, participate in dance recitals, and go to ballets where I could imagine that I was on that stage as a famous ballerina."

Phoebe stood up, placed the pillow back on the sofa and began to wander around the room. Barclay didn't say a word—he wanted her to tell her story at her own pace.

"I sort of had my time on the stage. I danced in several productions— and then *he* came into my world."

Barclay felt as if an arrow had just pierced his heart. He shouldn't have been surprised that Phoebe had had men in her life—after all, look at the number of women who had been part of his. But just to imagine anyone else with her was agonizing.

"He was an important public figure—still is. In fact, he's a judge— Judge Kraft on the state supreme court. Anyway, I met him at a gala that benefited the local ballet company. He was charming, and he knew all the right things to say. He was a great deal older than I and he certainly would not be considered handsome. While a little on the heavy side, he still made women turn their heads when they saw him. I was flattered that someone that powerful noticed me and I thought I was in love."

Phoebe paced a bit. She took a deep breath and said, "We started dating and the world became a much different place for me. We traveled. He bought me all kinds of things—things that I thought I would never have. My nineteen-year-old brain was much too immature to realize that it would appear to others that I was nothing more than a well-paid hooker. My parents objected strongly. But then I wrote them off as old fuddy-duddies and thought that I knew what was best for me. I can't believe that I ever let him touch me."

Phoebe sat down once again. "I began noticing things—late night calls, people coming and going. They would arrive at our doorway at all hours of the night. Packages would arrive that he would immediately take into his study—never revealing to me what the contents were. Then, there was his lackey—someone he called *The Man*. I never knew his real name. But I would find them in deep discussions that would always stop as soon as I entered the room. I wrote this off to legal business that he simply could not share with me. I would go shopping and bring home whatever I wanted. I started noticing that the sales clerks would bend over backwards for me. I'd get the best table in restaurants. He would let me decide where we would go on our next vacation, and, somehow, he made me aware that dancing was over. While I still wanted to dance, I had sold myself for the so-called good life."

"After about a year, things began to change. He became more controlling and more demanding. At first, I thought it was my fault and I tried to placate him whenever I could. When he began questioning who I was with and what I was doing, even when I had his permission, I was afraid that I might do something to upset him. He didn't hesitate to remind me that he would not tolerate my leaving him and making him look like a fool. He told me stories of how some individuals, who had displeased him, simply disappeared from sight and were never seen again. I had never experienced such fear. The cold look in his eyes was enough to let me know that he was serious. His jowls would shake and his eyes would fill with anger. Then, he would apologize, shower me with luxurious gifts and tender love-making sessions, and I would tell myself that this time he meant what he said. But, in a short period of time, the ugliness would begin again."

Phoebe took a few deep breaths. "Then, when I got the call that my father had died, I saw another side of him—uglier than before. He said that I could go to the funeral only if I promised to make certain that I would be getting the farm when my mother died. I didn't argue. When I arrived in Burlington, my Uncle Wilson took me under his wing. He explained that my father had been angry with me for living with Kraft, and as a result, he had stipulated that I was not to get anything until I turned twenty-five. Until that time, Uncle Wilson was to take care of the expenses for my mother. He assured me that he did not need any of the money nor did he want to run the tree farm. So, the two of us decided that he should put the farm up for sale. Meanwhile, he would have his bank make the monthly payments to the nursing home for my mother. I knew this arrangement would not sit well with the judge."

Barclay wanted to take her in his arms and let her know that he loved her no matter what. But, he thought it best to let her move ahead on her own terms.

"I can still see the judge's face when I explained what happened. He was livid. He started calling me names, all the time waving his arms in the air like a maniac. He called me *stupid*. He stomped around the living room and began hurling things around. With each tirade, his face became more and more flushed. I could see the sweat running down his forehead. I tried to calm him down. He then called me an *imbecile*. Suddenly, he fell to the floor in a heap. The Man and I rushed him to the hospital. The judge had had a heart attack and the doctor said he would be hospitalized for about ten days."

Phoebe looked down at the floor. She was afraid to look directly at Barclay. "I began thinking that what happened to the judge was my fault. I blamed myself for not handling the situation better. I told myself, that when he got home, the judge would once again apologize for his behavior, and maybe, just maybe, things between the two of us would be different. As I sat in the waiting room at the hospital, The Man came in and approached me. We had seldom talked so his nearness unnerved me. He sat down beside me and leaned over. Very quietly, he told me that if

I walked out on the judge, he would dispose of the collateral damage—I realized quickly that he meant me—in a heartbeat."

Phoebe got up and paced a bit. She suddenly turned around and said, "God, Barclay, this is hard."

"Then stop. I don't need to know, Phoebe. I mean it."

"It must be now; I can't live with this any longer. "I went back to the judge's house to clear my head. I felt that no one would believe me if I told them the judge would kill me. It was during that time that I discovered what was going on right under my stupid nose. I was alone in the house that I had started thinking was mine, when I wandered into his den. I knew that there was a safe behind one of the pictures and, for some reason, I pulled the picture away to discover that the safe wasn't locked. I took out a yellow plastic binder and sat down behind his desk. I started looking at the papers, feeling like a traitor and a snoop. It took me some time to put the pieces together, but I did. My lover, the man that I thought would someday be my husband, was taking thousands of dollars in kickbacks and was even involved in the drug trade."

"Oh, darling, that had to be devastating," Barclay said.

"The only thing I could think of was to run away. I couldn't stay. I knew I wouldn't be able to hide from him the fact that I knew some of his dirty secrets. But, where to go? Uncle Wilson was on another photo assignment around the world. It was then that I thought of Amanda. I had met her a few years prior at a conference for tree growers and we formed an instant friendship. In my screwed up pattern of thinking, I decided that if I took the binder with me, it could be my safety net. I rejected the idea of turning the packet over to the police—I couldn't do that. I thought I still loved him. At the same time, I also despised him. There were stacks of money in the safe. I didn't take any. I wanted to get far away from him. I struggled at first, financially, but Amanda was most gracious."

"I longed to see my mother. I kept thinking about her. I tried to put the threats that the judge and The Man had made in the back of my mind. On my first break at The Haven, I decided to take a chance and I drove to Burlington. I took along a nurse's uniform, dark glasses, and a cloche for my head. In my disguise, I slipped into the backdoor of the nursing home. As I was talking with my mother, I glanced out the window and spotted The Man coming up the walkway. I hurried into the bathroom that was jointly used by my mother and the lady in the next room. I slipped out the door that led to the next room. I breathed easier when I realized that the patient in that room was sound asleep. I waited in that room for an hour before I was brave enough to go back to my mother. I kissed her and tucked her in bed. She had no idea who I was. I realized later that the judge probably had had a contact in the nursing home, so I never went back again."

The tears began to flow. It was then that Barclay pulled her into his arms. "No, Barclay, there is more. Let me finish. I kept the binder that I had taken from the judge's safe in the little chest in my dance studio at The Haven. About a month or so ago, I noticed that some costumes that I had piled on the top had been moved. And, when I opened the trunk, the binder was gone."

"Gone?"

"Yes. I thought that maybe the man, who peered in my studio window that night, might have come back and had taken the binder. And, perhaps, the judge had ordered him to come back to punish me—or even to kill me. I couldn't tell you—I wanted to, but I was afraid."

"Afraid? Of the judge?"

"Yes."

"Phoebe, he's a judge. Do you really think he'd hurt you?"

"He swore that he would get even. He said that he could track me down and get rid of me and nobody would know what happened to me. Yes, he would hurt me if he had the opportunity. Right now, I'm not afraid. But once the contest is over, whether my class wins or not, there will be press coverage of the contest. That's when he'll know for certain where I am."

"Let's think about this. You don't have the documents. That means that you have no proof that he did anything illegal, so going to the authorities is out. If he *does* have the documents, he has no need to harm you. Phoebe. I guess it would be a dumb idea just to pick up the phone and call him."

"Don't ask me to do that," Phoebe pleaded. "But he might not know that I don't have them."

"Well, you're safe for now. I'll be with you every step of the way when you take the girls to Pittsburgh. Maybe we should hire someone to protect you until we know for certain that no harm will come to you. I'm not going to let you go through life being afraid, Phoebe. If it means that I face this famous judge in person, then that's what I'll do. I'm not taking any chances with you."

"Barclay, I don't want a body guard. Please, don't hire one," Phoebe pleaded.

"Okay, for now. Let's not overlook Roberto. Darcy said he's on an assignment right now, but she thinks he'll be back before too long. Let's talk with him. Meanwhile, don't say anything to anyone about the documents or the judge. Roberto might be our answer."

CHAPTER 34

Russ didn't know why Quentin and Amanda wanted to see him, but it seemed that Lady Luck was on his side because he had some ideas that he wanted to run by them. He had been mulling over ways that The Haven could increase business, but he hadn't been certain that he'd be able to present his plans to Amanda in a manner that wouldn't come off as pushy. Amanda hadn't announced any changes in The Haven as a result of her upcoming marriage, and he didn't want to appear to be a leech. As he drove along in the gentle rain, he kept practicing how he would open up the dialog. However, each version seemed worse than the last one. He hadn't noticed that the rain had stopped until his windshield wipers began dragging over the glass, creating an annoying squeak. Then, as he started climbing the little hill leading to The Haven, the sun began shining, creating a bright canvas on which to view the beautiful trees and flowers along the lane. As he stepped out of his car, Russ spied a rainbow that seemed to hover right over The Haven—surely a sign that all would go well.

"Good to see you again, Russ," Quentin said, "Please have a seat. Amanda and I have been discussing our honeymoon and the subject of who would manage The Haven while we are away came up. We both immediately thought of you. What do you think?"

"What an honor. Of course, I will do what I can," Russ responded.

"I want you to meet with my accountant, Russ, so you can sign documents that will allow you to make decisions, pay bills, and so forth while we're gone." Amanda said. "In this way, you'll be protected since you'll be the acting manager. Since we're not having a summer session, except for Phoebe's July class, it will be fairly quiet around here. But you know how it is—who knows what concerns and problems might arise? You should see the applications coming in already for Barclay's class! Since the article about Barclay was in the paper, everyone wants to become a writer," Amanda said. "And, there are some classroom adjustments that must be made, too."

"All of this borders on what I wanted to discuss with you. For some time now, I have been thinking about ways to expand the services that we offer at The Haven. I hope you don't think this is too bold of me," Russ said.

"Russ, you're family. I'm excited that you've given this some thought. Tell me about your ideas," Amanda said.

"I think we should enlarge the gift shop and keep it open all year. I would like to suggest that the store specialize in things for Christmas. People seem to shop for Christmas all year round now. In addition, we could possibly do away with that one storage area behind Fifi to create an office. You really should have a place to meet with students and vendors alike."

"My goodness, Russ. This sounds exciting. I love the idea. Quentin, what do you think?" Amanda asked.

"The idea of a Christmas shop is certainly an excellent one," Quentin said. "Homer could start on some of the work this summer. We'll probably need some building permits and such."

"I recommend that you give me parameters as far as the budget is concerned. I don't want to cause financial problems," Russ said.

"You and Amanda can talk that over. But, since I'll be her financial backer, she has carte blanche from me," Quentin said.

"I would like to recommend that we have a logo for the shop. As soon as I saw the necklace you gave Amanda—the Christmas tree one—I thought it would be great to have such a piece in our shop. My students could create the trees, using birthstones for the tree topper. We could even put the logo on our shopping bags."

"Oh, Russ, I love it," Amanda said excitedly.

"I have another suggestion. I think we should add some artists. For instance, photography—especially with all these high-tech gadgets that are on the market. I'm certain that many people need help. Look what phones can do now—everything but wash the dishes," Russ said. "Some people have inquired about the possibility of a pottery class, but I don't know anything about that field at all. Tell you what, while you're gone, Amanda, I'll draft some ideas and maybe your accountant can help me cost them out for your consideration when you return," Russ said.

"Alright. Start with photography. See where that goes," Amanda said. "This assignment may just lead to something more permanent, Russ. As you are aware, I consider the tree farm a true haven. It's been for me, as well as Phoebe and Ana. If we can continue providing sanctuary for those who need it, The Haven with its aura will not only prosper, but will continue to fulfill its destiny."

Russ drove away with a renewed sense of purpose. The idea of running The Haven's gift shop and the classes even for a short period of time really appealed to him. He became excited over the thought of adding managerial responsibilities to his resume. Now, the next thing he would have to do was to get rid of Roberto one way or another. As silly scenarios for ways to do this entered his mind, he chuckled. Well, he thought, how about another explosion?

CHAPTER 35

Darcy ran up the front steps of The Haven. She was late once again. She could tell that Phoebe and Hannah were already there since their cars were parked out front. She had several shopping bags over her arms that were filled with paper wedding bells and silk flowers—her contribution to the decorations needed for Amanda's wedding. Just as the front door opened and Hannah stepped out on the porch, Darcy's cell phone rang. Darcy hurriedly gave Hannah the bags and walked to the far end of the porch and sat down on a wicker rocker. Turning her back toward Hannah, she excitedly said, "Hello."

Hannah got the message that Darcy wanted her privacy so she went inside and shut the front door.

'Baby, it's me."

Darcy's heart skipped a beat. She hadn't spoken to Roberto for several days and she missed hearing his voice.

"Darling, I was hoping that it was you. God, I miss you," she said.

"Not as much as I miss you, baby. Is everything okay?" Ray asked.

"Well, right after you left for your trip, there was a car explosion up on the highway."

"My God. Was anyone hurt?"

"At first, they didn't know who, if anyone, was in the car. As luck would have it, some teenagers had been parked right where the car was found. They had been chased away by a man who had threatened to kill them. They were able to describe the man to the police and they put a sketch of the man in the paper. When Phoebe saw the sketch, she claimed that it was the same man who had been peeking in her window. Later on, they identified the guy from some tags they found in the debris. It's the talk of the town," Darcy explained. "I hope he doesn't have any friends who are still around here who just might…"

"Listen, I cannot explain, but, no, he doesn't have any friends who can harm you. He was just a small-time hood. I told you before that I took care of the matter, now relax and just go about your normal life."

"My life cannot be normal without you. Do you know when you'll be back?"

"Not yet. This case is a bit complex. But I can tell you that my heart aches for you, baby."

Darcy started to cry. "Roberto, I love you."

"Don't cry, sweetie. You are helping me so much by taking good care of the documents that I gave you for safe keeping," Ray said.

"I found a great place for them. I put the whole folder in a burlap bag and put the bag under the floor boards in a small closet behind Fifi."

"Who's Fifi?"

Darcy laughed. "You know, that metal statue in the reception area of The Haven. I think at one time it had been used as a clothes closet. Well, any way, it's been empty for a long time—it's full of cobwebs. So, the bundle will be safe there."

Ray laughed. He thought it was ironic that he had taken the documents out of The Haven and now they were right back there, just in a different place. "That's my girl," Ray said. "I hate to say this, Darcy, but my life could be in the balance if anything happens to those documents."

"I'll guard them, Roberto. But I want you to come home."

"Well, that will take a bit longer. You better give some thought to where you want to live when I get back. Darcy, I would like us to start our life together somewhere where neither one of us has been. You know, a clean slate—just you and me. Don't say anything to anyone about this, just think about it, baby. Anywhere. Even overseas."

"I'm beginning to feel like Juliet and you are my Romeo," Darcy replied happily.

"Got to go. I have a plane to catch. I'll call you as soon as I can. Bye, my love."

The line went dead. Darcy sat there for a few minutes. Her happiness was short-lived. She jumped when she heard a car door slam. Russ came running up the steps. "Hey, pumpkin, what are you doing all alone out here?" he asked.

"Oh, I was just talking with Roberto."

"He coming home soon?"

"Not just yet. He's still working on an assignment. By the way, Russ, congratulations on your temporary appointment. I think you'll do a great job for Amanda."

"I'm looking forward to it. How about that, Darcy, I'll be your boss for a few weeks," Russ said jokingly.

"Russ, I'm really frightened. Ooh!" said Darcy as she laughed.

It looked like chaos in the salon as the women dug into the boxes and bags they brought, and tried to decide what decorations to put where. The arbor that Homer had made was off to one side where Hannah was already applying lovely silk flowers.

"Did I tell you that I made covers for the chairs that we'll put out on the lawn for the guests?" Hannah said proudly.

"My God, Hannah, do you ever leave your sewing machine? You must sew twenty-four hours a day," Darcy teased.

"I just love to do it. The covers will be ivory satin tied with large organza bows in the back," Hannah said excitedly.

"Hey, Russ, why are you taking measurements in the sun porch?" Darcy asked.

"We're exploring the idea of expanding the gift shop. I'm going to develop several ideas and then run them by Amanda. What do you guys think about changing our gift shop to a Christmas shop that's open all year round?"

"Splendid," Phoebe said. "I think that it will be well received."

"Well, Barclay, it's about time you arrived. I have to keep fighting off these women; they just won't leave me alone," Russ said as his friend entered the salon.

"Sorry, guys. What do you want me to do? I'm not a bit artistic, so I'll need plenty of supervision," Barclay said.

"If you ladies can do without him, I'd like to borrow Barclay to help me take more measurements," Russ said.

"What measurements?" Barclay asked.

"Russ said they might be expanding our gift shop," Phoebe said.

"Okay, you men get out of here and let us get our work done," Darcy said.

Slowly, the salon was taking on a different look. While the wedding was going to be held outside, the luncheon was going to be held in the salon area instead of the formal dining room. The ladies decided that they would draw a sketch for the florist to use when placing the baskets of flowers that they had ordered. Darcy was immediately appointed to make the drawing. She ran to her studio and grabbed a pad and markers. As she re-entered the reception area, she stopped dead in her tracks. She saw Russ and Barclay pushing Fifi away from the closet door. Her eyes opened wide as Russ began pulling on the closet doorknob. She had to do something—but what?

"This closet is much smaller than I had thought," Russ said. "I was hoping that we could use the space for an office but that won't work." Russ put his hands on his hips and stood back for a minute. "Well, we'll just keep this area in mind as we move ahead with our plans. If we do take the space, however, we'll have to find a new spot for Fifi."

Darcy stood behind Russ with her eyes glued to the loose floor board. "Russ, Fifi has stood here for years. I'm not too sure that Amanda would want her moved. Perhaps you may want to rethink that idea. You know how sentimental Amanda is. Besides, we don't use the cloak room that's on the other wall. That should give you plenty of room for an office."

"Good suggestion, Darcy. Let's put Miss Fifi back where she was."

****

Ray smiled as he put his cell phone back in his jacket pocket after talking with Darcy. Everything was going extremely well. He was disappointed in himself since he had forgotten about those damn dog tags Fat Tony wore around his neck.

Ray had just completed another job that he had been given by The Man—one that paid very well. And, in the past few days, he had worked out a plot to get rid of The Man so that Ray could deal directly with the judge. This plan might also get the judge to forget about getting rid of Phoebe—something Ray would rather not do. However, if the judge insisted, then he would have to complete the hit.

Ray's future was getting brighter with each passing day. Once he met with Judge Kraft, and planted the seed of distrust for The Man in the judge's mind, Ray could possibly take The Man's place. And if that didn't work out, he was ready to lay low, where he had a great deal of money stashed away—and that was the Cayman Islands.

It was time to work out the last detail in his plan—getting in to see Judge Kraft without The Man knowing anything about it. He paced his hotel room for some time. He had to figure this out before he returned to The Haven for the documents. He leaned on the dresser and looked into the mirror. He liked what he saw. Not only did he believe that he was handsome, even with the scar, he was pleased that he was now using his brain to move up the ladder economically. Sliding his hand into his jacket, he could feel the wad of money that he had just received, and it felt good. One more deposit, the big one, and Ray could fly to his new home. All Darcy had to do was take care of the documents.

CHAPTER 36

It was the last Saturday in June and it was the day that Amanda and Quentin were to be married. Homer, Russ, and Barclay were in Phoebe's studio to move the flower-covered arbor out onto the lawn. Hannah hovered over them to make certain that they wouldn't bump the arbor against anything that might ruin all the work that she had put into covering it with silk flowers.

The weather could not have been nicer: blue skies and a gentle breeze. After Darcy and Phoebe had arranged the folding chairs outside for the guests, Hannah moved from one seat to another, sliding the covers over the backs of the chairs and then tying the organza bows to keep them in place. Homer, following Hannah's instructions, then placed baskets of white lilies, daises, roses, and hydrangeas at the end of each row. The handyman had made a small platform for the harpist so she would have a level area for her instrument and he placed it next to the arbor.

The caterers arrived and began taking their things inside. Hannah quickly followed them. It wasn't long before they too knew that she was in charge of all arrangements. Since they were also responsible for an ice sculpture, they waited for Hannah to tell them where to place it. And, her choice was perfect—a table in front of a large mirror where it reflected across the room, creating a myriad of sparkling lights. On the other side of the room was a lovely fountain, where melted chocolate would soon be flowing down so guests could put the delicious treat over pieces of fresh fruit.

A smaller table for gifts was placed beside the front door. A white leather guest book, with a feathered pen, attached with a white satin ribbon, lay at the end of the table. Tables and chairs to accommodate thirty-six people were positioned around the room where lunch would be served after the ceremony. Hannah had not forgotten Fifi. She had Homer remove the lamp that Fifi normally carried in her right hand and replace it with a basket of white hydrangeas with long satin ribbons flowing down to her knees. The wedding was scheduled to begin at eleven so that the ceremony would be over before the sun might make it too hot for the honored couple and their guests.

"Everything looks so beautiful," Darcy sighed. "I can't wait until Amanda sees what we've done. When I first learned that Liz Becker couldn't serve as Wedding Coordinator, I was worried about how this would come together. But, Hannah, you stepped in and you are doing a fantastic job."

"Well, when I heard that Liz had to fly to California to take care of her mother, I was happy to do it. Oh, my, I didn't mean that I was happy that her mother was sick. I meant that since I used to help her from time to time, I was happy to step in," Hannah explained.

"What time will the photographer be here?" Darcy asked.

"He should be arriving shortly," Phoebe responded. "He'll be videotaping everything. He's bringing his helper along so they can also take dozens of digital pictures."

"Things seem to be under control," Russ said. "This place looks fantastic."

"So many pretty ladies in one place," Barclay said. "You have not only outdone yourselves getting The Haven ready for the wedding, but all of you are gorgeous."

"Well, Barclay, I have never seen you in a shirt and tie. What's the matter? Don't they make wedding clothes in plaid or flannel?" Russ said as he laughed.

"Excuse me, folks, I must meet the limo so that I can escort the bride down the aisle," Barclay said proudly.

"I think some of the guests are arriving. We need to be outside to greet them," Hannah said.

"Yes, dear," Russ said as he winked at Hannah.

The harpist had arrived and she was playing as the first guests were being seated. Hannah couldn't help herself. Even though the wedding hadn't started yet, she was already tearing up. She started feeling nervous about the gift that Homer and she had planned on giving the couple. Surprisingly, though, Homer seemed very cool and confident.

"Here they come," Russ said as he spotted Quentin's car pulling into the parking lot. "Oh, it's Quentin and the pastor. There's Ana and Jennie, too, but not the bride."

As Quentin joined the group, he said, "Amanda didn't want to come with me. She said that I'm not supposed to see her before the wedding. So I arranged a limo for her."

"Wow, Quentin, you're already sounding like a henpecked husband," Russ teased.

"As long as Amanda's the wife, I'm willing to act like one," Quentin said.

"Quentin, when we spy Amanda, you'll have to stand in the back of the arbor and close your eyes—no peeking at the bride until she starts coming down the aisle. I'll let you know when you may open them," Hannah said gently. "Here comes the limo."

Quentin did as Hannah directed. He could hear the *oohs* and *ahs* and assumed that they were for his beautiful bride. As soon as the harpist began playing *I Found You,* Hannah leaned toward the groom and whispered, "Okay, Quentin, open your eyes."

Although Quentin already considered Amanda beautiful, he was overwhelmed when he saw her. She was poised on Barclay's arm, looking radiant and carrying a single calla lily in her hands. A small, sparkling tiara was nestled in her hair which was combed straight back from her face. Her ankle-length dress was stunning. Small diamond earrings, the ones he had given her for Christmas, dangled from her earlobes. Her smile was captivating. No man could have asked for more. Barclay then took Amanda's hand and placed it in Quentin's. The groom suddenly became aware that the ceremony had begun. But it was over all too quickly. When he heard the words, *"You may now kiss your bride"* he came to life. When the harpist began playing Mendelsohn's *Wedding March,* Amanda placed her hand on Quentin's arm and they walked down the aisle and into The Haven.

As the guests moved inside, Homer helped the harpist get her instrument in the doorway and positioned where she could play during lunch. The tables were covered with white linens. Matching napkins, encircled with colorful rings made of different gem stones, were perched alongside each plate. Russ' creations didn't stop there. The bride and groom's napkin rings were made of crystals and pearls and were amazing pieces of artistic work. Tall vases, filled with white roses, stood in the center of each of the six round tables. The scene was breathtakingly beautiful.

When the champagne glasses were filled, Barclay and Russ stood up to make toasts. "What a lovely day this is. Two wonderful people are now joined as one. Amanda, Quentin—all of us here wish you many years of happiness and health. You are loved by all of us," Barclay said,

"Let's raise our glasses high, folks. To Mr. and Mrs. Quentin Toth," Russ said.

"Don't forget Fifi," Amanda said.

"Fifi, sorry, we love you, too," Russ said, as he sat down beside Darcy.

Darcy leaned over to Russ and quietly said, "See, Russ, she loves that statue."

"I just want you to know that we're still not sure where we're going to place Amanda's office. We have three locations in mind," Russ said. "But I'll take Fifi into consideration."

"Ladies and gentlemen, we have a surprise for the happy couple. Hannah and Homer will be singing a duet as their gift to the newlyweds," Barclay said. Homer reached for Hannah's hand and they took their places alongside the harpist. When the strains of *Because* were heard, the guests showed obvious delight. All faces were turned to the performers, but Homer didn't look back at the audience. He kept his eyes glued on Hannah. The crowd was mesmerized with their perfectly pitched voices filling the air. When the duet was over, all the guests applauded loudly.

Amanda stood up. "Hannah, Homer, thank you for your very special gift. Quentin and I will long remember your marvelous rendition." The flustered couple then walked over to the bride and groom and exchanged hugs and well wishes.

Darcy, however, could only think about the closet door behind Fifi. It was obvious that the statue was now very close to the door. How was she going to be able to get those documents from underneath the floor boards before Russ stumbled upon them?

CHAPTER 37

On Monday, Ray arrived at Judge Kraft's office. Last night, he had sent a text to The Man to get him out of Kraft's office in the morning. It was quite a clever ruse. He asked The Man to meet him so that he could him give him some vital information about the last job they did together. Ray wanted to meet with Kraft without any interference from the judge's sidekick.

Ray had conducted some online research since he knew next to nothing about the Pennsylvania Supreme Court. He discovered that Judge Kraft had been appointed to the bench and then had been elected to his post by the voters. Therefore, he could possibly hold that position for life. It bothered Ray that the old fart would be collecting a monthly pension of ten K when he retired. The bastard was dirty. Ray would love to blow the whistle on the infamous Judge Horace Kraft. Well, depending on how well his scheme worked maybe Ray could do just that. That thought made him chuckle.

It stuck in Ray's craw that Kraft, from the time that he had been appointed, had positioned himself out there as an advocate for children and families. When Ray thought about this, he could not help but be amused. The bastard was not only on the take, he was also heavily involved in the transport of drugs into the Commonwealth. But Ray knew that he probably had this one-time-only to convince Kraft that he, not the judge, held the royal flush.

"Do you have an appointment?" the receptionist asked.

"No, but just hand this to the judge. This is a very confidential matter."

Ray was relieved that there were no signs of The Man.

The young woman took the note from Ray and went into the judge's office. She glanced at the note—*yellow binder* was all that it said.

In short order he was ushered into Kraft's office.

The judge looked at Ray. "And you are?"

"For the purpose of this meeting just call me Ray," Ray said as he held out his hand.

The judge merely looked at Ray—never extending his hand. "And, why are you here?"

"I have some things you need and want. I'm here to conduct business with you. I believe that you're a reasonable man. You lost some things several years ago—some money, a few papers and, even a woman," Ray said, all the while watching the judge's eyes as they started twitching. Ray sat down without an invitation.

"I'm not sure that I remember losing such items," Kraft replied woodenly.

"Let me put it this way. The papers are in my possession. I have read them. I have not shown them to anyone. I wanted to give you first rights in getting them back."

"Stand up. Open your jacket and your shirt."

Ray followed his request. "You can take me down to my underwear— I'm not wired. I'm a business man."

"You said I lost money?" Kraft said as he clasped his hands across his wide girth.

"I know that you did. But the person who took your documents is not the same person who took your money. I know because I know where Florence is and, while she admitted taking the papers, she claimed that she did not take the money." Ray was now ready to point fingers at The Man without any evidence at all. "She suggested that you ask The Man what he did with the money. She said that when she left that day, the money was still in the safe," Ray stated emphatically. When Ray saw the concern on Kraft's face, he was delighted.

The judge was quiet for a few minutes. Ray knew now that he had him.

"Where did Florence live as a child?" Kraft asked.

"On a tree farm in Vermont. Come on now—no more fucking games. I'm not interested in hurting your career. But I do think I deserve a nice reward for finding the papers. By the way, if you get your papers, all of them, there may not be a need to go any further."

"These are some serious charges, young man. How do I know you're telling me the truth?" the judge asked, now obviously concerned. "You may be making some incorrect assumptions. Papers may just be that—papers and nothing more."

"One of the documents is on light blue paper and holds the signature of a well-known, shall we say, unsavory character. Another one has little black check marks here and there—shall I go on? Listen, if you still want the girl out of the picture, I can handle that. But without those papers, if she tells anyone what she knows, she won't be believed without proof."

"I'm still bothered about the money. Can you prove that she didn't take my cash?"

This question took Ray by surprise. He needed to come up with a story fast. He remembered a few things that Phoebe had told him, but he needed to appear to be on Kraft's side. He would rather not have to whack the dancer, since he wanted to get the money and then to get the hell out of the country quickly without the fuzz looking for him.

Ray took his time. He slouched back in his chair. "Well, she was destitute when she got a job. Her employer, who I also know very well, took care of her until she began making a salary. Florence told me that she regretted taking the documents. She said that she had loved you very much, and she realized that she could never harm you. But now I have the papers and I'm not as generous as she is. I would advise you to check The Man out. Who knows what he may have taken right from under your nose," Ray said convincingly.

Kraft stood up and began pacing. "Did The Man hire you to find her?"

"Yeah, he did. I couldn't go to him to get in to see you since I know he was the one who took your money. I knew that he would never allow me to speak with you."

After several silent minutes, the judge said, "Okay, we have a deal. But, I want the girl gone. She betrayed me. No one plays me for a fool. I don't care how you do it—just do it."

"How can you guarantee that I'll get my money?" Ray asked.

"As soon as you can, bring me the documents. I know exactly what should be in that folder. When I see that they are all there, you will get half of what The Man told you. When you eliminate the girl, you get the other half. But, I'll need proof. Do you agree to these terms?"

"What if I can take care of both your concerns at one time?"

"Then you get it all at once. She always wore an ugly opal ring on her little finger. I hated that ring, but in spite of all that I did for her, she insisted on wearing the damn thing. Get me that ring," Kraft demanded.

"I have one condition."

"And that is?"

"Do not share this with The Man. How you deal with him in the future is your business. But I don't want him coming after me when he realizes that I told you about his disrespecting you."

"Deal."

For a long time after Ray left his office, Kraft was lost in deep thought. Maybe the time had come to get out of Pennsylvania and perhaps even the US. He had known that he would have to face this one day, but he was surprised that it came sooner than he had expected. He had to make sure that he covered all his tracks. If he resigned his position, he wanted to make certain that he would take his cushy pension with him. He needed to begin his charade. He'd start by buying a walker and using it everywhere he went. Pain—that's it—he'll claim excruciating pain in his back.

He should get rid of The Man—but then why burn a bridge? He'd keep him around to clean up any messes that might surface here in the states—including Florence.

CHAPTER 38

Darcy was driving to The Haven to help put the wedding decorations away, but more importantly, she wanted to keep her eye on the closet where she had hidden the documents she was trying to protect for Roberto. When she had first discovered the forgotten closet that was behind Fifi, she was certain that it would make an ideal hiding place. Apparently, no one had used the closet for years since it was filled with cobwebs. But when she discovered that Russ knew about the closet and that he was considering using it to make an office for Amanda, she knew that she had to retrieve the documents and put them somewhere else. And, to make matters worse, when Russ had moved Fifi, he had placed her much closer to the door of the closet than she had been before—making it almost impossible for Darcy to get the closet door open far enough to pull the bundle out.

As she was about to turn into The Haven, her cell phone rang. She pulled her car over immediately since she saw Roberto's name on the screen. "Hello, Roberto," she said with a little sob in her voice.

"Hey, babe, are you okay? You don't sound like yourself."

"I'm fine, sweetie. Just tired from the wedding and all. How are you, my darling? I miss you so much," Darcy replied.

"This case is moving along, but I need to explain some things to you," Ray said.

"This sounds ominous," Darcy said.

"Maybe not ominous, but extremely important. First, are the documents ready for me?'

Darcy swallowed hard. "Certainly."

"Good, I'll be there tomorrow night for them."

"By the way, Barclay wants you to get in touch with him. I think it has to do with Phoebe. But he left for a book signing tour and I'm not sure when he'll be back. Do you want him to call you?"

"No! Darcy, if I don't even give you my number, I certainly don't want anyone else to have it either," Ray said with a tinge of annoyance in his voice.

"I'm sorry, Roberto, I didn't want to upset you," Darcy replied weakly.

"No, I'm the one who should be sorry. Darcy, things are getting difficult with this government case right now and I am a bit on edge. Forgive me?"

"Of course, sweetie."

"Do me a favor. Stay away from The Haven for a few days. I'm not certain but there's a possibility that something may occur there. Say nothing to anyone. Stay home. Will you do that for me, babe? But first I must ask, do you still love me?"

"Do I still love you? Let's see now—yes and yes and yes."

"That's my girl. Now I need to know exactly what will be going on at The Haven for the next few days."

"We should have all the wedding things put away today. The only teacher who will be there tomorrow is Phoebe. She has some kind of special class, meeting three days a week during July. The others won't be getting their classrooms ready for another three weeks or so. Russ may be in and out—by the way he's in charge until Amanda gets back from her honeymoon. Russ is going to be doing some remodeling for Amanda but the plans haven't even been chosen yet."

"Plans for what?"

"They're going to make the gift shop larger. It'll be a Christmas shop that will be open all year round. I think it was Russ' idea."

"Russ again? Darcy, must I worry about him?"

"Heavens no, darling. Russ is like a big brother to me."

"Well, I don't want to be your big brother," Ray said.

"What do you want to be?" Darcy asked coyly.

"Babe, wait until I get ahold of you tomorrow night. You better be ready for an all-nighter."

"You naughty boy," Darcy teased.

"I never heard a complaint from you before," Ray replied.

166

"I'd move the moon for you, Roberto."

"Don't do that. The moon may come in handy tomorrow night," Ray said. "Got to run, babe. Be ready for me tomorrow night. Bye, my love." Ray said right before he hung up.

Darcy could hardly contain herself. Now, she had to get those documents no matter what it would take. She heard someone honking a horn and turned to see Hannah's smiling face as the seamstress hurried up the hill to The Haven.

When the two women met in the parking lot, they greeted one another with a hug.

"Darcy, I was just about to turn around and come back down the hill in case you were having trouble with your mini-van," Hannah said.

"No car trouble. I was talking on my cell phone," she explained.

"I wish more people would do that. We'd probably have fewer accidents."

Homer was just coming out the front door with a ladder slung over his back. "Morning ladies," he said as he tipped his hat.

"Morning, Homer," Darcy said. "How are things going in there?"

"Fine, Miss Darcy. Mr. Russ is stacking the folding chairs and the tables now. Hannah, you better get in there. I'm afraid they might mess up your pretty chair covers," Homer said as he put the ladder down and held the door open.

Hannah gave Homer a sweet smile as she lifted her skirt a bit to get up over the doorsill. Homer followed them and said, "I'll stay here and help. Some of those boxes may be too heavy for you ladies to lift."

Phoebe was sitting on the floor with a marker in her hand. "I'll label the boxes so when we need them for the next wedding we'll know where things are," she said as she looked directly at Hannah.

Hannah blushed. "Oh, go on, Phoebe."

Darcy took over the vacuuming of the salon while Russ polished the hardwood floors. In no time at all, the salon looked as it had before the wedding.

"Russ, how about moving Fifi about a foot forward. I don't think she's standing exactly where she was before. Beside, I'm certain your contractor will want to inspect the closet anyway. I'd feel more comfortable if you guys would move her rather than some stranger who doesn't realize how important Fifi is to all of us," Darcy explained.

"Your heard the lady, Homer, give me a hand here," Russ said. "I thought I was the boss, but you see I'm not."

"Oh, Russ. It was just a suggestion," Darcy said.

"I know," Russ said. "We bosses hate to admit that our workers are sometimes smarter than we are."

"Workers!" they all shouted.

"That was just a term," Russ said playfully.

"How's that, Darcy?" Russ asked as the two men slid Fifi forward.

"Perfect. You guys sure do good work," Darcy teased.

"Homer, Miss Phoebe will be holding classes for the next three weeks every Monday, Wednesday and Friday. Make sure you keep an eye out for her and her little ones," Russ said.

"My goodness, I can take care of my own class," Phoebe said.

"Miss Phoebe," Homer said. "I'll stay out of your way, but just in case you need me, I'll be close by," Homer said.

"I think I'll sort out some things in my studio," Darcy said. "I've been meaning to select some additional pieces to send to my friend in Philadelphia. It seems he's having a fall art show and he's willing to take on more of my paintings."

"Darcy, that's great," Phoebe said. "I wish you luck."

"I'm off to my studio. I'll see all of you later," Darcy said as she walked down the hall.

Darcy was relived. She waved goodbye to them as she headed to her studio. After twenty minutes of moving art work around and rearranging this and that, she scurried back to the reception area. She checked out the window. Her car was the only one parked out front. Moving over to Fifi, she walked to the closet door. Slowly, she turned the handle. Locked— the damn thing was locked! She started pulling on the knob and almost jumped out of her skin when she heard Homer's voice behind her.

"You need to get in there, Miss Darcy?"

"Yes, Homer. I put some things in there for safekeeping that I need," Darcy said.

"No problem. I have a master key."

"Homer, you're a life saver," a relieved Darcy said.

"There you go. When you get your things, just push that little button on the back of the knob," Homer instructed.

Darcy waited until Homer went out the front door before she lifted the floor boards up and took the burlap-wrapped package out. She pushed the little button and shut the door. Hurrying to her studio, her heart was beating rapidly. Tossing the packet into a large tote bag, she grabbed her purse and left the building. She was exhilarated. She was part of a government operation—just like Roberto.

Early the next morning, Russ and his contractor entered The Haven with tools in their hands. "We'll start by taking that closet door off and we'll go from there," Russ said. "While it might be too small for an office, I thought it could be a great place to put a showcase—you know for trophies, awards and such. I wonder if there are any other secret places like this one in The Haven."

CHAPTER 39

Ray arrived at The Haven and was pleased to see only one car in the parking lot. He wanted to meet with Phoebe, and he really didn't want too many others around in case things didn't go as he planned. Since Darcy had told him that Barclay wouldn't be around to interfere with his dealings with Phoebe, this meeting shouldn't take too long. Phoebe should be a pushover. But, he had to get that opal ring. If she didn't give it to him willingly, then he would be forced, one way or another to take it. Just as he was walking up the front steps, he heard another car pulling in. He kept his head down, but then he heard someone calling him. He was irritated when he saw that it was Hannah. He stopped in his tracks. That fucking old broad is always around.

"Well, hello Hannah, How are you today?" Ray said as politely as he could muster.

"I'm fine, thank you, Roberto. I don't think Darcy will be here today. I just stopped by to pick up some yard goods and then I'll be on my way. However, Phoebe is here. That's her car over there," she said.

Ray's mind was racing. Now that Hannah has seen him once again when he didn't want to be seen, he might be forced to get rid of her, too. Damn her. He didn't like this situation. It was getting too messy. But, a hit was a hit and if it turned out to be two instead of one, so be it.

Ray followed Hannah inside. As she climbed the steps to her studio, he said, "Have a nice day, Hannah."

Just then, Phoebe came out of her studio and said, "Roberto, you're right on time. I was so pleased to get your call last night. Barclay said that you would be able to help us."

"Well, Phoebe, I'll do my best. Where should we talk?"

"In my studio."

170

Ray looked up when he heard Hannah coming down the staircase. "Finished already?"

"I just needed this material," Hannah said as she hurried out the front door.

Phoebe closed the door to her studio. "I don't know where to begin, Roberto. I have so much to explain to you."

Ray smiled. The ballerina had no idea how much he already knew about her—her past history and her dalliance with Kraft. But he put on his best face, and while she was talking, every so often he would ask a question. He had been right about the money in Kraft's safe. Phoebe had not taken it. As Phoebe described how the documents looked when she last saw them, she had no idea that he knew exactly where they were.

"Look, Phoebe, you don't know this, but we have been investigating Kraft for some time now. I was sent to The Haven to make sure you were okay. We knew the judge has been looking for a person to snuff you out and get his stuff back."

Phoebe's eyes opened wide. "What!"

"We have you protected, Phoebe. However, you cannot share this information with anyone. We are after him, big time. He is very familiar with me. But, not as an agent. He thinks I'm a hired killer."

"My God, you don't mean…"

Ray shook his head. "Yes, he offered me a deal."

Phoebe grabbed Ray's arm. "Heavens, I'm still not safe," she whispered.

"Not to worry," Ray said as he patted Phoebe's hand. "You're safe. The government can guarantee that. I met with Kraft. He wants his documents and he wants you dead."

"But I don't know where they are. Honestly, I don't," Phoebe cried.

"We know that, Phoebe. We have the documents."

'This is so hard to accept. But I'm pleased that the government has them. Oh, look at the mess I have created," Phoebe said as she start to cry.

"Phoebe, don't cry. You are being protected. I can't give you all the details, but I can tell you that you will not be harmed," Ray said gently.

"Barclay has hired someone to look after me," Phoebe said.

"That really wasn't necessary. I'm telling you that you're safe; that should be enough," an irritated Ray said. "Who is he and where is he?"

"He won't be here until noon. It seems that he's coming from Harrisburg. He will escort me to and from The Haven and where ever else I need to go until Barclay gets back. His name is Frank but I can't remember his last name."

Ray checked his watch. He better get the hell out of here before Frank arrived.

"My head is spinning. I can't take all of this in. I wish Barclay were here." Phoebe said softly.

"Do me one favor. Don't tell anyone, not even Barclay, what I have shared with you. I can't afford to have anything go wrong with what the Feds arranged. When does he return from his book tour?"

"I believe he'll be back in two to three days."

"Oh, by then it will be okay to tell him. But do not use the phone, email, or any social media to tell him. Kraft has access to an unbelievable amount of information. Tell Barclay, but only in person. But absolutely, *tell no one else.* In two weeks or so, after we arrest Kraft, then you will be free to tell anyone. I know this sounds like it came right out of a TV crime show, but, Phoebe, we're dealing with bad people here. You are very lucky that you got away."

"But am I safe right now?"

"Yes. Now, steel yourself. I have more to share with you. I promised Kraft that I would do the hit and get rid of your body. He then instructed me to bring him proof that you are indeed dead."

"How are you going to do that?" she whispered.

"Your little opal ring."

Phoebe held up her hand. "My ring?"

"Yes, he told me he hated that cheap ring, but that you would not stop wearing it. So, if I show him the ring, he'll be certain that I went through with the hit."

Phoebe was quiet for a minute. Slowly, she pulled the ring off her finger and put it in Ray's outstretched hand.

"Phoebe, once we have Kraft behind bars, the government will return your ring."

****

That night, Ray paced the floor in Darcy's bedroom. He couldn't sleep. He knew that he had to leave soon. Every once in a while he would pause and look down at her. There was something different about this woman. It was a sensation that he had never felt before with any of the other women in his life. He wasn't sure that he liked the feeling at all. It seemed to threaten his way of life—coming and going—never worrying about the collateral damage that he would leave behind once he had taken all he could from each one. Maybe this was what some would call *love—a complication* he really didn't want. Love would only get in the way of his plans. His off-shore account was growing rapidly and, after he collected his reward from the judge, he would have enough to live comfortably for quite some time. He reminded himself that the only reason he came back to Darcy was to get the documents.

Darcy stirred, "Roberto," she said softly.

"I'm here, love."

Ray sat down on the bed. "I must go," he said as Darcy reached for him.

"I know, I know," she said as she wrapped her arms around him. They sat side by side, clinging to one another, just like lovers all over the world. Ray's head was spinning. He wasn't sure that he should allow himself to feel this way. Feelings of tenderness were strange to him and he didn't know how to interpret them.

"Don't make it hard for me, baby. I don't want to go, but I must. Remember, do not mention that I was here. And, stay away from Russ."

Darcy smiled. "Why, Roberto, I do believe you're jealous," she said coyly.

"Well, after what went on here in this bedroom tonight, I need to protect my woman. Darcy, you did a great job. Thank you, love," Ray said as he gently laid her down on her pillow and disappeared into the darkness. In just a few more hours, he would be meeting with Kraft again. But this time he'd walk away with a small fortune. All Ray could think about at the moment was that life was sure good to him.

CHAPTER 40

Judge Kraft was all alone in his office. He needed time to think—time to make a very important decision. He had to put Ray in his place. He had to show him that no one, and that included that bitch Florence, who disrespected him, lived a long life.

But things were getting a bit too hot and unless all went well, everything could explode at any minute. He had to decide what he was going to do about Ray. While he needed those documents back in his hands, Kraft despised that fact that this no-account, two-bit crook seemingly had him over a barrel. He wanted Ray to think that he had disposed of The Man, but in reality, The Man was ready to follow Ray as soon as he left the judge's chambers with his ill-gotten gain.

As far as his career was concerned, Kraft narrowed his choices down to two: one, to stay right where he was and continue his operations as if nothing had happened and hang in there until he reached the mandatory retirement age of 70; or, two, to simply retire, citing health problems and take off for the Cayman Islands. There he could live out his life in style without the worry of being arrested and sent to prison. He had no wife to worry about and no steady girlfriend—he was a free man in that respect. And, he wanted to stay that way. But he really liked his job. He was important and powerful. He was respected by many rich and influential people. He would hate to give all that up. However, this whole mess—this thing with this upstart Ray—could very well bring him down in flames. Perhaps it was just as well to get out now. With what he had in his off-shore account, along with a $10,000 monthly pension, he could live a world of ease and contentment. After all, he deserved that much.

It would be quite easy to retire, feigning illness. Since his brother was a doctor, he'd have no problem getting all kinds of reports indicating that his health was in jeopardy. And, he did have a heart attack a few years ago. But, he had to get those documents from Ray first. And, he wanted to be certain that Florence paid the ultimate price for her betrayal. After all that he had done for her, he just couldn't fathom how she could disrespect him in such a manner. She was nothing more than a country bumpkin when he had found her. He had given her everything that she had asked for. Perhaps she was no longer a worry. Ray was coming to see him today and maybe he had already taken care of the bitch. But he wouldn't give Ray another opportunity to blackmail him. The Man would see to that. Kraft felt that he could be in the Caymans by next week.

Kraft buzzed for his secretary. "Please cancel all my appointments for the day with the exception of Mr. Caltigarone. I'm not feeling too well today."

"Judge, shall I call the doctor?" she responded.

"No. I'll see him later."

Kraft had made his decision. He was going to retire. He needed to take steps to be certain that there were no incriminating papers left in his personal files. Above all, he needed to stay focused and get this sonofabitch out of his life. No more. He would deal with this man no more.

The office door opened and Ray stepped in with a bundle under his arm.

"Judge, how nice to see you again," Ray said as he sat down on a leather chair.

"Look, Ray, we have business to take care of. So, let's get down to the nitty-gritty."

Ray put the bundle down on Kraft's desk. "Take a look. Examine it carefully."

"You mean to tell me that you've been carrying these papers around in a plastic bag? You apparently have spared no expense," the judge said sarcastically.

"Hey, you have them now. What more do you want?"

"How can I be certain that you haven't made copies of anything?"

"I made a deal with you. You get the papers and I get the money. I did not make any copies since I will have no use for them. I'll be leaving the country very shortly, and I don't plan on returning."

Kraft opened the plastic bag. He reached in and pulled out the yellow binder, shoving the plastic bag onto the floor. He hurriedly opened the cord and rifled through all the papers. After a few minutes, he took the papers and put them in his bottom desk drawer.

"May I ask where you're going?" the judge asked.

"No, I don't want you sending anyone after me. By the way, what happened to The Man?" Ray asked. "He's usually in your shadows somewhere."

"I really don't know. No one seems to know. I think he probably ran away with someone else's wife. He was that kind, you know. He was a bastard, a fucking bastard," the judge replied.

"I have no such plans, Judge. But I'll be leaving as soon as I get my reward."

"You haven't told me whether or not you took care of my second problem."

"Oh, she's run away, too. Isn't that *odd* how many people are simply running away?"

"Did the whore leave anything behind?"

"Funny you should ask. Yes, she did. She told me that you would want this," Ray said as he placed Phoebe's little opal ring in the judge's hand.

"Oh, how nice of her to remember me in this way," he said as he slid the ring into his pocket. "Where can I send her a thank you card for her generosity?"

"They don't have any mailboxes where Florence is now," Ray said as he smiled at the judge.

"No one can reach her?" the judge probed.

"Oh, no. That's impossible," Ray replied. "One would have to be a very clever gopher to visit Florence."

"I must remind you, Ray, I don't like being taken for a fool. You want a good life and you don't want to be looking over your shoulder all the time. So, what you have told me is the truth?"

"I too am a businessman. So, where's my reward?"

"Our little arrangement has been quite innocuous, wouldn't you say?"

"Nice try, judge. I know what that means—nothing more than a win-win situation for the both of us. You truly think that you're so much smarter than everyone else. Now that we both know that you're not, where's my fucking money?"

Kraft pointed to a suitcase sitting in the corner of his office. "I thought that since you'll be traveling that you may need a new suitcase. I hope you like the color," he said.

Ray jumped up, grabbed the tan suitcase and put it on his lap. He snapped it open and almost stopped breathing when he got his first glimpse of the money all in neat little stacks. "Well done, Big Cheese, well done." And, with that, he rushed out the door.

Kraft coolly picked up the phone. "He's on his way out of the building. Now, don't lose the sonofabitch. I want that dammed suitcase back in my office before dark. No excuses."

He sat still for a few minutes. It worried him that he only had Ray's word for it that Florence had met her just reward. He leaned over and picked up the white plastic bag that Ray used to carry the documents. He was about to toss it in the waste can when something fell out of the bag. Curious, he picked it up. It didn't take him long to determine that he had just found out where Florence was. The brochure he held in his hand was an advertisement for a place called The Haven. Lo and behold, they were offering classes in ballet. The ballerina pictured in the ad had her head down, but he instinctively knew that it was Florence. This won't take long to check out—if Florence is not already dead, she soon will be.

****

Kraft's happiness was shattered two hours later.

"What the hell do you mean you lost him?" Kraft yelled at The Man who was standing in front of him. "What happened?"

"As soon as he came out of the building he jumped into a cab. I was ready, so I followed him. The cab took him to Moyer's Travel on Elm. He jumped out and hurried into the building. The cab stayed there, so I figured the bastard would return shortly. I waited for a while and then I went inside. He wasn't anywhere. I questioned the clerk, but he claimed that he didn't see anyone like I described. Hell, there are twelve floors of offices in that place, so I didn't know where else to look. Boss, I thought he was gonna pick up travel tickets."

"You jackass! Don't you realize that there's a helicopter port on the rooftop? You dumb sonofabitch. He flew away with my money," Kraft seethed.

"I didn't know that, Boss. I'll go back and see what I can find out," The Man said hoping to placate the angry judge.

"No. I'll make some calls. So help me, I'm tired of having to deal with nincompoops. Must I do everything myself in order to get anything done right? Just get out of my sight. I'll deal with you later."

Kraft was livid. He was counting on having that money back in his possession by now. He began pacing his office. He had to calm down. Getting so angry surely couldn't be good for his heart condition. The first person he called was the owner of the building where Ray had managed to fly away like a damned bird. He was able to extract a promise from the owner to find out where Ray was taken. At least that would give him a starting point to look for that thief.

Maybe he should have gotten rid of The Man a long time ago. But now he needed to concentrate on Florence and Ray. Maybe he could use The Man anyway. He paced the office, trying to make up his mind. Reluctantly, Kraft picked up the phone once again. "We have two problems that need to be handled. I'll meet you in an hour at our place."

Kraft grabbed his walker and stomped out of the office and down the hall.

CHAPTER 41

It was almost two weeks since the wedding and Russ still had some of Amanda's wedding gifts in his trunk, so he decided to drop them off at the cottage for safe keeping. Using the key Amanda had given him, he let himself in. He had to make two trips since the one package was very large and cumbersome. As he was about to leave, the phone rang.

Taking advantage of his new position, he decided to answer it. "Hello."

"Quentin?" a voice asked.

"No, this is the temporary manager, Russ."

"Oh, hi Russ. This is Steve, your California buddy who worked with you on the Ash sting. Wasn't that a hoot?" Steve asked.

"You can say that again. We sure made a good team. We got that damned guy good. I understand that the trial won't begin until early next year," Russ replied.

"Well, his ass is sitting in jail I'm sure Quentin will keep me posted when all of that goes down. I didn't think Amanda or Quentin would be there—honeymoon time—but I was going to leave a message. This is better. I can explain to you what I found out about another one of our buddies," Steve said.

"One of our buddies?" Russ asked.

"Let me start at the beginning. When I was back East, Quentin mentioned that perhaps Roberto could play the lead in Barclay's movie. Of course, that would be out of the question. But I got to thinking about that, and, out of pure curiosity, I decided to do some investigating on my own on our so-called government agent. However, Roberto does have the look I'm after."

With that, Russ rolled his eyes.

"Well, anyway, I began to investigate him and you'll never believe what I found."

"I hate that guy, so I hope it's something bad," Russ said.

"Your instincts are on target. Apparently one of the ways he makes a living is by romancing rich ladies. But, that's not the only thing. He seems to change names frequently. One of his gimmicks is to present himself as a government agent of one kind or another. He's wanted in two states for bail jumping. I'm sure there's more out there on this guy, but I just wanted to warn you people in case he's still hanging around. Tell you what. I'll fax these reports to Quentin. I'm certain that he'll want to see all of them when he gets back next week," Steve said.

"Roberto's in a relationship with one of our teachers. I knew he was a no-good bum, but others thought that I was just carrying my big brother routine a bit too far." Russ said strongly.

"Are you going to tell her?" Steve asked.

"I don't want to, but I think I must. It'll break her heart. She's crazy about him."

"It'll only get worse if you don't, Russ. Is there a woman who could tell her? It may come better from a female," Steve suggested.

"Perhaps I could wait another week and ask Amanda to talk with her. But suppose he comes back in the meantime?" Russ said. "The guy's like a yo-yo. He suddenly shows up and, just as suddenly, he disappears. That damned bastard."

"I hate that I have to be the bearer of such bad news. But I knew that I owed it to all of you to let you know that you have a fox in the henhouse."

After he hung up, Russ collapsed in an overstuffed chair. As much as he disliked Roberto, he simply could not imagine telling Darcy that he was a fraud. He usually played the part of a cut-up, and used his sense of humor to entertain people. But there was nothing entertaining about this sorry state of affairs. He decided that it was too late to do anything about it tonight. He would sleep on it. Perhaps, in the morning light, he'd be able to come up with the right words to tell Darcy. Maybe he should talk it over with Barclay. Now there's a man that's good with words.

CHAPTER 42

"Thanks for meeting me for breakfast, Barclay. I have a rather sticky situation to talk over with you," Russ said.

"Okay. You sound worried. What's wrong?" Barclay asked.

"This has to do with Roberto. Remember when we were all at Quentin's house after we pulled off that sting with Ash?"

"Sure. That was a fun time."

"Damn, it sure was! Well, anyway, Steve got to thinking about Roberto playing the part of the killer in the movie. He knew it was out of the question, but for some reason, he decided to do an online search on the bastard," Russ said.

"I didn't think too much of that idea, but I have to admit that he sure looks like my character," Barclay said.

"Everyone thinks he's so damned good-looking—it pisses me off," Russ said, obviously agitated.

"Sorry, Russ. But he is."

"Okay, okay. Now let me explain what Steve discovered. The bastard's been making a living off rich ladies for years. He also masquerades as some type of government agent and has his fingers in plenty of dirty stuff. He's even wanted in a couple of states."

"Darcy said that he works for the government. Are you sure what Steve said is true?"

"Well that's the line our handsome Romeo appears to be using with everyone. I'm sure Darcy doesn't know about the rich ladies, and I'm almost positive that she knows nothing about him being a wanted man," Russ said.

"Damn, Russ, this really is bad news for Darcy."

"I agree. But I believe she needs to know," Russ said.

"She'll take this pretty hard, Russ. Do you really want to be the one to tell her?" Barclay asked.

"There's the sticky wicket. One of two things will happen. If she already knows, she has accepted him anyway; or, she won't believe me and she'll hate me for the rest of my life. What do you think?" Russ asked.

"She'll be devastated either way. If she does know, she'll hate that we all know, too. If she doesn't, she certainly will hate the messenger," Barclay said.

"Don't be so helpful," Russ said wryly.

"Russ, you have to face the truth. Darcy's going to get hurt either way. What if we just don't tell her?"

"We can't do that. We don't know what he has planned for her. He comes in and out of her life as he pleases. I couldn't sleep at all last night. I wish Amanda were here. She would know how to handle this, but she won't be back until next week." Russ said. "I don't know Hannah well enough to judge whether she could handle such a delicate situation. I think it would be better if all of this came from a woman."

"We can't ask Phoebe to do this, Russ. Right now she's dealing with some emotional issues of her own. I'd offer to go with you, but then Darcy might resent us ganging up on her. I think you're right. Darcy needs to know. Then she can make up her own mind regarding her reactions. I don't envy you. She's special to you, but you can't keep her from getting hurt."

"Friends don't desert friends. I wish Roberto had never come into our lives. But, he's here and she loves him. I'd take a bullet for her, but she doesn't know that either. She has needed me, Barclay; oh not in a romantic sense, but she has really needed me as a friend. Now here I am, faced with having to break her heart. A good friend I turned out to be," Russ said sadly.

Later that day, Russ still didn't know how he was going to begin the conversation with Darcy. How does one prepare to destroy another person's happiness? He sat in his car outside Darcy's apartment for some time before he finally opened the car door. Somehow he felt like a dead man walking as he headed up the sidewalk. Was he really doing this because he disliked Roberto so much? Or, was he glad that he could expose him for the brutal cad that he was? No, he wanted Darcy to know the truth—at least that's what kept rolling around in his head. How many times had he heard the saying '*don't kill the messenger*'? Oh, how he wished he could have turned this task over to Amanda.

When Darcy opened the door, she looked so happy. "Why Russ. How nice. I was about to have a glass of iced tea. Would you like some?"

Darcy's apartment looked the same. Stacks of paintings behind the sofa, in the corners and even under her one good occasional chair. But he spied something new. Right above the television set was a painting of Roberto. He had to admit that Darcy had captured Roberto's likeness in an expert manner. He was looking at the rendition when Darcy said, "How do you like it?"

"Great, Darcy. You did an excellent job. I think I'll take you up on that glass of tea," Russ said as he followed her into the small, brightly-lit kitchen.

Darcy put ice cubes in two tall glasses and filled them with tea. "Here's some of those delicious cheese pretzels that I know you like."

"Thanks, Darcy," Russ said as he started munching on one.

"Okay, Russ, I can tell that something's wrong. What's up?"

"I have some information about Roberto. I want you to keep an open mind about what I'm going to share with you. Don't get angry with me, Darcy. Just listen to what I have to tell you."

"My God, Russ. Has he been hurt? He just left here a few hours ago," Darcy said as her eyes opened wide.

"No, no, he's okay," Russ said. "At least I think so." He took a few deep breaths, all the while wishing that he didn't have to do this. "Do you remember when we were all together after the Ash take down?"

"Certainly. Is he involved in this?" Darcy asked incredulously.

"No, please, just listen to me. When we were together, Quentin had mentioned he thought that Roberto would be an ideal person to play the killer in Barclay's movie. Well, Steve—you know, that guy from Hollywood—well, he started mulling that idea over. As a result, he knew that if he would go that route, he better know a little more about the man."

"Oh, don't tell me that Roberto's going to be a movie star," Darcy shouted.

"Don't jump ahead of me, Darcy. Well, Steve found out some things about Roberto that I think you should know," Russ said as he kept a wary eye on her.

Darcy smiled. "What did he find out?"

"Darcy, I'm not kidding. This is no laughing matter. This is some serious stuff," Russ said, a bit taken back with Darcy's casual attitude.

"Okay, let me see. He's a bad person with a shady past. Is that what you're going to tell me?" Darcy asked as she put her hand on Russ's arm.

Russ didn't know how to react. He couldn't believe that she knew all about the man and had accepted him anyway. "Darcy, he lives off rich women and he's wanted in several states for skipping bail."

"Russ, there are things that I know about Roberto that I cannot tell you. I can, however, share with you that he does investigative work for the government. To protect him, they lay false paper trails about him. But that's all that I'm at liberty to say. Trust me, Russ. Roberto's a kind, loving, gentle person."

Russ stood up. "Darcy, Darcy, this guy's got you hook, line, and sinker. I'm telling you…"

Darcy held up her hand. "You're a dear friend, Russ. But, you've got to know that I'm in love with Roberto and nothing and no one's going to change that. He has explained all of that to me and it just isn't true."

Russ then knew that no matter what he would say, Darcy wouldn't believe him. He had failed. "You say he was here overnight?"

Darcy smiled. "I didn't say overnight, but, yes, he was. Russ, dear Russ, you're very special to me. I know you only want to protect me. But, I'm just fine. Roberto and I tell one another everything. I know the kinds of things he does for the government. So, please, don't worry about what Steve said. It only means that the strategy to protect Roberto is working. All of this will become very clear in just a few more weeks."

As Russ headed to the door, he turned and faced Darcy. "Darcy, all I can say is please be careful. We have been good friends since we met, and you have become an important part of my life. I only want what is good for you. Remember, when you need me, and you will, I'll be there for you."

Darcy watched Russ as he got into his car and drove away. She had a special place in her heart for him. Someday, when Roberto no longer worked for the government, Russ would get to know the man that she loved.

CHAPTER 43

"Barclay, I don't know why you're upset with me," Phoebe said. "I didn't think there was anything wrong with my meeting with Roberto. You're the one who suggested that he might be able to help me. Besides, you were on your book tour. What was wrong with what I did?"

"I just don't want you going anywhere where you could put yourself in danger," Barclay grumbled. "I now know some things about Roberto that I didn't know before."

"What on earth is going on, Barclay? I know I can't criticize anyone for keeping secrets, but I thought that after what I shared with you that we didn't…"

"You're right, Phoebe. Russ found out some information about Roberto that puts a whole new light on that man. It seems that he's actually a wanted man. A background check that Steve ran on him uncovered some unsavory things about Roberto, if that's his real name. It appears that he's been a con man for quite some time."

"Oh, no," Phoebe said, as she covered her mouth with her hand in disbelief. "Does Darcy know?"

"Russ told her what he knew and it didn't go well. It appears that Darcy still believes in her man. She maintains that he's a government operative."

"No wonder she passed me by in the hall this morning without even looking at me. She must be hurting, Barclay. I need to go to her."

"In a minute, Phoebe. Let's go over what Roberto told you when you met with him two days ago."

"He told me that Judge Kraft was happy to get the documents back, but he wanted revenge. He wanted Roberto to kill me. So, Roberto said that he would tell Kraft that he killed me and that he took the ring off my finger as proof before he disposed of my body. Oh, Barclay, all of this makes me sick to my stomach," Phoebe said weakly.

"Did Roberto tell you how he came across the documents?"

"No, but…God, it was him! He was the one who took them out of my trunk," Phoebe said, almost in a whisper.

"That sounds logical. You must be very careful what you say to Darcy about any of this," Barclay cautioned. "I think it would be better if you avoided her for a while; at least, until we know what's true and what's not."

"Darcy wouldn't…."

"She's in love with the man, Phoebe."

"I know that. But she's my friend and right now that's probably what she needs the most—a friend. Roberto also told me that, after Kraft was arrested, he would see to it that I got my opal ring back. I guess that wasn't true either," Phoebe said despondently.

"If Kraft had been arrested, it would have been all over the news by now. Phoebe, I don't want you going anywhere without me. If Kraft is not involved in this bizarre plot, and it was all Roberto's idea, then you have nothing to worry about. However, if he is the main source of this plot that seems to be ripped out of a bad movie, we have a big problem."

"I don't want to live in the shadows any more. I want to assume my real identity. I caused all these problems when I ran off with those damned documents. If only I had just faced him before I left. I'm sorry I brought all of this to your doorstep, Barclay," Phoebe said.

Barclay took her in his arms. "Look, darling, I love you. Nothing will change that. We'll work this out. Besides, I'm hoping that your name will change again very shortly."

Phoebe lifted her head off Barclay's shoulder and said, "Do you realize that then I will become Florence Henderson? That's the name of an actress."

Barclay smiled. "Well, how about becoming Phoebe Henderson? You said that you liked the name *Phoebe* better. It's good to see a smile on your face. We have a problem, Phoebe, but we will solve it. I promise you."

"Barclay, today is the deadline for me to fax the application for the dance troupe to participate in the contest next week. I must register as Florence Gibble, since I was known as that during my training period. The application also states that no 'stage' names may be used to avoid bias. I can easily explain to my students and parents why Phoebe Snowden will not appear on the program. What do you think about that?"

"Sounds good to me. Your students and their parents don't need to know about your past. I'm going to be with you in Pittsburgh, just to be certain that you are safe. When you're ready to leave, Phoebe, give me a ring—I'll be upstairs."

"Hello. We're back," Amanda called out as the honeymooners came down the hall.

As the newlyweds entered Phoebe's studio, Quentin said, "Everything here seems so calm and serene, just as it was when we left."

Phoebe and Barclay looked at one another. "Welcome home," Barclay said. "I guess you missed us so much you had to come back early," Barclay teased. "You two better sit down and make yourself comfortable. We have lots to tell you."

****

Meanwhile, Darcy was in her studio, feeling upset and isolated. She was beginning to feel like an outsider at The Haven. Russ has probably told everyone about Roberto. She hadn't been able to convince Russ that all those things he thought he had learned about Roberto were nothing more than false trails that the government created to protect her man. She was worried that since the others had already heard Russ' side, they may not believe her. She could understand, and perhaps even accept, why Russ felt that way—he was looking for anything to put Roberto down. He never liked him. While Russ had been a dear friend of hers, he simply had a blind spot when it came to Roberto. Darcy kept telling herself that as soon as Roberto had finished his assignment, they would all know what a wonderful person he was. In her heart, she knew that she would have to wait it out. Easier said than done.

She wished that Roberto would call. He should have been finished with his government assignments by now and be on his way home. When she heard Amanda's voice, she quickly shut her studio door. While Amanda had always been her friend, Darcy was in no mood to hear about the honeymoon. When Phoebe hadn't come into Darcy's studio this morning to give her usual warm good-morning message, Darcy felt rejected. She could feel herself slipping into that dark abyss, where she would go whenever she felt perhaps Roberto was not fully committed to her.

Picking up her I-phone, Darcy was thrilled to see that there was a message from Roberto. She read it over and over again. *Hi, babe, all is well. Thanks for everything.* She stared at the little screen, unable to interpret the meaning of the words. It sounded more like a good-bye—forever kind of message. There was no indication that he would be returning soon—no *I love you*—just thanks. She could hear her heart beating in her ears. She had been dumped often enough to read even the lines that were not there. Russ' words echoed in her head. She whispered *no, no, no,* over and over. Clutching the phone in her hand, she bowed her head and wept. In her heart she knew that she was going to have to get used to being all alone. Roberto, Roberto, I love you.

CHAPTER 44

Later that night, Barclay arrived at Quentin's home in response to a phone call he had received. All he knew was that Quentin wanted to talk with him alone about the problem with Judge Kraft. Before he left Phoebe's apartment, he reminded her not to open the door for anyone. He was glad that his friend Frank had been Phoebe's escort for the past two days. Maybe he was seeing ghosts behind every tree, but Barclay had no idea whether or not Phoebe was in danger and he wasn't taking any chances.

Quentin opened the door and greeted Barclay warmly. "Thanks for coming, Barclay. I have an idea regarding Judge Kraft. Sit down, please. Amanda's not here; she's with Ana and Jennie. I felt that we needed to be alone to discuss this issue. Hope you don't mind."

"No, I really need help. I had a friend of mind take Phoebe back and forth while I was on the book tour. She said she didn't need a babysitter, but I insisted. I don't know where to turn. Should we be talking with the Sheriff?"

"Well, maybe we might have to but let me share my idea with you first. I'm very disturbed about what you and Phoebe told me about Judge Kraft. While I don't know the man on a personal level, I served with him on the Frank Lloyd Wright Board for a short period of time. The Board is dedicated to Wright's genius, and we oversee projects that involve him or any of his buildings. I've been trying to wrap my head around Phoebe's very vivid experience with him. Kraft is well known for his charitable work, and he's never been the subject of any gossip. Now, I'm not saying that I don't believe what Phoebe said—I'm trying to understand how the man I know could have threatened to kill *anyone*."

It was quiet for a minute or two. "Phoebe seemed believable. On the other hand, we have Roberto in the middle of all this and we now know, thanks to Steve, that he should never have been trusted in the first place. I have an idea that I want to run by you—this may sound crazy, but it just might work," Quentin said. "Suppose I call him?"

"Who? Kraft? Call him! Do you think he'll really talk with you? If he did put a hit out on Phoebe, he surely isn't going to tell you," Barclay stated firmly. "What we have here is a 'he said'—'he said' situation. Who are we to believe? Regardless. I believe Phoebe."

"Barclay, don't get upset; stay with me. Here's what I'm proposing. I'll begin by telling him that one of our teachers is Florence Gibble. He may react at once. But, if he doesn't, then I will tell him what Roberto told her. I'll have him on speaker phone. That way the both of us can weigh his reactions. I think it's worth a try. Look at it this way—if he's guilty of planning a hit, he'll surely back off after this call. If he isn't, then we know that this was Roberto's plan for some ungodly, perverted reason. Let's give it a try. What do you think?"

"I want to do anything I can to protect her. While it does sound strange, we might get somewhere with this whole thing. We can't reach Roberto. Darcy claims that she doesn't know where he is. She insists that he's a government agent and that she cannot contact him," Barclay said reluctantly. After thinking it over, Barclay finally said, "Okay, let's try it."

After Quentin flipped through his files, he said, "Ah, here's his number. I feel invigorated. I guess Steve was right—I will always act like a director."

Barclay still had his doubts, but he was willing to put his trust in Quentin.

"Hello, Judge, this is an old, old, friend calling,"

"My God, Quentin! You old dog. How the hell are you doing? According to the newspaper, you just married a lovely woman. What on earth did she see in an old relic like you?" the judge said as he laughed.

"She simply has good taste, that's why she chose me," Quentin deadpanned.

"I hope you have better luck with your choice of a younger woman than I had with mine," the judge replied.

"That's why I'm calling you. I have a delicate situation here and I need your advice. You have to promise me that you aren't going to get angry and hang up on me. I'm relying on the friendship we developed by serving on the Wright Board together," Quentin said.

"I'd never get angry with you; you should know that. Now, what's the problem?"

"Okay, here we go. This may sound like I've lost my mind, but I'll tell you what I know. My bride owns Amanda's Tree Farm. She also runs a school where several artists can practice their trades and teach their crafts as well. One of our teachers here is your Florence Gibble,"

"Florence?" the judge responded. "I haven't heard from her ever since she left. What does all of this have to do with me? She ran away from me—you know that."

"The situation here is a bit convoluted. Well, anyway, one of our other teachers is involved with someone who calls himself Roberto Pellagrino. We found out that his real name is Ray Caltigarone."

"Wait a minute. He's a sonofabitch, Quentin. That no-good bastard brought me the papers that Florence took out of my safe, and I had to pay to get them back. While he was here, he offered to dispose of her for a tidy sum of money. He kept pushing me, urging me to get back at her. My God, Quentin, you don't really think I would put out a hit on someone that I loved so much, do you?"

"We're trying to sort it all out. Apparently, Ray told Florence that you paid him to kill her and that he had to bring her opal ring to you for proof that she was dead."

"Why would I want that cheap ring? That man is crazy. I know that Florence took those papers so how did Ray get them? He's a thief, a liar, and someone who wants to become a hired killer. This is so unbelievable that I cannot even fathom why Florence would think so little of me that she would accuse me—someone who loved her dearly—of wanting her dead," Kraft said convincingly.

"That SOB could very well have taken those papers out of Florence's studio. At that time, he had the trust of most of us here at The Haven. My Amanda tried to caution me about him," Quentin said.

"Let me tell you about those papers. They involved nothing more than a few favors I did for some friends. They were not illegal, but they could be misconstrued as a conflict of interest. Surely, what I did for those people certainly did not rise to the level of criminal intent," the judge said firmly. "Remember, my friend, judges merely interpret laws, we don't make them."

"Nothing involving drugs?" Quentin asked.

"Come on, Quentin. You know how I feel about that. After dealing with my drug-addicted nephew for so long, do you think for one minute that I would get involved in that game? I can assure you that Florence never had a reason to fear me. While I hate her for running away, I love her at the same time. I could never hurt her. You better find out where that Roberto, or Ray, or whatever the hell he calls himself is and hang him up by his balls."

"I appreciate this, Judge," Quentin said.

"Okay, now for some good news-bad news about me. I'll be resigning my post in the morning. I've been experiencing severe back pain. So severe, in fact, that I've even spent time in a pain clinic. The general public will be told only that I'm ill. I don't want a pity party from anyone. I've been looking into various places and that part is quite entertaining. I'm not sure that I could face another winter in Pennsylvania. Damn, I just can't take the cold anymore without almost falling on my knees with pain. My secretary thinks that I should look at the Cayman Islands. Can you see me on the beach? Hell, no," Kraft chuckled, "but I'm not ready for some damned old folks home. I just may ask my real estate agent to look for a place for me in Hawaii. That's more to my liking. You know, Quentin, don't tell her this, but I'd take Florence back in a minute if she asked me. Now, that's the sign of a real old fool," Kraft said with an audible sigh.

"Oh, God, I'm sorry to hear that you're leaving the bench. You've been such a strong advocate for family values," Quentin said. "I apologize for adding to your problems, but I feel so much better now. I appreciate your talking with me about this."

"Do me a favor, Quentin. Give Florence a message for me. Tell her that I'm sorry we didn't work out and that I will always love her." And, with that, the judge hung up.

CHAPTER 45

Phoebe was totally relaxed as she and Barclay walked hand-in-hand up the front steps of The Haven. When Barclay had gotten home last night after his meeting with Quentin, he had nothing but good news to share with her. Both Quentin and he were convinced that she had nothing to fear from Judge Kraft. The memories that she had of a scowling, hateful man could now be tossed aside. Perhaps she had over-reacted all along.

As they entered The Haven, Barclay gave her a kiss on the cheek and said, "When you're ready for lunch just give me a buzz," he said as he bounded up the staircase.

Phoebe was looking forward to getting her little dance troupe ready for the contest in Pittsburgh. These six girls were, by far, the best dancers from all her previous classes. As she walked by Fifi, she automatically reached out and touched the statue's hand, her usual good luck ritual.

When she placed her tote bag on top of the trunk, Phoebe felt an icy vibe. Apparently, it had been Roberto who took the documents. Well, if she hadn't run away from Kraft, then she wouldn't have met Barclay. A little smile appeared as she thought about the first time that she had laid eyes on him. She could still see him on the day he had arrived at The Haven. There he was, getting out of his truck, work boots and all, with a cigarette hanging out of his mouth. She had been certain that she wouldn't like such a rough-looking man—but here she was now, totally in love. And those eyes, those gorgeous blue eyes that made her melt every time he looked at her.

Her thoughts were interrupted as her studio filled with giggling girls and attentive mothers. Each girl found one excuse or another to approach Phoebe, to touch her, to get her attention. Phoebe relished every moment.

Phoebe had the girls sit on the floor in a circle around her. "Let me tell you about this wonderful contest. We will be traveling there in a small bus. You will each be allowed to take one suitcase with you. Miss Hannah and I will take care of your costumes. Now girls, when you pack your suitcases, please don't try to bring your entire bedroom along with you. You'll need a change of clothes to wear to come home, and, of course, your night clothes. I have prepared folders with all this information for your parents."

"Miss Phoebe, what are we gonna wear in the contest?" one student asked.

"Girls, you're going to love this. You're all familiar with the music that we will be using, *Serenade for Strings* by Tchaikovsky. To complement our village theme, you'll be wearing white peasant blouses and chiffon skirts that will be the color of your choice."

"Yippee!" one girl said.

"However, I do want you to work with Miss Hannah on this, since we need to have colors that blend beautifully and look vibrant on stage. Our costumes will count for twenty percent of our score."

"Miss Phoebe, are these costumes going to be expensive?" another girl asked.

"Our costumes are being paid for by Mr. Toth," Phoebe replied.

"Oh, that's Miss Amanda's new husband," giggled one of the girls.

"We'll be practicing for one hour every Monday, Wednesday, and Friday. That will give you time off just for fun. Our music will be on tape, and you'll hear it often during our rehearsals. Our entire routine will be about three minutes long."

"Prizes….what will the prizes be?"

The first place group will receive a trophy for their studio. And, each dancer will receive a framed certificate as well as a little medal on a ribbon. But when we arrive home after the contest, no matter where we place in the contest, there will be a party held here in The Haven for the dancers, parents and friends. Oh, here comes Miss Hannah now," Phoebe said.

With her arms filled with bolts of lovely, stone-washed chiffon fabric, Hannah placed the fabric on the table and motioned for the girls to take a look.

"But, how do we decide who gets what color?"

"Ladies, and you are all young ladies, I believe that you're old enough to meet and sort that out for yourselves," Phoebe replied. Let me know when you have decided. My only suggestion is that no more than two girls wear the same color."

In no time at all, the girls called out to Phoebe. "We've decided. Mary and Joanne get the purple, Sue and Rosalie get the teal, and Wilma and I get the peach" Germaine announced proudly.

"Miss Phoebe, I'm so excited I could die," one girl said.

"If you die, you won't be going along," another girl teased.

"After class, please go upstairs with your parents and Miss Hannah will take your measurements. Now, we must forget about costumes, colors and such and get down to the basics."

Phoebe then switched into her teaching modality. She put the girls through their exercise routine first. After they had reviewed the parts of their routine that they already knew, Phoebe then demonstrated the rest of the dance for them.

"Now, before you are dismissed, I need to talk with all of you, along with your parents. When you get your programs in Pittsburgh, you'll see the name Florence Gibble listed as the dance instructor for the girls from The Haven. You see, Phoebe Snowden is my stage name, and I use that in my work. However, no stage names may be used in this contest so that no one can be swayed by the instructor's reputation and success on the stage. I will see you on Wednesday, ladies," Phoebe said.

As her studio emptied out, Phoebe felt elated. All was going well. She was now safe. Her little dancers were excited and she was in love. What more could she ask for? Now it was time to pay Darcy a visit in her studio.

****

Darcy was seated at her easel. She wanted to put her feelings onto canvas and perhaps, then, her heart wouldn't hurt so much. She had heard the chatter as Phoebe's studio emptied out and thought perhaps Phoebe would come over to see her. Darcy was certain that by now everyone at The Haven had heard the gossip about Roberto. She couldn't understand why they were all so willing to take Steve's word for anything—after all, he wasn't one of them. As she picked up her brush, the strokes began coming, from where she had no idea, but it was if some unknown muse was guiding her hand. The blues began fading into grays and a feeling of healing began sweeping through her body. She was working rapidly now. Here and there was a streak of brilliant red—just like pieces of her heart joining the sadness on the canvas. When the pale yellows appeared, they represented hope—hope that Roberto would come back one day and then they would all know exactly how marvelous he really was. At last she laid her brush down. There it was—all her emotions—all her pain—surrounded by streaks of hope. For the first time that day, Darcy smiled.

"Wow, it sure is good to see you smiling, Darcy," Phoebe said as she entered the studio. "And, you're working again. How wonderful."

Darcy's face brightened when she heard Phoebe's voice.

"Tell me what you see in my abstract painting, Phoebe," Darcy asked, as she turned the easel around.

"You know, I'm not very good at that," Phoebe said.

"Just try. You constantly ask me what I see in the dances your students perform. Now, it's my turn to hear how you interpret my work," Darcy said.

Phoebe looked at the painting for a while. "First, I think I see sadness, but then I'm thrown off when my eye goes to the yellows. The red reminds me of a sharp pain."

Darcy leapt out of her chair. "Phoebe, you got it. I guess it paid for me to give you lessons in art when we were at the Art Museum," a delighted Darcy said.

"Well, I love it," Phoebe said. "Now, you tell me what you wanted to say with your brushes."

Darcy pursued her lips. "You hit the mark—I'm sad. I'm sad because Roberto is not here. I'm sad because I know that all of you are now thinking the worst of the man I love. I'm sad because I want things to be different. But you're right about the yellows. I still have hope. I have hope that Roberto meant everything he ever told me. I'm hoping that Roberto comes back and proves Russ wrong."

"Darcy, I think we're all trying to figure things out. It's not easy for me, either. I know what the judge said to me. I heard his threats loud and clear. Now, however, even Barclay, although he doesn't admit it, seems to believe every word that the judge told Quentin on the phone. Darcy you and I are in the same boat. You know Roberto better than any of us. But isn't it strange that the men are more easily swayed by what the other men say than by what we tell them?"

Phoebe walked over to Darcy and wrapped her arms around her. "Darcy, I'm rooting for you and Roberto. I thought you knew that. I really don't know what to fully believe about my own situation, but I, too, am hoping for the best. You and I are like two birds sitting on a wire together. Both of us are hurting, but we are hanging onto the wire. I wonder why we don't fly away."

"Wow, Phoebe. That would make a good dance routine," Darcy said.

"What about you?" Phoebe asked.

"What do you mean?" Darcy asked.

"For your next painting, perhaps you could paint two birds sitting on that wire of hope. I need the encouragement of hope, too."

"Got a question—can a bird fly with only one wing?" Darcy asked.

"If that bird really wants to fly, it will fly—broken wing and all."

CHAPTER 46

Three weeks later, there was mild chaos at The Haven. The dancers and their chaperones were getting ready to leave for Pittsburgh. Suitcases were lined up at the edge of the parking lot. Homer was picking up each one and carefully placing it in the bus through the rear door. Hannah was hovering nearby with her eye fastened on the costume rack. Although there were only six teen-agers on the bus, the noise level was quite high. The young girls were all talking at the same time. They were obviously thrilled to be going to the classical ballet contest in Pittsburgh.

During the ride, Phoebe took the opportunity to talk with her students. She put her hands up in the air and, amazingly, they became quiet.

"Ladies, we have a few rules about your cell phones, I-pads, or any other electronic devices that you may have brought with you. You may use them tonight up to nine. Then, you must turn them off. You need to get a good night's sleep if you are to perform at your highest level tomorrow afternoon. In the morning, Mr. Barclay will collect all those devices for safe-keeping until the contest is over. That way, your mind will be on your performance, and not on what Johnny, or Mikey, or Bobby is doing back home."

"Oh, Miss Phoebe, we're not that *boy-cray*," the girl sitting beside Hannah said. "We need to call our *mains*,"

Hannah wrinkled her eyes and looked at the girl.

"Oh, *cray* means *crazy* and *mains* means *family*," Hannah's seat partner explained.

"Miss Hannah," said the girl behind her. "Don't mind Germaine. She talks like Bieber and Kanye because she thinks they're *styll* which means *cool*."

"I remember *cool*. That I understand," Hannah said as she laughed.

Phoebe put her hands up again. "Since this is the very first contest of this kind held by the Youth Ballet Society of Pittsburgh, they want to make certain that we'll be as true to our art as possible. You already know that your technical expertise will be judged, and we have reviewed all the required positions on which your scores will be rated. You're ready for this contest, ladies. You know the routine. I'm certain that we'll be given further instructions when we arrive at the hotel, and I'll call you together to share that information with you. Now, for some fun stuff—tonight there will be a dinner with entertainment. Some group called *Four Headless Horsemen* will be performing."

With that, the screams went up and the girls became even more excited.

"No, not them!" the one girl shouted. "I love them!"

Germaine yelled, "*Swag*!"

Hannah merely shrugged her shoulders.

"Oh, Miss Hannah, they're super good. You'll love them, too!" Germaine said, "They're great. While we don't perform ballet to their music, at least not in a classical fashion, they're super entertainers."

Hannah didn't know too much about ballet. She had gotten on the computer in recent weeks and did a bit of research. She didn't want to appear completely clueless when it came to the ballet. She already loved the music. Phoebe would often take the time to explain the various pieces of classical music that she used in her studio. Phoebe had been kind enough to perform parts of *Swan Lake* for her one night and, ever since, she was eager to learn more. While Hannah knew that she had barely scratched the surface of ballet, she was a willing student. She had even begun to introduce what she had learned to Homer. Perhaps, after this trip, Homer might be willing to go with her to see *The Nutcracker* this Christmas.

"Girls, we'll be arriving at our hotel in just a few minutes. Please stay together in the lobby while I check in. We'll be getting adjoining rooms, each with four beds. Miss Hannah and three girls will be in one room and three girls and I will be in the other. There's a door between the rooms that we can have open at all times so you can all go back and forth. And last, you'll be meeting young ladies from other dance studios. Remember, be friendly and outgoing. While I know that you want to win the contest, manners are still extremely important for young ladies of the ballet."

Germaine chimed in, "Girls, in other words don't be *rachel!*" Then she whispered to Hannah, "That means *rude.*"

****

After the party that evening, the dancers and their chaperones headed for the elevator.

"This was the best night of my life," Germaine said. "Did you see what happened to me when I walked on stage to collect my door prize? Did you see that?" she asked Hannah, as she held a framed photo of the *Four Headless Horsemen* for all to see.

"Yes, dear, the guitar player kissed you on the cheek. I was shocked to see that. I thought that was rather brazen of him," Hannah replied.

"No, that was okay, Miss Hannah. I'm never gonna wash my face again," the excited girl said.

"Come on, now," one of the girls teased. "You can't go through life without washing your face."

"Oh, yes I can," Germaine said.

"Girls, will you all please come here? It's time for a little chat," Phoebe said.

"Am I in trouble?" Germaine asked.

"No one's in trouble. I want to compliment you on how you conducted yourselves tonight. I was very proud of you. Even when that one dancer was a bit rude, you didn't react. That means that you are sophisticated young ladies. Now, for our schedule for tomorrow. There will be six groups of dancers competing in classical ballet. We will be the fifth group to be called to the stage. That means that you will have to remain patient and confident in yourselves. Remember, each troupe is here to win and they will all be doing their best. They too have practiced diligently. Now, you have one hour to use your electronic devices and to prepare for bedtime. If for any reason, you need help at any time during the night, Miss Hannah and I will be right by your side, so don't hesitate to wake us. Okay, the clock is ticking. In one hour, the lights will go out."

The girls scampered away in a flurry of activity.

"Phoebe, the girls are having the time of their lives. You certainly have made them very happy by bringing them here," Hannah said.

"Well, they earned this trip. They've worked hard and now they deserve to have some fun."

Just then the phone rang. Phoebe answered. "Who did you say this is?" she asked.

"Mr. Maurice Williams. I'm one of the judges. You seem to have missed something on your application so you'll need to come down to the desk to make certain that we have the right information for your troupe."

"Can you come up to our room?" Phoebe asked.

"I'm afraid that I'm not allowed to do that. You see, I cannot be near any of the contestants before they appear on stage. This will only take a minute."

"I'll be right down. I'll meet you at the front desk," Phoebe said.

"Something wrong?" Hannah asked.

"Just some missing information on our application. This should only take a few minutes. That's funny, though, because I thought I was careful with the application. Will you be alright with taking care of all the girls?"

"Certainly. I love being with them. Take your time, Phoebe."

Phoebe left the room, went down the hall to Barclay's room and rapped on his door.

"Well, young lady, what can I do for you?" Barclay asked jokingly as he leaned against the opened door.

"I need to go down to the desk to take care of some missing information on our application, so I thought I should let you know. Hannah is with the girls."

"I'm going down with you," Barclay said.

When they got to the elevator, Barclay said, "Wow, why an orange traffic cone?"

"Barclay, there's a note. What does it say?" Phoebe asked.

"It states that the elevator is out of order and we should use the stairway. Phoebe, I smell a rat. I don't like the looks of this. Quick, knock on Homer's door and tell him I need him right away."

Phoebe did as she was asked and in just a couple of minutes Homer, in his pajamas, was at Barclay's side.

"We have a problem?" Homer asked.

"I can't be certain, but this is strange. Phoebe, stay right here. Homer, I'll go in the stairway to check things out. But I want you to stay with Phoebe. If all is well, I'll let you know."

Phoebe pushed her back to the wall and with her eyes wide open, she watched as Barclay slowly opened the door to the stairway. The staircase looked unusually dark—as if some of the lights had been removed. Barclay stood still for a few seconds to let his eyes get used to the darkness. As he started down the steps, he saw a shadowy figure move toward him.

"Damn," someone said. "You ain't her."

Barclay managed to get a choke hold on the dark figure. "Homer," he yelled. "Come here!" he shouted.

For a second, Homer hesitated. Barclay had told him to stay with Phoebe, but Barclay was apparently in some kind of trouble. "Phoebe, stay right here," Homer said as he flung the door open and raced to Barclay's side.

"Homer, it appears that we have someone here who doesn't want to be seen. So, the first thing we will do is take his mask off," Barclay said as he ripped the mask off the man's face.

"Okay, buddy, who the hell are you and what the hell do you want?" Barclay demanded.

"Nothing, I don't want nothing."

"Nothing? You were in this stairwell for a purpose. And I know what that was. But it didn't work. What's your boss going to say about your feeble attempt to hurt a woman?"

"I don't know what you're talking about," the man said rather nervously.

"Okay, I guess I'll have to turn you over to the cops. If you want to get out of this mess, you better start telling me the truth or you'll find yourself locked up very shortly." Barclay stated firmly.

The intruder put his head down. "Look, I really didn't want to do this, but I needed the money," he pleaded.

"Who hired you to do this?"

"Some guy I met at the bar last night. He asked me if I wanted easy money. He said that, if I brought the girl to him in the parking lot, I could earn a thousand bucks."

"Where in the parking lot?" Barclay demanded.

"He's in a white van with Jersey plates. That's all I know. Honest, that's all. I don't even know his name. I thought it was some kind of domestic problem. He gave me my instructions—look, here—see?" the man said as he shoved a wrinkled piece of paper in Barclay's hand.

By now Homer had tightened the two light bulbs along the wall that had been loosened by the intruder. Barclay read the note.

"Homer, let's take this fellow up to my room. I have an idea." Barclay said.

Phoebe was amazed when Barclay and Homer came through the stairwell door, pushing a bedraggled man ahead of them.

"Phoebe, don't worry. We have things under control. Go to your girls; say nothing about this to anyone," Barclay said.

As soon as they entered Barclay's room, the intruder started crying.

"Look, buddy, I'm sorry. I wouldn't have hurt that lady, honest. I just needed the damned money so badly that I agreed to get her to the van. I thought that it could be just a lover's quarrel."

"I'll give you one chance—and only one. I want to know all about the person who hired you and exactly what he told you to do. If you do, then perhaps I'll let you go," Barclay said.

The man wiped the tears from his face. "I meet this guy in the bar, see? He buys me a couple of drinks. Then he gives me a proposition. He says he wants to talk with a woman who is staying at the hotel, but he don't want anyone to see him there. I saw him a little while ago in the parking lot. He takes me to his van and opens the back door. There's a damned plastic traffic cone. I spot a gun sticking out from underneath a blanket and there is also a shovel on the floor. He pulls the traffic cone out and hands it to me. I ask him what that is for. Then, he tells me to put it in front of the elevator on the third floor and to make sure that the note stays on. He tells me to hide in the stairwell and make a call to the woman. He then hands me that piece of paper and goes over what I am supposed to say to her."

"How were you going to get her out of the building?"

"He had the van parked in the space right in front of the emergency door on the side of the hotel. He said that the door led to the stairwell. All I had to do was get her to the door and then he would take over. All I could think of at the time was the money I would be getting. I really need it.

"You had to get her down three flights of steps. How did you plan on doing that without hurting her?"

"I was going to pretend that I had a gun. That's why I have a billy club in my pocket. You've got to believe me. I wouldn't have harmed her. I need money, but I wouldn't have done that," the man pleaded.

"Did he say anything, anything at all, that convinced you that he even had a thousand bucks to give you?"

"No. I don't think…now wait a minute, when we were drinking, he did say that he used to work for a judge."

"Bingo!" shouted Barclay. "Now it's time to call 911."

"You're not letting me go?" the frightened man asked.

"Oh, I'm going to let you go, but not just yet. I want to make sure that I get a happy ending out of this escapade."

The man suddenly wrapped his arms around his body and began to rock back and forth.

Barclay dialed 911. "I want to report a suspicious person, who is parked on the east side of the Forbes Hotel up against the emergency exit door. He's in a white van and he's been there for some time. The van has Jersey plates. I'm one of the chaperones for a group of young girls, who are in a dance contest, and I'm concerned about the safety of all these young girls…….Yes, I won't go near the van…..Yes, my name is Barclay Henderson….alright, thank you."

The intruder just stared at Barclay. "What if they don't arrest him? He'll come after me."

"Oh, I don't think they will let him go. If you saw a gun, the cops will, too."

They sat in silence. After about ten minutes, there was a knock on Barclay's door. Barclay motioned for the intruder to go into the bathroom.

"Officer," Barclay said.

"Are you Mr. Henderson?" the officer asked.

"Yes, sir."

"Well, I want to thank you for calling 911. Your suspicions were correct. We have the driver in custody, and we'll be interviewing him when we get him to the station. He's a strange one, that's for sure. He was armed."

"Did he say why he was parked there?"

"I can't really tell you that, sir, but he's in a heap of trouble. He made me laugh, though. When I asked him his name, he told me to just call him The Man."

Barclay shook hands with the officer. "Thank you, officer." He waited a few minutes to give him time to leave the hotel. When Barclay finally opened the bathroom door, the man almost fell into his arms. Handing the disheveled man some money, Barclay said, "Here I know you need this. It isn't much, but maybe it will help"

The man stood there for a few seconds. "How can I thank you?"

"By getting out of here, now. And, from now on, be careful with whom you do business."

CHAPTER 47

Phoebe and Hannah were a bit bleared-eyed, since they had had a late night meeting with Barclay and Homer. They kept glancing at one another, really wanting to talk about what they had learned regarding the intruder and The Man, but, right now, they had to concentrate on the six, very excited dancers. Both women were extremely proud of their men and how they handled what could have been a very tragic incident. It was finally time to take the dancers downstairs to wait their turn to perform.

The theater was filling up rapidly. Hannah had found a spot in the wing where she could look out over the crowd without being noticed. She was excited. Last evening she had had an opportunity to meet people representing other dance troupes, and she was thrilled that they seemed to like her even though she didn't know as much about ballet as some of them. While Hannah would certainly be rooting for the girls from The Haven, this exposure made her realize that it was not going to be an easy task to walk away with the first-place trophy. She smiled when she spotted Homer in the crowd. Wearing the new sport coat that Hannah had picked out for him, he looked so very handsome. He surely looked the part of *Hero*.

Each troupe was warming up in their own assigned waiting area behind the curtain. While they would be able to hear the music for each group, they would not be able to watch the performances. Hannah left her spot to help Phoebe and the girls prepare for their big moment. Suddenly, they heard the host of the event welcome everyone and, before too long, the music of *Midsummer Night's Dream* made them realize that the contest had begun. Phoebe had given Hannah a copy of the program so she could follow along and be ready for when it was their turn on the stage. It didn't surprise Hannah when she heard music from the *Nutcracker Suite* since Phoebe had told her that someone would probably choose that ballet.

When the music for the third group began, Hannah needed to check the program to see what was playing. Apparently, this piece was from *Sleeping Beauty*. When the fourth group took the stage, Hannah immediately recognized music from *Swan Lake* since this was Phoebe's favorite. Hannah closed her eyes as she envisioned Phoebe dancing across the floor of her own studio. The girls from The Haven were on their feet—they were next.

Hannah didn't know if she could take much more pressure. When she heard *Serenade for Strings* she quickly moved to the wing so she could see the girls. Her breath was almost taken away as she saw her little ones, in their chiffon skirts, that seemed to float on air as they danced. Nothing that she had ever seen had affected her this way. She knew full well that it had been Phoebe, not her, who was responsible for the girls maturing into such fine little ballerinas. But she also knew that she had put every stitch in their costumes with love—so, in essence, they belonged to her, too. Their three-minute performance was over and the applause indicated that the spectators thoroughly enjoyed what they had just seen. Hannah didn't wait to hear the music for the last troupe, she hurried to the dressing room area to hug and kiss each of the young dancers.

"What do you think, Miss Hannah?" Germaine asked.

"Spectacular, my little angels, spectacular! I'm so proud of you. Congratulations, Phoebe, your troupe did a superb job," Hannah said as she enveloped Phoebe in her arms.

"Girls, we must all go on stage in a moment. Remember, stay together, and, no matter what the results are, I want to see smiles. You have never performed so well, my darlings. You didn't miss a position and you hit all your cues right on target," Phoebe said. "In other words, my precious ones, you were perfect."

Just then, the stage manager motioned to Phoebe. "Please lead your girls on stage and have them stand about three feet away from the group you are following."

When all the girls were lined up on the stage, the spectators stood up and gave them a rousing round of applause. Hannah was once again hanging onto the side of the curtain.

The president of the Youth Ballet Society of Pittsburgh approached the microphone. "Ladies and gentlemen, what you have witnessed here today is very hard to put into words. To observe these wonderful, young dancers perform classical ballet with such grace and expertise was indeed a rare privilege. At this time, I would like the teachers to step forward so we can honor them for their dedication to the art and for their patience and diligence in helping these ladies develop their skills."

Then, coming from behind the curtain, six little eight-year-old girls, in pink tutus, came forward, each one carrying a bouquet of flowers. As they presented their beautiful gifts to the teachers, the crowd, once again, came to their feet and applauded.

"Now, for the moment you have all been waiting for. This was a very difficult task for our five judges. Let's give them a round of applause, too." Once the applause died down, an almost deathly quiet came over the audience. "Now, the troupe receiving the runner-up award is the Johnson Dance Studio. Come forward, ladies."

Hannah's heart seemed to be in her throat. She crossed her fingers and closed her eyes.

"Now, first-place goes to the troupe from The Haven."

Phoebe exhaled and broke out into a smile. She turned to her girls and held out her arms. They instantly ran toward her and a group hug ensued. After the girls lined up, the president of the Society approached them and placed medals around each of their necks.

"Will Florence Gibble, the instructor for the group, step forward?"

Phoebe wasn't used to hearing her real name spoken out loud, and it took her a second or two to pull herself together.

"This trophy, which we hope is only the beginning of an annual event, is presented to you and your troupe. A great deal of work must go into teaching classical ballet. Patience, dedication to the art, and a true love of the art are all necessary components for ballet instructors. We hope you will proudly display this trophy in your studio, not only for what your troupe has done here today, but for promoting this art form."

Barclay was seated in the back next to Homer. When the first-place winner was announced, he grabbed Homer's arm and squeezed it tightly. He could hardly sit still. He wanted to run up on that stage and sweep Phoebe off her feet. He could now breathe. Phoebe had won. The Man was in jail. Kraft was probably far away. Now they could look forward to peace and quiet at The Haven.

CHAPTER 48

During the past month, there had been a flurry of activities going on at The Haven. After the dancers returned from Pittsburgh wearing their first-place medals, they were feted with a party for all the students in Phoebe's classes and their parents. Now their trophy was resting in the brand new exhibit case that Homer had built. Russ and his renovation crew were moving ahead on creating the new Christmas shop. Amanda had moved her things into Quentin's beautiful home and seemed quite content in her new surroundings. The little cottage had sat empty for a few weeks, but it was now occupied by Ana and her little Jennie. Things seemed to be normal and everyone, except Darcy, seemed to be happy and content. Darcy, more and more, was becoming reclusive, only putting herself out there with the students in her art classes. She refused to believe that Roberto was not coming back. But, every day it was getting harder and harder for her to go on thinking, hoping, praying that he would.

Barclay could think of no better time to propose to Phoebe. He wanted to do something special for her. It was then that he thought of his grandmother's pendant—an Australian crystal opal set in rose gold. Slipping the blue velvet box into his jacket pocket, he hurried over to the new gift shop to meet with Russ to see what he thought of the idea.

Russ was standing behind the counter with a large sheet of paper in front of him. He was laying out the plans for shelves and alcoves that he envisioned making the shop something really special. He was lost in thought when Barclay approached him.

"Hey there, fellow, can you spare a minute?" Barclay said light-heartedly.

"Barclay, if you come in here, I'm gonna put you to work. Can writers do anything else but play with words?" Russ teased.

"No, I'm afraid not," Barclay responded. He then opened the box and dangled the pendant in front of Russ.

"Where the hell did you get that? That's a remarkable piece," Russ said as he reached out to take the pendant out of Barclay's hand.

"It was my grandmother's," Barclay said proudly. "She was a special lady in my life."

Russ twirled the pendant around. He then took it over to the window and pulled out his jeweler's glass. "The more I look at this, the more I fall in love with it. Would you want to sell this piece?"

"God, no. I would like to give this to Phoebe instead of an engagement ring, but I don't know how she'll react. It means a great deal to me—in fact it's priceless. But I really don't know what it's worth. What do you think?"

"Of course, you have to replace the chain. I have several upstairs that you can choose from. But the pendant itself is probably worth about five grand. Phoebe will love this. She's a delicate little flower. She's not into garish things and modern-day nonsense. If you want her to say *yes* to your proposal, this will seal the deal. Let's go upstairs and get a chain that is truly worthy of holding this lovely piece of work," Russ said. "By the way, you wouldn't have any more jewelry laying around, would you?"

Just then Ana and Jennie entered the shop. "Good morning, Mr. Weber," Ana said.

"Ana, didn't I tell you yesterday—no Mr. Weber. Just call me Russ," Russ said as he reached for Jennie. "Come here, my little one, Uncle Russ has a present for you," he said as he took her over to the stuffed toys and picked out a Santa Claus doll and gave it to her.

"Russ, you're spoiling her." Ana said.

"That's what uncles are for—spoiling little ones."

"Hannah's right behind me," Ana said. "She wants to take Jennie to her place, so I'll be free to start to tag things. I'm so excited about my new job. To think that I'll be here in this lovely shop every day, and I can easily walk to work."

"How do you like living in the cottage?" Barclay asked.

"I love it. I cannot begin to ever repay Amanda for what she's done for us. I have not been this happy for a long, long, time," Ana said. "And, Quentin told me that his lawyer is certain that he can get my inheritance back for me. If he does, that will be Jennie's college fund money," Ana said excitedly.

"How's my little precious?" Hannah asked as she took Jennie out of Russ's arms.

"Hey, woman, that's kidnapping," Russ said.

Jennie immediately nestled into Hannah arms. "She loves her Nanna Hannah."

"Hey, that's funny, Nanna Hannah," Russ said as he laughed.

"Just take your time, Ana. Jennie and I have lots to do today. First, we must have milk and cookies. Then we must roll the ball around the yard—oh, so many things to do. Jennie, we must get going," Hannah said as she took off with the child.

"Ana, I want to make certain that you understand you'll eventually be in charge of all the buying and selling. Once you feel comfortable handling these responsibilities, you will no longer have to consult with me for anything. Amanda and I want to give you the opportunity to run the shop as you see fit."

"I hope that I can live up to your expectations, Russ. I'm only now beginning to feel like a real person with my own ideas and purposes. I'll try not to let you down."

****

Barclay felt nervous. He knew, or rather he hoped, that Phoebe was ready for this. He would not tell her just yet that Steve had assured him that the film, based on his book, would begin shooting in the spring. While he was proud that this was happening, the only thing he wanted to talk about tonight was Phoebe wanting to marry him.

When she opened the door of her apartment, he saw that she had dimmed the lights and had placed lighted candles around the room. How could she have known that this would be the night?

"Hello, sir, and who are you?" Phoebe teased.

"Well, young lady, I'm Sir Galahad. I tackle ferocious enemies and bring them to the ground with a bang. I also sometimes make a fool of myself, but only for my lady love," Barclay said.

"And who would that be?"

Barclay stepped inside, took Phoebe in his arms, and said, "Don't tell anyone, but that would be you."

On the coffee table was a bottle of wine in a bucket and two glasses.

"If I wouldn't know better, I would think that you're prepared for some kind of celebration," Barclay said.

"Perhaps."

"Phoebe, while I probably should have written you a letter—since I'm better at writing than I am at speaking—I didn't think that that would be romantic at all. Phoebe will you marry me?"

Phoebe smiled. "You will never believe this, but I was prepared to propose to *you* tonight. Yes, my darling, I will marry you."

They were wrapped in each other's arms for a long time—not wanting to lose a moment of sheer bliss.

Barclay pulled out the velvet box. "Phoebe, I have often mentioned my grandmother and how important she was in my life. Well, you see, I thought.....," Barclay mumbled as he held the box in his hands, half afraid to open it, half afraid she might not like the pendant. He pulled the pendant out and gently nestled it in his palm.

Phoebe was stunned. "God, that's beautiful, Barclay. Did that belong to her?"

"Yes," he said weakly.

Phoebe looked at the piece as it lay curled in her lover's hand. "Barclay, are you certain that you want me to have it?"

"I thought it would mean more than a ring I would purchase," he said as he stood up and placed the pendant around her neck. "There," he said, "A beautiful pendant for a beautiful lady."

Phoebe hurried over to the mirror and studied the gemstone. "Oh, Barclay, no wonder I love you! How precious of you!" Scurrying back to him, she tenderly placed her hands on his shoulders. She lifted her face and sighed as he kissed her. The two were locked in an embrace—neither one ready to break away.

Finally, Phoebe said, "I love you, Barclay. More than I ever thought would be possible."

"I love you, Phoebe. I have since the first day I met you. From the time I first saw you dance, you took possession of my heart," Barclay hesitated. "One more surprise for you, Phoebe—Steve got the funding to film my book!"

Chapter 49

It was just four weeks until Thanksgiving and it was the day of the grand opening of the new Christmas shop at The Haven. Homer had been working diligently making sure that the porch, sidewalks and parking lots were in good condition. He didn't think that a store opening was such a big deal, but Hannah thought it was, so he pitched in by helping to park cars and to direct customers to the shop.

Inside the front door of The Haven were the six young girls who had won first place in the ballet contest. They wore the medals they won around their necks. As they moved about in their colorful costumes, they made an impressive sight for the shoppers. To the right of Fifi, stood a display case that Homer had made, and it held the two-foot trophy that they had won. The girls invited the shoppers to view their trophy and encouraged them to sign the register book and to fill out door prize slips. They each had some brochures about The Haven and all it had to offer, which they handed out, especially to those parents who had children with them.

Here and there were bouquets of flowers, sent by friends wishing Amanda good luck with her new Christmas shop. On one side of the room was a long table holding punch bowls and goodies for the shoppers. Quentin mingled with the crowd, proudly serving as ambassador for The Haven.

Russ and his crew had done a fantastic job. The ambience was mesmerizing. The shop was so much more than shelves lined with merchandise. Here and there were small alcoves, each holding an item that only added to the holiday theme. While there were hundreds of items, the store did not seem overloaded. Ana was introducing herself to the visitors and, even though she was extremely busy, she didn't appear to mind the commotion at all.

It seemed that none of the customers really wanted to leave. They enjoyed the goodies and talking with the girls. And, their arms were full of things that they had purchased in the shop. Music was playing softly in the background. Several of Darcy's paintings were resting on easels, attracting a great deal of attention. One customer spotted Darcy's abstract entitled *Hope* and immediately said, "I must have that painting."

Suddenly, Barclay came into the room and headed right for Quentin. "Did you hear the news?" he whispered softly.

"No, what happened?"

"The Judge—Kraft—was found dead on the beach in the Caymans. It was just on CNN," Barclay said.

"What? Do they know what happened?" Quentin asked as his eyes opened wide in disbelief.

"The homicide police are handling the case, so it apparently looks suspicious. But the police indicated that they didn't have much to go on. I've got to find Phoebe."

"The last time I saw her she was taking some people on a tour of her studio," Quentin said.

"Could it have been, you know—him?"

"Roberto? I guess it could have, but we can't even suggest that near Darcy. Remember, Barclay, we have two people to be concerned about—Phoebe and Darcy. Let's not drag Roberto into this just yet. If Kraft was dirty, then there could be many people who might have wanted him dead," Quentin said. "Let's keep this to ourselves, and then, later, we can talk with both of them. They need to know, but not right now."

Just then, a flustered Phoebe came rushing out of her studio. Barclay knew immediately that she had heard about Kraft. He quickly took her arm and led her down the hall to Amanda's new office.

"Phoebe, you heard?"

"Yes. My God. Barclay. What on earth happened? A man that was taking a tour of my studio was telling someone that he had heard it on the news. I hated Kraft, but this is horrible!"

"It could take a long time before we know the true story. But, Phoebe, you are not to blame for this. From what we know, and we surely don't know everything, there were others who wanted him out of the picture.

Come, let's take a walk outside where we can talk in private. We don't want to spoil Russ' grand opening."

When Amanda arrived carrying a stack of envelopes in her hand, Quentin immediately took her into her office, closed the door, and told her about Kraft. She was quiet for a few minutes. Then she asked, "Quentin, I hate to say this, but does this mean that Phoebe is free of this man at last? You know, can she truly feel safe? Or is that a terrible thing to say when someone has been killed?"

"Terrible? No. my dear. But it can be considered good news for her."

"Is Darcy here?"

"So far she's a no-show," Quentin replied.

"For her sake, I hope that Roberto was not involved. Now, I'm going to try to bring a bit of joy to this day by handing out our dinner party invitations to the staff. That will give us all something happy to talk about," Amanda said as she headed for the gift shop.

As she met with each of her staff members, Amanda said, "Quentin and I are having a small party for the staff on the Sunday before Thanksgiving. We want to share our plans for The Haven with all of you at the same time," she explained to each one. "It will be our own little Thanksgiving dinner."

The rest of the day just flew by. When Amanda became aware that Ana was having a difficult time keeping up with all the customers, she went behind the counter to help. Finally, when Russ closed the door to the shop, ending business for the day, they all breathed a sigh of relief.

"What a great day!" Russ said as he looked around the shop. "If business is as good on Black Friday as it was today, our shelves may be quite empty."

"Quentin, what do you think about Kraft's death?" Barclay asked.

"As I said before, it could be any number of people depending on how involved he was with the wrong side of the law. For Darcy's sake, I hope it wasn't Roberto."

"For every rat you see, there are a dozen that you don't," Russ said. "But, if I were a betting man, I'd put all I own on handsome Roberto. It's been my experience that he was just a bit too perfect to be true. I'll cool it around Darcy, though. And, I'll be here to help her pick up the pieces when he breaks her heart."

As Quentin was holding the front door open for Amanda, he saw Sheriff Wagner's car pulling into the lot. "I wonder what he wants," Quentin said.

As Wagner hurried up the walkway, he said, "I have news for you. When they picked up The Man in Pittsburgh, he really spilled his guts. As a result, Ray Caltigarone, or as we know him, Roberto Pellagrino, has been indicted in absentia under the RICO Act. So, if he got out of the country, and comes back, as soon as he puts one foot in the US, he'll be arrested. You sure know some nice people," Wagner said as he patted Quentin on the back.

CHAPTER 50

Darcy was annoyed. She had hoped that it had bothered them that she hadn't shown up for the opening of the Christmas Shop. But even that thought didn't make her feel any better. While no one had said anything directly to her about Judge Kraft, she knew what they were all thinking. Although Quentin had assured her that the staff at The Haven did not believe that Roberto had anything to do with the judge's demise, she didn't believe him. And Russ—well he had a hard time looking Darcy in the eyes since that time. She hated the government for making Roberto do under-cover work. If Roberto was involved with the judge, he had done it at the behest of some high government official.

Pulling her easel closer to her side, she began putting the finishing touches on the painting that would perhaps free her soul. Her heart was heavy. She had been certain that Roberto would come for her before Thanksgiving, but now that too seemed impossible. After an hour of work, she was at last satisfied. Darcy stood up, walked across the room, and looked at the painting. Her first reaction was sadness, over-whelming sadness. However, quite suddenly she felt a vibrant sense of hope, springing forth, covering the sadness. Yes, she had captured her feelings that only Phoebe and she would fully understand.

On one hand, she wanted to rush into Phoebe's studio and show her the painting right now. But, she rejected that temptation since she now wanted to be alone. Gathering her things, she walked down the hallway to the front door as quietly as she could. She didn't want to run into anyone. As she neared Fifi, her hand went out instinctively to touch her. But she stopped. Fifi was supposed to bring her good luck, but she had only brought her sadness. Rage filled her. Darcy looked around. She was alone in the hall. She stepped right up to Fifi, looked the statue in the eye and spit on her. Just then she thought she heard Phoebe call out to her, but she just kept on going. And, she surely didn't want to attend the little dinner party that Amanda and Quentin were giving tomorrow night in the formal dining room at The Haven. As Darcy approached her mini-van, an UPS truck pulled up and a young man with a manila envelope in his hand approached her.

"Hi, there. Is this The Haven School? I'm looking for Darcy Hamilton. I stopped at the little cottage down the hill and that lady told me to come up here."

For the first time all day, Darcy smiled. "This is your lucky day, that's me," she said.

"Well, great. This is my first run up here. Sure is nice," he said as he looked around. "You need to sign here and then I'll be on my way."

Darcy was almost speechless. It had to be from Roberto—it just had to be. As the delivery man jumped back into his truck, Darcy shouted, "Thank you—thank you so much."

Darcy's hands were shaking so badly she hardly had the strength to open her van door. She looked around. She didn't want to share this moment with anyone. Slowly she examined the envelope—The Cayman Islands. Turning the envelope over and over in her hands, she could almost see his face. Perhaps she should wait until she got home to open it. She laid it on the seat beside her. But anxiety got the best of her and she picked it up once again. It was taped all around—that would be a problem. Rummaging through her tote bag, she found a nail file. She looked around once again to make certain that no one could interrupt her. It seemed as if her heart was trying to jump out of her chest. She knew it—she knew that he had not forgotten her. There were two sheets of paper and a small envelope with Phoebe's name on it. Now she was confused. For Phoebe? Why Phoebe?

Trying hard not to cry, she began reading the letter. *Darcy, my love. It is time to come to me. All is ready. I have reserved a first-class ticket for you at the Pittsburgh Airport. The first thing you must do is call the airline and confirm the date of your departure. Pack lightly. After all, a bride deserves lots of pretty new clothes. Bring your passport, your birth certificate and any valuable jewelry that you have. Close your bank accounts and sell the mini-van. Tell no one where you are going. This is a test for you, Darcy. If you really love me, you'll come. If you're not here by the end of the month, I'll know that you no longer care. All my love, Roberto. PS Get rid of the painting in your living room!*

Darcy was dumb-struck. A bride—she was going to be a bride. Just the thought of that overwhelmed her. She certainly loved Roberto with every fiber of her being. But was she ready to leave all behind and join him no matter what he had done? Her answer was a resounding *yes!*

Trying to keep from driving too fast, Darcy hurried to her apartment. She had much to do. As she threw things on her bed, she looked at the little envelope that had Phoebe's name on it. What would it hurt if she opened it? Phoebe would never know. She ripped the envelope open and Phoebe's little opal ring fell out. Darcy was even more proud of her man than ever. He had promised to get Phoebe's ring back and he did. What a remarkable man. She called the airline to verify her reservation. She felt a bit nervous since she would have only one day to prepare for the trip and get to Pittsburgh for her flight. She decided that she would take only one suitcase for clothes and use her tote bag for the few pieces of jewelry that she wanted to take with her. Rifling through her desk, she located her safe deposit box key and her money market statement. Luckily, she also found the title to her car.

She sat down at her computer and wrote directions for the disposition of the items that she would be leaving behind. She addressed it to her cousin and explained that everything in the apartment was hers and that she was free to do whatever she wanted with the furniture and clothing. She laid out her plans for tomorrow. First, she would stop at Happy Harry's Auto Sales and sell her van. Next, she would walk across the street to the bank to withdraw her funds and close her accounts. Then, she would call for a limo to take her to the airport. She would stay overnight at the Hilton. The next morning, before she boarded the shuttle to take her to the airport, she would make two calls: one to her cousin and one to Russ. She would ask Russ to come to her apartment and, using the key that she would place under the mat, retrieve the little gift bag she had for Phoebe She spent the next hour going over and over her plans to make certain that she had covered all bases. Suddenly, she remember the painting. Putting her hands on the frame, she pulled it off the wall. Laying it on the kitchen table, she took black paint and covered the entire painting. She carried it outside and tossed it into the dumpster behind her apartment.

She would miss Phoebe and Amanda, as well as Hannah and little Jennie, but Roberto was far more important. He was her destiny. No matter what Roberto had done, she would still love him. Of that she was certain.

****

The next day, when the phone rang at seven in the morning, Russ was tempted not to answer. Begrudgingly, he reached across his pillows and picked up the receiver.

"Hello," he croaked. "This better be important."

"Russ, this is Darcy. I have a favor to ask."

"Darcy, are you having problems with your mini-van already?" Russ asked.

Darcy laughed. "No, Russ. I don't need a ride. I need you to go to my apartment, get the key from under the mat and go in and pick up the little gift bag that you'll find on the coffee table and give it to Phoebe. It's from Roberto. Also, please remember to tell her that I have a gift for her in my studio. She'll find it on the easel near the back window."

"Is Roberto back again?"

"No, he's not."

"My God, Darcy, are you going to him?" Russ said as he sat up straight in his bed.

"I don't have much time to talk so, please, no more questions—just listen. Please don't lose that little gift bag. It will mean a lot to Phoebe and tell her I will miss her," Darcy said.

"What do you mean…?"

"I'm going away. So, Russ, if you have any feelings left for me, please do as I ask. I cannot explain. Maybe I'll see you some day, but I can't promise. Russ, remember, I love you as a friend. I know I can count on you to help me with this."

"Wait, Darcy, wait, what do you…."

The line went dead. Russ sat for some time just holding on to the receiver. He was hoping this was only a bad dream, but he realized that it wasn't. He knew in his heart that he would never hear Darcy's voice again.

Should he call Amanda? What should he do? The special dinner at The Haven was scheduled for six with cocktails at five. Everyone would be scurrying around his morning, trying to get things accomplished before the party. He would just have to wait—but that was going to be hard. Darcy was gone and he didn't know where. At noon, he decided he would go to Darcy's apartment. Maybe that would ease his frazzled nerves. He found the key under the mat. With a heavy heart, he opened the door. He spotted the gift bag immediately. As he turned around, he felt as though something was different—suddenly he became aware that Roberto's painting was gone. Why was it missing? Where could it be? He never dreamed that it was laying in the dumpster behind the apartment house.

When he arrived at The Haven he noticed that the only cars parked there were in front of the Christmas Shop. In all his concern about Darcy, he had forgotten that the world moved on. He ran into the shop to check on Ana. As usual, she had everything under control. He opened the front door and stood in the foyer for a few seconds, looking at Fifi. Making certain that he locked the door behind him, he was about to climb the steps to his classroom when he remembered what Darcy told him about her gift for Phoebe. Eager to see what it was, he walked down the hall and pushed the door open to Darcy's studio. He could hardly bear to enter. He would never see Darcy again. He stood there, in the center of the studio, for a few minutes, just listening to the silence. She was visible in so many ways. Her paintings, her smocks hanging on hooks right inside the door, an extra pair of shoes sitting on a chair, and her paintings—sad and happy scenes, all lined up along the one wall. How was he ever going to get along without her? *What a terrible big brother I made.* He forced himself to walk to the back of the studio. He spotted the painting that Darcy was giving to Phoebe. He didn't understand its meaning, but he was certain that Phoebe would.

He left Darcy's studio and slowly climbed the stairs to his own classroom. He sat down at his jeweler's bench and mechanically began working on some of his orders. After several hours, he finally heard the sound of cars. The caterers were the first to arrive and he was about to run downstairs to let them in when he saw Amanda and Quentin pulling into the parking lot. He decided that he would wait awhile before joining them. He just wasn't ready to share the news about Darcy—at least not yet.

Finally, Russ turned the lights off in his studio and went downstairs. He saw that all the invited guests were in the salon just milling about. With the gift bag in his hand, he walked into the salon lethargically.

"Russ, what's that?" Amanda asked, as she pointed to the little bag.

"Guys, come here a minute. I have news—unbelievable news," Russ said forlornly.

"What's wrong, Russ?" Quentin asked.

"Darcy's gone, but I don't know where."

"What?" they said in unison.

"She called me this morning. She said that she was leaving, but she wouldn't tell me where she was going. She asked me to go to her apartment and pick this up and give it to Phoebe. That's all I know," Russ said sadly.

They huddled together, not wanting to believe what Russ had just told them.

"Maybe she just needed some time away from all of this," Hannah suggested.

"It can't be," Phoebe said. "It just can't be."

"Oh, my God," Amanda said. "Where else would she have gone if not to Roberto?"

Russ pointed to the small gift bag. "She said it's from Roberto."

"Roberto. Is he back?" Quentin asked.

"No. But I have a feeling that she's going to him wherever the rat bastard is," Russ said angrily.

"Open the little bag. Perhaps that will tell us. Open it, Phoebe," Amanda urged.

Phoebe held the gift bag in her hands. A little piece of red ribbon was hanging out of the bag and Phoebe began pulling on it. "My opal! My opal!" she said as the ring swayed back and forth in the air. "Roberto said he'd get it back for me. I'm confused. What do you think, Russ?"

"I think you should go into Darcy's studio and see the painting she left there for you. It may be another clue as to where she went. I didn't understand it, but I'm sure you will," Russ said hopefully.

They all followed Phoebe to Darcy's studio. Phoebe walked over to the easel and turned it around.

"She's not coming back," Phoebe said mournfully. She stared at the painting, while her hand clutched her heart. "I know this painting; we talked about it. We agreed that we were like two birds sitting on a wire, hanging on for dear life, afraid to let go, afraid that we couldn't fly by ourselves. She asked me if a bird with a broken wing could fly. I told her that if the bird wanted to fly badly enough, it would. You see, the bird in the air, the one that's flying, only has one wing. She's gone to him. She's on her way to Roberto."

"Look, this is a shock for all of us. But Darcy is a grown woman and she has the right to make her own decisions. All we can do is to be here for her. She may decide to come back," Amanda said.

"I don't think she will," Russ stated dejectedly.

"Let's go back to the salon, Quentin suggested. "It's time to begin our Thanksgiving celebration."

Quentin took Amanda's hand and the two of them stood alongside of Fifi. "Welcome, family, make yourselves comfortable. Cocktails will be served shortly."

They were taken back by the lovely decorations that had been placed in the salon while they were in Darcy's studio. Wicker baskets, filled with bright yellow mums, pine cones, and large orange satin bows, were positioned around the room.

"Oh, Amanda," Hannah said. "This is such a nice surprise. Your little elves must have been here. Look, Jennie," Hannah said as she knelt down so the little one could see too. "Pretty flowers, sweetie."

After everyone had a drink in their hands, Amanda said, "I would like to take this opportunity to thank everyone for such a successful year here at The Haven. Let's raise our glasses to one and all."

"We have not only accomplished much this year, but we have instituted changes that we feel will guarantee an even more successful one next year. Our class rosters were filled to capacity and our spring semester applications are pouring in. Russ has done a fantastic job with the renovations he made to our shop. Ana, bless you so much, for taking over the management of the shop with such professionalism that it astounds me. Phoebe, oh what can I say about her? Well, her students brought home a wonderful trophy which attests to her ability as our teacher of dance."

"Here, here," Barclay said.

"And you, Barclay, not only did your book land on the best-sellers' list, Hollywood is already working on a movie. No too shabby, Barclay."

Everyone started applauding.

"Hannah, or should I say Nanna Hannah," Amanda teased, "Not only can you work your needles to produce anything we need, but you cook and bake too. Hannah was responsible for the gorgeous costumes that Phoebe's students wore in the contest."

"And I cannot fail to mention the work all of you did for our wedding. Homer, the trellis you made was absolutely beautiful. And, by the way, the trophy case you made is remarkable. That was a lucky day when I found you walking up the driveway."

Homer blushed. "Miss Amanda, I'm so happy to be here."

Just then, the caterers opened the pocket doors between the salon and the dining room.

"Looks like dinner is being served," Quentin said as he stood up.

The dining room table had been arranged in a square with a seasonal, circular flower arrangement in the center, set off with tall candles that were sparkling under the crystal chandelier.

"Breathtaking," Phoebe said.

"It's the most beautiful Thanksgiving table I've ever seen," Hannah said as she held Homer's hand. "And the dinnerware! I'm so happy to see Mrs. Nesbit's original china on the table. How thoughtful of you, Amanda."

"I simply had to use them," Amanda said. "A long time ago, one day when I was in the kitchen with her, she lit candles and then served peanut butter and jelly sandwiches. She maintained that, while the food may be elegant or simple, the ambience should always be lovely."

"Ana, where do you want the high-chair?" Quentin asked.

"Oh, Jennie will fuss if she's not next to her Nanna Hannah," Ana said pleasantly.

"Okay then. Homer, you sit here on this side, and Hannah, you sit next to him. Then we can put Jennie next to her and then Ana. How will that be?" Quentin asked. "Phoebe, Barclay, and Russ you sit on the other side."

"I have one request," Russ said as he smiled. "Please put Phoebe in the middle. That way I can enjoy the company of a lovely lady rather than having to talk with a grumpy author."

"Hey, you old coot! I'm not grumpy. I'm just particular about my friends," Barclay said as he held the chair out for Phoebe.

One spot at the table was not taken. Suddenly, Darcy was on everyone's mind. As the server was starting to remove that place setting, Amanda said, "No, please, let all of that there. While I sincerely doubt that Darcy will be here, in case she would miraculously walk through the doorway, we need to be ready for her."

"Hannah, would you do us the honor of saying grace?" Quentin asked. "Let's all join hands."

Hannah bowed her head. "Lord, thank you for the food in which we are about to partake. Bless our little family and help us continue to walk in Your ways. And, Lord, wherever Darcy is, keep her safe from harm and, if it be Thy will, bring her back to us. Amen."

The conversation during dinner was lively and upbeat. Laughter filled the air. As serving dishes were passed around the table, it was obvious that they were enjoying themselves. When it appeared that the guests had had their fill, Amanda said, "I invite you to move to the salon where we can continue our conversations. Dessert will be served by the fireplace."

Barclay and Russ rearranged the chairs in the salon so everyone could enjoy watching the logs burn.

When they were seated, Amanda said, "I think this would be a good time for each one of us to share what we are thankful for on this special occasion."

"That sounds wonderful, Amanda," Phoebe said. "I know that I have much to be thankful for."

"Would you like to start, Phoebe?" Amanda asked.

"Amanda gave me a job even though she knew that I was running away from something. She never pressured me—she just accepted me. I found a safe haven right here among the beautiful trees. I thank all of you for supporting me when my relationship with Kraft practically exploded in my face. You are my wonderful family. And you, Barclay, I am especially thankful I found you," Phoebe said as she leaned over and kissed him on his cheek.

They were surprised when Homer said, "I would like to go next. "I ain't used to talking in front of so many people. But there is something I have wanted to share for a long time. I owe all of you an apology. I brought the wrath of Adam Ash to this lovely place. You see, Ash paid for my mom's burial and, in exchange, I was supposed to spy on Miss Amanda. On my first day here, I was sneaking around her cottage. I even walked up on her back porch, but then I ran away. I became ashamed of myself and I went to Mr. Quentin and confessed. While he was disappointed in me, he forgave me and so did Miss Amanda. It took awhile, but I also told Hannah. You have all been so nice to me and I love working here. I did wrong—and I'm sorry."

They were all quiet for a few seconds. Then as one unit, they applauded. Hannah turned to Homer and said, "How nice of you to share that, Homer. You are a perfect gentleman. *Thankful* is such a lovely word. It brings such joy to our lives when we express thanks. First, I am thankful for being part of this family. I'm thankful for having so many wonderful friends. I usually have had a hard time when it came to associating with people, but not here. And, if I may be so bold, I am glad that Homer and I are such dear friends."

One could almost see Homer's chest expand with pride. In a whisper, he leaned toward Hannah, and said, "Thank you."

Barclay stood up. "When I first arrived here, I wasn't sure that I was going to be happy in the middle of so many trees. However, I was lucky enough to see Phoebe dancing in her candle-lit studio. In all my life I had never seen anything quite as breathtaking. All of you have made me feel welcome and I too look at you as family. For that I am truly grateful. While I am pleased that my book will be made into a movie, without all of you by my side, keeping me grounded, I don't know what I would do. Confidentially, I have even fallen in love with all these trees," Barclay said happily.

Russ stood up next. "Well, I can't speak like a writer, but I totally agree that you are now my family, too. Every day I remind myself how lucky I have been just to be here at The Haven. I am also thankful for the opportunity that Amanda and Quentin have given me to manage all that goes on in this marvelous edifice. I will try my best to keep The Haven the kind of place that Amanda has created. I will keep in mind that my top priority is to make certain that it remains a haven for everyone."

Ana hesitated. As tears filled her eyes, she said, "Words cannot express how thankful I am. I came here in the pouring rain and Amanda took Jennie and me in even though she knew who my husband was. She made a home for me. She provided me with a job. But, most importantly, she provided love. Jennie and I love all of you."

"Dear friends," Amanda said. "Thanks for participating in my little exercise. Quentin and I will treasure your remarks. You have a home here for as long as you like. While we all wish that Darcy was seated beside us, let's keep her in our Thanksgiving prayers and perhaps Fifi will bring her back to us. Now, Hannah has a surprise for us. She's made some of her famous desserts that she wants to serve herself."

Homer said, "I'll help you, Hannah."

After they had had their fill of chocolate cake, ginger cookies, banana cream pie, and mince pie, Hannah and Homer collected the dishes and disappeared into the kitchen. One by one, they ambled about to enjoy the comradery and fellowship of their new little family.

Quentin took notice that the caterers were leaving and loading up their van. He stepped out onto the porch to thank them for their service. After a few minutes, he came to the doorway and motioned for Amanda to join him. "Sweetheart," he said softly, "I know that you feel very bad about Darcy, but wait till you see what I spied as I walked out with the caterers." Quentin took Amanda's hand and led her to the window outside the kitchen. "Look, there's Hannah standing on a little step stool. And there's Homer, handing her the dishes, one at a time. They exude happiness. You know that you provided a safe haven for both of them. Don't they represent a picture of contentment?" They took a few more steps and stopped to look in the window of the salon. "There's Ana, reading a story to Jennie, who is curled up in her mother's lap. Two more people who you protected." When they came to the window that looked into Phoebe's studio, they were both mesmerized as they watched the loving couple, arms around one another, dancing. "They are lost in a moment of bliss as they dance as only lovers do. You worked your magic again and allowed them to develop a deep love affair."

They were both quiet as they looked into the window of Darcy's studio. Russ was sitting on a chair in the middle of the studio. He was slumped over with his head in his hands. "We know that this is a hard time for Russ, but you have given him a reason to go on. You and Fifi will help him heal his heart. Amanda, you are a remarkable woman. I love you." Quentin gathered her in his arms and kissed her.

"Do you think Darcy will ever come back?"

"I'd like to think so. However, if she did go to Roberto, I hope she finds happiness."

They turned and walked back in—hand in hand. They stopped in front of Fifi. Amanda was staring at the statue's face. "I wonder what stories Fifi could tell us. Perhaps she knows where Darcy went. If Fifi does have magical powers, Darcy may return. So, Fifi, my dear, it's all up to you."

EPILOGUE

The owner of Happy Harry's Auto Sales arrived at his lot bright and early Black Friday morning. Through grimy windows, he looked at the Toyota Sienna mini-van that he had featured on the automatic turn-table and smiled. When that pretty lady had driven it onto his lot a few days ago, he had sensed that she was in a hurry to sell. He immediately had seen dollar signs. So he had put on a show for her. He had scanned the title carefully to make it seem like he really didn't want to buy the car at all. Less than eight thousand miles were on the odometer—a great steal if he was careful. He had hemmed and hawed, while the lady had gotten nervous. He was curious why she would want to sell the mini-van, especially when he spotted a suitcase in the back. When he had offered her only $18,000 a fraction of its worth, she surprised him by taking the deal. As soon as she had the check in her hand, she grabbed her suitcase and hurried across the street to the bank. He was certain that he could make more than four thousand profit on this baby.

While the coffee brewed, he walked to the front door to pick up his newspaper. As he put his chunky body down in his ripped leather chair, he poured himself a cup of coffee and unfolded the paper. He almost dropped his coffee mug when he saw her picture. There she was, on the front page—the pretty lady whose car was spinning around and around on the turn-table. He began reading the article aloud. They had found her body in the Caymans, slumped over an easel with a gun next to her feet. It stated that she had probably been dead for more than forty-eight hours when she was discovered. She had been a resident of Sweetbriar and taught art at The Haven. After the shock wore off, Happy Harry remembered that just recently, some big muckety-muck had been found dead on a beach in the Caymans too. For a brief moment he felt sorry for her. Happy Harry was not a betting man, but he would wager all he had that the two were involved with one another in some way. But, after all, life does go on.

Suddenly, he spotted a couple standing in front of the turntable looking at the Toyota. He jumped up and hurried out the door. He was about to make his first sale of the day!